Why Did

by
James Kirkpatrick Davis

PublishAmerica
Baltimore

© 2005 by James Kirkpatrick Davis.
All rights reserved. No part of this book may be reproduced, stored in a retrieval system or transmitted in any form or by any means without the prior written permission of the publishers, except by a reviewer who may quote brief passages in a review to be printed in a newspaper, magazine or journal.

First printing

ISBN: 1-4137-6813-X
PUBLISHED BY PUBLISHAMERICA, LLLP
www.publishamerica.com
Baltimore

Printed in the United States of America

For:

Carter J. P. Davis III, DDS
and
Neva J. Patterson Davis

Acknowledgments

Thanks to family, friends and instructors along the way:
Whitney Davis Kretsinger, Mark Osborne, with *The Kansas City Star;*
Amy Lucas, Graduate Assistant, and Barbara J. Ryan, Professor of English,
both with the University of Missouri at Kansas City, for assistance with the
text; F. Scott Davis, Michael C. Davis, Julie E. Oliver, and Suzanne W.
Luginbill for encouragement.

Prologue

The woman appeared near death, as indeed she was. Although only in her early fifties, she looked much older. When the weather was mild, she would sometimes sit outside on a solitary upright metal chair next to her small apartment. Now, in the terminal stages of lung cancer, she would often appear outside, wrapped in layers of dark clothing, wearing sunglasses and a stocking cap. She enjoyed watching children having fun on a nearby playground. Her fascination with their fun was one of the few enjoyments left. The enigmatic woman was, to the children who often saw her from afar, old beyond count, maybe as old as the beginning of things. Her somber expression, from day to day, seemed joyless and unchanging. The children, after a time and sensing she was sad and perhaps ill, brought her a small assortment of marigolds and carnations one day. The woman managed a smile and was able to whisper thanks.

On this day, a Tuesday, with the weather chilly, the woman was too ill to sit outside. A flicker of life still burned within her, but it was barely discernible. Today, she rested on pillows and sat upright in bed, wrapped in blankets up to her neck. She was awake. Her deep-set watery eyes, bloodshot, were at half-mast. The small, dimly lighted yellowish room with a few pieces of old furniture had become a prison for the last stages of her life. Another stay at the hospital as a human pincushion, was out of the question. She wanted no more of it; she wanted to get it over with.

Her face, ravaged by time, by smoking, by alcohol and by debauchery was lined and emaciated. She had, after years of smoking, yellow stained teeth and fingers. A deep grating cough had lasted for years without medical attention. The room smelled of nicotine and disinfectant; prescription containers covered the small end table next to her bed.

Ruth Cahill remembered, as she often did, that summer of so many years ago, a wonderful golden summer in Stamford Bridge, Michigan, that sometimes seemed as if it might have happened only last week. Life in 1945 was more fun and somehow less complicated. Ruth worked in the resort town. The summer help lived in a boarding house, in sight of the beach. Ruth fell in love with one of the students. He was from a wealthy Chicago family and was heading to law school somewhere in the east. She often wondered, over the years, if he had any idea that she was pregnant at the end of that summer. He told Ruth he would write to her from law school. She never heard from him again.

Ruth knew, soon after her son was born, that she was not emotionally or financially equipped to raise him. She was very young in early 1946. Her parents were deceased. Ruth worked as a clerk at a nearby Woolworth's dime store, but could not afford a baby-sitter. In order to feed Brian, she often went without food. Her situation, trying to raise him by herself, was hopeless.

Her eyes flooded with tears as she remembered waving goodbye to her son for the last time. She remembered his large blue eyes and the quizzical look in his eyes as she left. He began to cry. He waved and waved until she was out of sight.

Her only companion on this day, this Tuesday, was Jim Sudbury, a hospice volunteer.

"Jimmy, do you have the package ready to go?" she asked in a whisper.

"It's right here, Ruth. It is ready to seal, and then I'll send it. You were going to write a letter or a note to him and put it in with the pictures. It would be more meaningful to him if you did. He may not know what the pictures by themselves are all about," the hospice volunteer replied.

"I can't do it, Jimmy. I started a letter. I can't finish it. I'm too exhausted. It's too late."

"Do you want to give me your thoughts, and I can write it for you and sign your name?"

"Jimmy," she whispered slowly, "I can't do it. I'm sorry, I just can't do it. I can't organize my thoughts. It's no good. It's too late. I don't know. So many years have passed. I started a letter a few times. It wasn't any good. I'm exhausted. Will you just do what I asked and send it?"

"Of course, Ruth."

"How did you find him after 28 years?"

"I don't know how our people found him, but it really is the Brian Cahill you have been looking for. There's no doubt about that. Brian should have the package by the end of this week. It's going right to the apartment where he lives. Also, I have a special surprise for you, Ruth."

"Jimmy, what are you talking about?" Ruth whispered.

"These people were able to get a picture of him as he was leaving his apartment one day, a couple of weeks ago. He was probably going to work."

"This was too much to hope for," she replied and fell into a violent coughing attack. The hospice volunteer held her hand. After wiping her forehead with a cold cloth, he gave her another tissue for her nose and mouth. Ruth recovered slowly. She took a small drink of water and asked the volunteer for the photograph.

She carefully took the photograph in both hands, with thumb and index finger on each corner and brought it up close to her eyes. She slowly whispered, "Well, well, Brian, my little boy, there you are. My, my, you did grow up to be a handsome young man. Oh God, I left you all of those years ago."

She fell into a violent sobbing. "Jimmy, please take my hand and hold it hard. It's the pain. It's the pain. Oh God! The pain in my heart, oh God, the sadness of what I've missed."

Jim Sudbury reached over and wiped her eyes, then her nose and mouth. He took the photo, placed it back in the envelope, and put it on the end table. Ruth, all passions spent, fell into a deep sleep. The volunteer turned off the lamp and sat down on a chair close to her bed. The wild emotion had passed. He fell asleep in the chair.

Ruth slept for several hours. As she was waking up, near midnight, she suddenly said, "Jimmy, when I'm gone, you know, after I've died, I want you to put the picture with me. Will you do that for me?"

Jim Sudbury had fallen asleep in the chair and was startled when Ruth made the statement. "Of course I will do that for you. That's no problem."

Ruth seemed calmer now after her rest. The small apartment was almost dark. One small lamp next to the end table provided the only light.

"Ruth, I think I should contact a priest. One could be here in about fifteen minutes," the volunteer said.

"I haven't taken the sacraments for 35 years," she whispered. "It's way too late for that."

"Ruth it's never to late. There's the matter of Absolution."

Ruth's breathing, with a deeper grating sound, was more difficult. "It's too late for that, Jimmy. With the life I've lived, a priest probably would not give me Absolution anyway."

Her response seemed to tire her and both were quiet for a few minutes.

"Ruth, you can't go off into eternity without Absolution."

"Jimmy, I think I'm damned anyway."

"Please don't say that, Ruth."

Her eyelids moved up and down, and breathing became very slow, until it seemed as if each breath might be her last. Her eyes opened and then closed. Her breathing stopped.

Chapter 1

The owner of The Promontory Inn, Penfield J. Meacham, a handsome man with pale gray-blue eyes and sandy skin, looked to be in his early fifties. Friends, family, and associates called him Pen. Those who worked at the Inn called him Mr. Pen. He was beginning to age; salt and pepper hair had thinned. Pen Meacham wore a blue shirt with sleeves rolled up to the elbows, threadbare khaki shorts, and tennis shoes.

Pen had been an indifferent student at Albion College and graduated in the lower part of his class. He met Geraldine Rose freshman year and they married after college and had two sons. The oldest, Graham, was in school at Loyola Marymount. Cooper lived at home with his parents in The Promontory Inn and attended Charing Cross School at Cornwall Bay.

Pen awakened at 5:30, Saturday morning, July 26. Geraldine still slept and Pen did not disturb her. Cooper had worked at the night desk until midnight and was asleep in his bedroom down the hall.

The Meachams' austere off-white bedroom had a hardwood floor. Wooden shutters covered bedroom windows facing the lake. Light at this early hour was seeping through. A floor-to-ceiling mirror covered the bedroom's north wall and chrome pedestal-mounted lamps on each side of the bed were turned off. Bed linens and blankets were white.

Pen savored the early morning solitude, and he paused to look down at the beach from a third-floor window. The damp lawn rolled out like a green carpet to the breakwater and he noticed the overgrown gravel path leading to a dilapidated old dock still in the water. Morning fog still obscured the horizon and tops of evergreens. Pen made his way past Cooper's room, down the hallway to the central stairwell and down to the hotel kitchen on the first floor. Kitchen walls were the color of eggshell. Stainless steel cabinets and work areas looked brand new. Utensils, pots, pans, condiments, dishes, cups, serving trays and glasses were put away. Geraldine had placed an orange Motherwell print over the main sink. It was the only bright object in the room.

Hotel guests were sleeping at this hour. Ida Mae, the hotel's food service manager, and the kitchen help would arrive in an hour. Guests would come down for breakfast in three hours. This was the peak of the summer season; tonight's party would begin early evening. The band would start playing in the dining room at nine. The hotel would be jammed with people by ten. Weather permitting, tables and chairs would be placed on the lawn.

On most mornings, Pen would have a cigar and coffee, review his list of projects and go to work. He smoked for a while today and then put his cigar out in a glass ashtray. A minute passed, and he poured a second coffee and lighted his first cigarette of the day. The table was bare, except for Pen's clipboard, coffee cup, and ashtray. He took a sip of coffee and rubbed his fingers slowly over the rim of the cup. Pen listened to the silence and picked up his pencil as if to write a note to himself and then set it down on the table.

Ida Mae and Geraldine kept the hotel account books, bought the liquor and soft drinks and analyzed food purchases every few days. Geraldine answered all correspondence and requests for reservations and kept the reservation ledger and the cash journal current. Almost all of the Inn's 32 guestrooms were reserved from May through September.

Nevertheless, Pen was worried about the hotel. Earlier this week, Ida Mae caught a college student waiter stealing from the commissary, and he was fired on the spot. Two other students had been fired in early June. Food and bar receipts declined for June and half of July. Pen, Geraldine, and Ida Mae knew the hotel receipts week by week, but they could not get a handle on what was wrong.

Pen pulled another cigarette from the pack and had a change of heart. Something else was wrong.

He rolled the cigarette around with his fingers and the smoke spiraled upward. He picked up the pencil, tapped it quietly on the table, and set it down again. His fingers touched the smooth surface of the worktable, and there were signals of uneasiness. Something out of his control was in the works. He turned to look at the lake. Thoughts of his own ineptitude and irrelevance folded themselves silently around him. Pen thought that something was going to happen today for the last time. The sunlight filtered toward him and a breeze made its way through the kitchen shutters.

Pen grew up in a wealthy Chicago neighborhood with his parents and twin brother, Paul. Pen and his brother were never close, even when they were boys. Paul, a superb student, was serious, introspective, and never popular. Pen was scatterbrained, a lackluster student, outgoing and always popular. The idea of going east with Paul to study law held no interest for Penfield and his decision caused permanent estrangement. Pen had had no contact, other than through Christmas and birthday cards, with his parents or his twin brother for years.

Pen had a worrisome career in advertising. After 26 years, he was apprehensive about the future. After a lifetime of second-guessing himself, there was no sense of fulfillment. In his forties, he began to panic. There was the recurring nightmare–near the end of his life, he would look in a mirror, and say, "Meacham, you failed at everything!"

The Promontory Inn, a handsome rambling affair with white horizontal clapboard siding and dark green shutters, was his effort for a sense of accomplishment–a legacy, he hoped, of style and taste for his boys. Pen wanted his family together. He wanted Graham to come back after graduate school to live in Stamford Bridge and practice law. He did not want Cooper to leave, except for college. He wanted his family to belong in Stamford Bridge–a quiet little resort town, located among evergreens and pine, birch and maple trees, near the top of a bluff above the Lake Michigan shore–a place where well to do families had spent summer vacations for generations.

Pen Meacham appeared carefree and his native intelligence was obvious. He laughed at himself and was popular. Episodes of depression and feelings of worthlessness were known only to him and Geraldine. After college, Pen worked for advertising agencies in Detroit. Each new job represented a move up someone's corporate ladder. Each new position led to longer hours and late nights. Drinking became a family problem, and Sundays were spent with hangovers. The Meachams, with two sons, lived in a Detroit suburb. They discovered that a house with a triple garage was no more satisfying than one with a double garage. The city was too big, and Geraldine drank in the afternoons. The boys were in trouble at school, cutting classes, stealing and getting into fights. The threads holding the Meachams together were coming apart. Penfield and Geraldine came to understand the isolation of living in Detroit–a city of millions, too vast to care about them. Graham and Cooper had only known life in a big city suburb. They were too young to know, but they did know, something wholly basic was missing from their lives.

One day in 1971, the obvious hit Pen between the eyes. His son, Graham, then 16, had grown up. Pen's work had taken all of his time. He had missed Graham's boyhood, and his older son would soon be ready for college. The same was happening with Cooper. Geraldine, past forty and home alone during the day, was heading for drinking problems. Aside from the equity in their home, they had saved nothing.

Later that year, Geraldine's father died. After years of estrangement, Harold Rose left his only living child a large inheritance. The family went to the funeral in Sutton's Bay. Harold Rose had been an old and cruel man for a long time, and his wife had been gone for almost 40 years. Six people attended the funeral, including two cousins Geraldine had never met. Harold Rose's hostility toward his daughter was never understood. Geraldine thought her father edged toward madness. Graham and Cooper had never met their grandfather, and they were not sad at his passing.

The family became wealthy overnight.

The inheritance was a watershed.

The Meachams saved their new assets, and Pen continued to work. They had no idea what they were looking for, only that what they were seeking did exist somewhere.

Four years ago, on a November afternoon in Detroit, Geraldine was making a bank deposit. She noticed a Michigan property catalog in the lobby and a classified ad for a resort hotel on Lake Michigan caught her eye. They bought an abandoned structure known as The Promontory Inn. The Meacham family paid cash for the building and moved across the state to Stamford Bridge. Neither Pen nor Geraldine had ever been there. Pen remembered that his twin brother, Paul, worked one summer, years ago in Stamford Bridge.

The telephone rang. Picotta's Produce said delivery would be 11:30, not

WHY DID I GROW SO COLD?

first thing. Pen left a note for Ida Mae, picked up his clipboard, and headed through the back door. This Saturday would be the perfect day for the Queen's Cup E-Scow sailing competition. Guests could watch the race from the Inn's front porch.

Pen looked at the horizon and could not escape the feeling that winds of change were coming his way. He was uneasy. He walked to the breakwater, where the Inn's handyman, Charlie Putnam, was already at work.

Chapter 2

Ida Mae Murphy, 61, a native of Stamford Bridge, was a timeless fixture in town. With a prominent nose, high cheekbones, thick eyebrows and a wide, often scowling mouth, Ida Mae was not attractive. As a plain, simple person, she had never used makeup, nor did she own jewelry. Ida Mae wore work clothes every day–a blue uniform with a white collar and black work shoes. Of average height and overweight, Ida Mae was a moderate drinker and heavy smoker.

Two generations ago, while in high school, Ida Mae had an unsuccessful love affair. She was deeply hurt. Two old movie ticket stubs were her only keepsakes. Neither she nor her parents had discussed the matter in more than 40 years. Since that time, she had never been involved with a man. She lived uneventfully with her parents in a small, one-story, thatched-roof house, surrounded by an old white picket fence, near Campbell Street. She was past middle-age and never considered living anywhere else. Her small bedroom had changed little in 60 years. There were a few mementos on an old dresser, a single bed, and a picture of her sixth-grade class on the wall. She read very little and often watched television in the living room with her parents.

Aside from her parents, Ida Mae was close with no other person. Her father and mother, retired for many years, were now almost 80, and she knew they would not live forever. Her parents would need care, and they would die, and the thought of living alone was disquieting to her; Ida Mae knew she would grow old, imprisoned alone in the small house.

For over 20 years, Ida Mae worked at Christie's restaurant, near Campbell Street on Ramsgate, as assistant manager. Four years ago,

WHY DID I GROW SO COLD?

Penfield Meacham offered her a job as food service manager at The Promontory Inn. She took the job and now managed the waitresses, the dining room and kitchen; she bought the food and planned the menus for all three meals every day. She was grateful to the Meachams and worked at the hotel every day. Aside from her parents, the Inn was the focus of her life.

Although successful at managing a staff, Ida Mae was distant. She often spent time in empty reflection, and early morning brought sadness to her unabated by work, cigarettes and alcohol. Now, after three generations, Ida Mae knew her die was largely cast. Morning melancholy would always be with her. She thought often about the darkness deep within her that others could not see and the absence of meaning. Work for the Meachams would continue for as long as they wanted her. Beyond that, there was nothing for her.

The classmates she had grown up with in Stamford Bridge moved away years ago. Few, if any, had returned, and there had never been a class reunion. For Ida Mae, it was just as well. Never popular, she sometimes looked out of her bedroom window and wondered what became of her classmates. *What did I miss by not leaving here 40 years ago?* she asked. There were moments before sleep when she saw an older and exhausted image of herself standing on the beach, holding hands with the boy who hurt her so many years ago.

Her high school graduation speaker said that her class would never again be together in one place. He was right. On that big night, most of her graduating classmates went to parties rumored to have lasted most of the night. Ida Mae walked home with her parents to a dinner of swiss steak. A new bathrobe was her graduation present. It was a quiet dinner and she soon went to bed.

At sunrise today she looked at the lake from her bedroom window. Ida Mae was troubled and did not know why. *Something was out there*, she thought, *on or near the horizon; perhaps it was a message of some kind.* It might have been her imagination, but she thought otherwise. She pondered the matter and finished a cigarette.

Ida Mae looked in on her parents and found both sleeping, and she left through the front door. Her thoughts turned to The Promontory Inn and the Saturday night party.

Chapter 3

Geraldine Meacham finished breakfast at 7:45 a.m.

On this day, her long black hair was tied with a red scarf. She wore a white blouse, blue denim slacks and deck shoes. Geraldine had hazel eyes and an attractive mouth that broke easily into a smile, followed with a skittish laugh. Her olive complexion, at 52, gave evidence of stress and smoking. Those who worked at the Inn were fond of her and called her Miz M; family and friends called her Gerry.

Geraldine was exhausted. The coming winter months would be dark and cold, and she would have time to be alone and read and sleep. Drinking haunted Geraldine and Pen for years, and Pen had been drinking heavily on Saturday nights all summer. It bothered Geraldine, and there might be one more scene before the summer was over. Cooper tested his mother often, and it made her angry. Pen was not firm with Cooper, and she often felt cornered by Cooper's assertiveness.

Geraldine slept late this Saturday. Pen was at work, Cooper was sleeping, and she ate alone. Guests had not come down for breakfast, and it was quiet. She smoked a cigarette. The Meachams' table was next to the west bay window. It faced the lake. The sweep of lawn from the Inn's front porch led down to the breakwater.

The dining room had a bright hardwood floor and could seat 60. Tables were covered with white linen tablecloths and napkins. Each table had a crystal vase filled with fresh flowers and ladder back chairs. The east wall was covered with a floor-to-ceiling mirror. Guests had a view of the lake, either facing west toward the lake, or east, with a mirrored view. One piece of art was displayed on the north wall–an Alexander Calder print.

Geraldine looked at the print, then at the lawn, back to the lake and back to the work of art. *Calder, so much in dialogue with the world–a perfect place for his work*, she thought. The wind was up and she saw the bright colors of a spinnaker on a fast moving sloop then just cresting the horizon. The sky was cloudless and waves tumbled onto the beach. A faint cadence echoed in her mind. She thought of her own life ebbing away.

She lit another cigarette.

Gerry and Charlie's flower garden was in the hotel's west side yard, and trees clustered around its circular path. It was a large, round garden with a cross-section of annuals and perennials in spherical rows. Flowers, presented to her this morning as a tapestry, were in bloom. *Flowers,* she thought, *spoke almost as a chorus, of splendor and hope.* Aldous Huxley, she remembered, had written that he once viewed a group of flowers in which the colors seemed to come from inside the flowers, rather than as objects illuminated by light. Huxley said that words like "grace" and "transfiguration" came to mind. Geraldine felt this morning as if she was somehow near the edge of a plateau, trapped by her inability to understand the nature of things in their entirety. The thought suddenly gave her a feeling that a message beyond understanding had come her way. *What was missing?,* she asked. *If the doors of my perception could be opened,* she wondered, *would everything appear as it must be–infinite?*

She poured another coffee.

Growing up in Sutton's Bay, Michigan, had been miserable. Her mother, whom she could barely remember, died when Geraldine was 4. Her brother, Graham, also almost lost in memory, died when Geraldine was 5. Her father was a large man who had made a great deal of money and retired young. Harold Rose was a cruel man, and Geraldine often wondered why her mother had married him.

After the death of Geraldine's mother and brother, Harold Rose retreated from the world. There was no sympathy for Geraldine's loss. Guests were not welcomed at the Rose home. The maid, Elsie, lived in a first-floor room by the kitchen. Elsie and two classmates were Geraldine's best friends. Holidays and birthdays were celebrated with cash left on her pillow. It was a large, cold house in Sutton's Bay. Geraldine rarely saw her father, who lived on the third floor. It was very quiet, and there were many shadows and dark hallways. Geraldine received a check at high school graduation; her father did not attend the ceremony.

Harold Rose would not discuss college with his daughter, and Geraldine enrolled at Albion College without his advice or consent. Geraldine placed the tuition statement on the kitchen table. Later, she found an envelope on her pillow, with a check covering first year costs. In the fall of her 18th year, she left for Albion College without a word from her father. Harold Rose missed his daughter's college graduation and her wedding.

With her mother and brother both gone, Geraldine's father had been her only relative. She neither loved nor liked him. Harold Rose's neglect wounded Geraldine. For years, she believed that all men were cruel and neglectful. Geraldine often looked back through the years to a deep, undefined feeling she had for her mother.

Geraldine met Pen Meacham at Albion College and married the only man she had ever loved. Pen's career began after their marriage, and for the next 26 years his advertising career moved upward. He worked very hard. Long hours, entertaining, drinking, and uncertainty of Pen's changing agency employment almost destroyed them.

Harold Rose died in 1971 and left an estate of almost two million dollars to Geraldine. She was stunned by the incongruity of God's mercy. Harold Rose was almost unknown to her for two generations and had treated her with contempt. She was thankful for the fortune, but why had her father hated her all these years, or had he? she asked. If he did not hate her, why had he acted as he did?

The family bought The Promontory Inn in 1971.

Ida Mae came to the dining room, said hello, and then said, "Miz M, sorry to interrupt, but Mimi says she needs to see you in housekeeping."

"Thanks, Ida Mae. I need to get going anyway. I'll get over there in a few minutes," Geraldine replied.

Chapter 4

Cooper Meacham sat up in bed, rubbed his face and ran his fingers through thick dishwater blond hair. His eyes were puffy, and his face was swollen from sleep. He pushed the covers to one side, and moved over the side of the bed and stood on the hardwood floor. Cooper was wearing gym shorts and a Charing Cross School football shirt. Sunlight filtered through narrow blinds, and the room had a melancholy feel. It was very quiet. Cooper blinked, scratched his head, and looked into the half-light. There were vague shadow outlines of things and he was oddly apprehensive.

"What the hell...?" he heard himself say aloud.

Cooper went to a bedroom window, opened the shutter, and looked out. It was a bright day. The fog had cleared, and there was a scent of mist. The lake water looked blue green to the skyline. White cottages along the north shoreline looked bright and crisp in the sunlight. To the south, clusters of pine and birch trees shaded the beach. Pockets of white sunlight in motion reflected off the water and Cooper could see the beach below from his third floor window. A dinghy had been pulled ashore and left near the beach grass. Its oars lay next to it on the sand. A tall man and two boys were throwing a beach ball back and forth. Several children were building something out of sand; black embers from last night's beach bonfire still formed a circle. The sky looked as if a thread had been suspended across the horizon, separating the sky from the water. A yellow catamaran was moving toward the skyline.

Is there something out there I'm not seeing? he wondered.

Cooper felt oddly disconnected from the moment that he opened his eyes. He stood at the window and stared at the horizon. Cooper shrugged his shoulders, closed the shutters, and turned to the mirror on the bedroom wall. He took his shirt off and did calisthenics for 20 minutes. Cooper stopped and wiped the sweat off his face with his hands. He looked in the mirror, "You're lookin' good today, Coops." He went to the shower.

Cooper's bedroom was down the hallway from his parents. The door to Graham's bedroom was closed, and the hallway was empty. Cooper's room was khaki color, two bedroom windows faced Lake Michigan. The room was small. A brown chair sat in the corner and a footstool was stacked with books and papers. Two bulletin boards were in one corner, and they were covered with photos of his girlfriend, Mary Meade Saltonstall. A small roll-top desk was the center of Cooper's room. A letter from Graham was lying open on the desk.

Cooper was co-captain of the football team, Canterbury Club president, an acolyte at Holy Cross, and an honor roll student. Football fascinated him. Pen thought Cooper should be a defensive player; he told Cooper it would be better to hit than to be hit. The coach saw Cooper's breakaway speed and made him into a running back.

"He's a natural runner," Charing Cross coach Bob Briggs told Pen. "We are going to get the ball to him as often as we can. He's not going to play defense, and no special teams. He's got too damn much offensive talent. He can take a hit–my God, that boy can take a hit. He's a good blocker, and he's got good hands. His real talent is running with the football. He's got speed and the ability to make people miss; nobody can catch him. He'll get better with every game! I wouldn't be surprised if you hear from some colleges next year. He'll need some more bulk to play college ball."

Cooper was probably smarter than his brother, Graham. College for Cooper was a year away. Life was busy, and he hoped high school would never end. Cooper looked like Pen. He was taller than his father, weighed probably 180 pounds. He had a wide face, a low hairline, and blue-gray eyes, set far apart.

Life with Cooper had been hell.

Cooper ran with the wrong kids in Detroit and got into trouble. After a third shoplifting offense, Pen took Cooper to the Detroit police department and asked a jailer to show his son a holding cell. The jailer took Pen and Cooper down a dark hallway to the lock-up. He showed them a cell packed with criminals waiting for trial. He asked Cooper if he would like to spend the night with these guys.

"If you're messin' up, young man," the jailer said, pointing his finger at Cooper," and I guess you are or you wouldn't be here, we've got a place for you. Mark my words, pretty boy, if you're off the straight and narrow, you better damn well straighten yourself right now, tonight, or you're going to be in here with these guys. Handsome white boy like you, these sonsabitches goin' to rape you first or knock your teeth out soon enough. Now listen to me, white boy, and listen good. Be damn thankful to God your father brought you down here. I'll tell you this. If I see you down here again, I'm going to smack you hard in the chops, and don't think I can't do it. Now go with your dad, and get the hell out of here. Don't ever come back!"

Cooper and his dad walked close to the cell and heard a cell door somewhere slam shut. Inmates whistled at Cooper and called him names. Cooper's eyes were wide open, and he was scared.

Stamford Bridge had been good for Cooper. Most problems were in the past, except for an incident three weeks ago. Geraldine had been talking to Cooper about seeing just one person in high school. "Have you thought about playing the field a little more and dating other girls?" Geraldine asked every few months.

"Why, Mom? I know lots of people, and Mary Meade is the one for me. I'm not going to see anyone else, and neither is she. That's it. We have a ton of fun together. We know everyone. We're popular. We both get good grades. We're in almost every activity there is. I help out here at the hotel, and so does she. We've even got a part-time job at the White Sands on Saturdays. We enjoy being together. Her folks talk about the same stupid thing. Mary Meade and I don't want to see anyone else. We really like each other. I don't know why you and Dad and the Saltonstalls can't understand that. Are you guys dense or something? Your comments and what Dad has been saying irritate the hell out of me!"

"Cooper, watch it!"

"Watch what, Mom? Watch what? That's what you and Dad did in college. You've told me that a hundred times. It's always sounded like you're proud of the fact that Dad was the only person you saw in college–or ever, I guess. The Saltonstalls did the same thing. We do our best. I think you'd be pleased. I'll be honest with you, Mom, this is really making me madder than hell–I mean madder than holy hell! Christ almighty, I think you'd be pleased that Mary Meade and I've found each other while we're still young. No matter how well Mary Meade and I are doing or whatever, the four of you seem to be sitting around finding a way to be critical of us. Well, I'm goddamn sick of it, and so is Mary Meade. You can tell Dad, or I will. I'm fed up with all of you. End of story," Cooper said.

"All I want is for you to be sure..." Geraldine started to say.

"All you want to do is to be critical," Cooper interrupted. "Mary Meade and I don't smoke. We suck a beer once in a great while. We're not out getting drunk. She's not pregnant, and we aren't fooling around. We don't drive fast. We're not flunking out. Between the two of us, we are in just about everything in school. We're both acolytes. We're both on the honor roll. No drugs. Tell me, what the hell do you guys want?" Cooper's face was red. "Christ almighty, what the hell do you and the Saltonstalls want? The four of you just can't wait for us to screw up! While you're waiting for that to happen, you begin to wonder if we should be together at all. That just sucks! Mom, that just sucks!"

"Don't you take that tone with me, Cooper. I'm trying–" Geraldine began.

"You're trying to make me madder than hell," Cooper interrupted again. "You've damn well done it. Congratulations, Mom, you've done it."

"Cooper, I told you to watch it!"

"Is that all you can say? Watch it! What the hell are you talking about? You'll never find two people anywhere trying any harder to do the right thing. If you find two people trying harder than us, then you all made a mistake bringing us into the world in the first place, so I'm real sorry. You and Dad shouldn't have messed around after Graham was born or something."

"You're way the hell out of line!" Geraldine said angrily.

"This's a bunch of crap, and you know it. Mary Meade and I have done more things in high school than the four of you in high school and college put together. And you know it! We've got better grades than all of you, and we don't deserve this bullshit from you or anybody else! Dad has always been proud of the fact that he was a lousy student. It's always been some kind of a stupid inside joke with Dad and Mr. Saltonstall. We've heard it a million times. Ha! Ha! Ha! Big joke! Boy, isn't that funny? The four of you have a big laugh over your martinis or whatever you guys drink to get sloppy or falling down or whatever. Wow! Isn't this all funny? How would you like it if we were crappy students, too? Then we could bore you with stupid, exaggerated stories of beer parties and dumb crap like that! How would you like it if we were proud that we were lousy students? What then? Remember all of the beer parties you and Dad have told us about all these years? Boy, that's real cool. If we carried on like the four of you say you did, you'd send us to jail or reform school. Well, I'm sorry if we've disappointed you and the others. You know what? I don't give a damn."

Cooper picked up a school notebook and threw it hard against his bedroom wall. He walked out of the room.

Geraldine flinched, and the notebook hit the wall. She was shocked and angry. She could not fault Cooper's logic. Telling Pen about this tirade would solve nothing.

Chapter 5

Julie's Hometown Restaurant near Saginaw, Michigan, was quiet, and the woman sitting alone finished breakfast. Shannon Fitsimmons looked through a travel brochure and put it in her bag. Her plan to stay in a bed and breakfast in Stamford Bridge was exciting; it meant a week away from the *Saginaw Journal*–where she worked as a general assignment reporter. Shannon paid her bill, checked her bags, map, books, and brochures, and left the restaurant. She pulled her green Ford Mustang onto Michigan Highway 56 and headed west to Stamford Bridge.

Shannon, 27, was tall and thin, and her long, sunshine bleached hair was tied with a blue scarf. A cross of St. George pendant, a gift from her mother, was attached to her gold necklace. She wore sunglasses, a yellow blouse, khaki shorts, and loafers. Sports gave her complexion brightness. Her almond-shaped eyes were blue, and she had high cheekbones, a beautifully shaped mouth and a freckle covered nose.

Shannon grew up in Wheatstone, a Kansas town of about 3,000 near the Colorado border. She had obvious athletic ability in gymnastics even as a young girl. It was during senior year at Wheatstone High that college recruiters made contact with Shannon and Ardith, her mother. Sports provided the money for college. Shannon's decision to attend college was the biggest of her life.

Even now, at 27, leaving Wheatstone and living away from Kansas was still underscored by homesickness. Did she want to live in Michigan? Could she go back home after all these years, now that both parents were gone? Friends had gone on with their lives without her, and if she did move back, would Wheatstone be as wonderful as she made it out to be? If she left Michigan and moved back to Kansas, would she miss Michigan? Shannon quietly missed the simple joy of life; she often wondered what it was that one actually lived for.

Shannon remembered scholarship offers from colleges, and none were near Kansas. A few of her classmates planned to attend junior colleges. None planned to leave the state. Several at graduation were married, and some had children. Most had no college plans, and none graduated from college.

Shannon had been close with Wheatstone classmates since kindergarten. The last summer in Kansas after high school was lodged in the twilight of memory; it was probably more marvelous now than it ever was. She remembered working part-time, a few parties, a first hangover, and sunsets at the edge of the prairie. Time slipped away that summer as the season changed into fall, and Shannon and her mother went to the Labor Day picnic at Ruder Park. Shannon said goodbye to her friends and their parents. As the sun was setting, leaves from trees around the town square fell on brick streets and sidewalks. The county courthouse was closed for the long weekend and parking places were empty. Few cars were on the streets, stores were closed, and summer was over. Lawns were turning, and locusts were in full sound. School would begin the next day, and most at the picnic had left early. Soon, only the picnic tables and swings were left. Shannon and her mother walked through the park, around the town square and then up the single-lane road to the hillside in Providence Cemetery, where Shannon said goodbye to her dad.

The thought of leaving her mother alone in the house on Oakley bothered Shannon; she had never been away from her mother. Ardith Fitsimmons appeared to ignore the prospect of loneliness and told Shannon to take advantage of this once-in-a-lifetime offer. Shannon did not look forward to life at a university larger than Wheatstone–a setting in a harsh and bitter northern climate where students were known by numbers.

The memory of saying goodbye to her mother on the day she left for college would always be with her. Her Aunt Suzanne, also a widow, lived a block away and came to the Fitsimmons' house that morning. It was a clear day in September. Shannon's Aunt Neva, a retired English instructor, and her cousin Whitney drove over from Garden City. Ardith met her niece, both sisters and Shannon in the front yard. Shannon was packed and ready to leave. All five walked down the sidewalk, and they stopped before reaching the street.

"Shannon," her mother said, "your father isn't here to say goodbye, so I'll say it for both of us. I know you'll do your best. We'll be waiting till you come home for Christmas. Don't worry about me. I'm in good company. We'll all stay busy. I'm proud of you. I'll miss you. We'll all miss you. Call me tonight, and let me know where you are staying. I packed a lunch for you and put it in the back seat. Suzanne brought you some cookies."

Her mother's eyes flooded with tears. Shannon hugged her mother, both aunts, her cousin, and said goodbye. She looked up at her second-story bedroom window.

Shannon remembered seeing them standing on the front sidewalk. They stood together and waved until she could no longer see them in her rearview mirror.

Chapter 6

Brian Cahill received a package from Seattle on Friday. He discovered it resting against the front door of his apartment. The package was the size of a shirt box and addressed to him in longhand. It was wrapped in brown paper, sealed with tape and had no return address; Brian did not recognize the handwriting.

He went inside and set the package and mail on the front hall table. Brian went to the bedroom and changed clothes. He put his business suit and tie on wooden hangers, set his shoes inside the closet and closed the door. His white shirt went into the laundry bag in the back hall. Brian put on khaki walking shorts, a faded 1st Cavalry sweatshirt and made his way to the kitchen.

The small apartment had hardwood floors and was spotless—a place for him to regroup and dwell erratically on the past. Everything was in place, reflecting careful decorating habits. A narrow dining room, with a wooden game table and four high back chairs with blue pillows, served also as a library. Bookshelves were mounted on dining room walls.

Brian's Veteran's Administration psychiatrist prescribed exercise to reduce the symptoms of post-traumatic stress disorder. There had been other treatments—hypnosis, medication, vitamin therapy, bio-feedback, acupuncture, psychoanalysis, group therapy and others—to help deal with the horror of Vietnam. Most were a waste of time. Brian had some confidence in the physician who recommended exercise. Other VA physicians probably meant well, but they had not been in Vietnam; they had not seen their platoon annihilated in the jungle, and they had not been there when the enemy was so close at night that the Americans called in artillery fire on top of their own position.

Vietnam haunted him, and sometimes the enemy seemed only yards away. Brian could smell napalm and hear screaming in the darkness. American artillery was deafening, and his M-16 would be firing on full automatic. At times, he was afraid to look in the mirror. Trauma came in the night with periods of rage and flashbacks.

The depression caused by a stay at the Veteran's hospital to treat a bronchial infection nearly ended his life. Without a workout schedule, the depression was nearly unbearable. The side effects of drugs–Prozac, lithium, and others–were worse than the depression itself. Brian had seen what such drugs had done to other vets, and he knew it was a blind alley.

Brian combed his black hair straight back from the hairline. His eyes were hazel, sometimes at half-mast when listening, and his nose was narrow. His mouth revealed straight white teeth when he smiled or laughed. With ruddy skin, he looked healthy. Brian could be engaging in conversation and profound after two or three beers. To his few friends, he seemed happy. Brian's psychiatrist described his behavior as reaction formation–Brian acted in a manner opposite of the way he felt; he needed friends to avoid remembering what he had seen.

Women enjoyed being with Brian, and he was serious with one, Charmon Le Carre. Brian and Charmon slept together from the beginning. They went on a California vacation and traveled to New York. Brian often spent weekends at her apartment. Charmon, a lawyer with a downtown Chicago firm, was tall, athletic, and attractive. They played racquetball together every week, and she fell in love with Brian. Sometimes, Brian would look in her eyes, put his arms around her and hold her so close he could feel her heart beating. Often they would lie together, Brian would touch her face, and Charmon would close her eyes. They liked to wake in the night and find each other and know they were no longer alone. Charmon always knew that part of Brian was beyond her reach and, after a year, he started to break off their relationship with no explanation. Charmon was hysterical.

"Brian, what are you saying?" she screamed.

"I said maybe we should see less of each other," he replied.

"But, why? Why are you saying that?"

WHY DID I GROW SO COLD?

"I was just thinking that maybe we should take a breather."

"A breather? What are you talking about?"

"A breather means we would see less of each other."

"I know what it means, Brian."

"Well, okay, just forget I said anything."

"Forget you said anything? I thought we were planning to spend the rest of our lives together. Was I wrong?"

"No, just forget it," he replied.

"Forget it! Is that what you said again? My life is in the balance, and you're saying to forget it. Is there someone else? That's what it is, isn't it?"

"There's no one else. How could there be? You and I are together all the time we are not at work. That's not it."

"It must be somebody at your work."

"Charmon, you're not listening to me. There is no other person, and there never has been!"

"You've hurt me, Brian. I've given you everything. You're my life, and you've hurt me. That isn't like you," Charmon screamed as she broke down.

Brian stood next to her and put his hands on her shoulders. He started to say he was sorry, but she interrupted. "Stop it! Damn, stop it! Don't say anything. Just go ahead and kill me."

"Charmon I was going to…"

"Shut up!" she screamed. "Just get out of here. Get your hands off me. I don't understand what I've done. Why do you want to leave me?" Charmon slammed the door shut and fell to the floor, sobbing, "Oh God, Brian. Oh God, Brian, what have I done?"

Charmon was awake that night and missed work the next day and the next. She did not answer the telephone and did not pick up her mail. She stayed in bed until late afternoon, but sleep was impossible. Three days later she recovered and called Brian at work. She said she would wait for him, no matter what. Brian told her he did not intend to see anyone else.

She called Brian every night, and weeks later, they talked for a long time. Vietnam, the killing, and the terrible atrocities had destroyed any sense of well-being. The orphanage brutalized him, and he felt incapable of giving himself to another person, even Charmon. No other person, other than his doctor, he said, knew that Vietnam caused such suffering or that his early life caused such anguish. No one else knew that Brian could explode and kill again. Charmon did not draw back from him. Much she already knew–his voice in the night said things she did not understand, and sometimes Charmon saw the look of terror in his eyes. Sometimes she did not recognize him, and Charmon knew he would never be well.

Brian's life had been a nightmare.

He had no memory of his mother, and he did not know her name or if she was alive. Brian had no idea who his father was or if he was alive. He was raised in an orphanage. His mother had placed him there when he was two. Beyond that, he knew nothing. The discipline at the orphanage was harsh; Brian did not have a room of his own, and he owned nothing. No one ever visited him, and Brian thought his parents did not care if he lived or died. He hated them.

Brian grew up with few friends, now forgotten or in prison or dead. He remembered fighting, always fighting. His nose was broken twice, his ribs had been cracked, and he broke knuckles on his right hand attacking a gay truant officer. There had been conflicts with teachers, the courts, police and court-appointed attorneys, and all those around him. The court finally gave him the option of prison or the Army. Brian joined the Army.

Brian completed two combat tours in Vietnam. An officer told Brian to think about college. It was the first time that anyone had ever said an encouraging word to him. After Vietnam, a small college in a Chicago suburb provisionally accepted him–tuition was paid by the Army. Brian applied himself and discovered his intelligence. College took five years, and he now worked at an accounting firm in Chicago.

Brian made a drink and sat down on the living room couch, across from the small fireplace. The apartment was quiet. Brian opened the package and set the wrapping paper on the couch beside him. He found a photo album with a worn cover. There was no message. A metal binder held the album together. Brian lifted the album out of the box and opened to the first page. He found old photographs mounted on black paper. The paper was brittle and the photos yellow with age.

He saw a photo of a woman in a white uniform holding a child of perhaps two or three months. "New Baby Cahill, September 1907" was the caption. Another photograph was of a man wearing a straw hat, apparently holding the same child. "Dad Cahill with New Little One, September 1907" was the caption. "At the Lake, Fall, 1907" captioned two photographs of the same man, evidently with the same child and an unnamed woman, standing on a beach.

"What is all this?" he said.

Brian got up from the couch, walked to the living room window and looked at the Chicago streets below. The windows were closed, and the quietness was undisturbed. Brian picked up his glass and went to the kitchen. He made another drink and came back to the couch. He picked up the scrapbook again.

"Who are these people?" Brian said.

The album paper was very old. As Brian turned each page, there was a cracking sound as small pieces of black paper splintered and broke off near the metal binder. The next page featured six photographs of the same people, perhaps a few years older, standing by an unidentified lake. The captions were obscure.

"Mom, Dad, and MacKenzie Cahill, Our Big Trip to Texas, 1912" was the caption under four larger snapshots on the following page of the same three individuals. They were standing next to luggage and apparently getting ready to board a train. The child was about five years old, and her hair was tied in a bow. The man in the picture looked tall, with a mustache and a long face. He was wearing a suit, white shirt, tie, and hat. The woman looked thin. She was wearing a simple, long dress, which reached almost to her feet. They looked somber.

A studio portrait was mounted on the following page. The description read, "We Three, 1922." The names of individuals Brian guessed to be MacKenzie's parents were not listed. Mackenzie appeared to be about 15 years old. She was almost as tall as her parents and the familial resemblance was obvious. "The Cahills Picking Berries in Northern Michigan, 1924," captioned four photographs showing the same family in coveralls standing next to a pickup. Each was holding a bucket, and all three looked worn out.

Several pages were devoted to Mackenzie Cahill. Brian saw a woman of about 18: "Mackenzie Swimming at LM," "Mackenzie and Friends Birthday Party, 1925," "Mackenzie Starting High School," "Mackenzie and Dad Cahill Fishing Up North" and "Mackenzie/High School Band, 1926."

The next page had no photographs and there was a message in a different writing style, "Mom, Dad died last Sunday in a boating accident off of Port Huron. The funeral was Friday. God, how horrible, I loved them so. The pain in my heart is terrible. I am alone. I don't know what I will do. I am very frightened and alone. Mackenzie Cahill, April 1, 1926."

The next page featured a snapshot of Mackenzie Cahill, a year later, holding a newly born child. The caption said, "Ruth Cahill, First Birthday, April 25, 1928." Snapshots over the next pages were devoted to Ruth Cahill. There was "Ruthie Playing in The Yard, Summer, Tacoma," "Ruthie and her New Dog, Chopper, Fall, 1932," "Ruthie and Mom Cahill at the California Beach, 1933."

The next snapshots were apparently taken 12 years later. The first was a larger photo of Ruth Cahill, about 18, sitting on the lap of an unidentified man. The picture was taken in front of what looked like a boarding or apartment house. Brian could make out the letters "WS" over the front door. Next to this picture was a blank spot where a photo had apparently fallen out or had been removed. The caption read, "Ruth and Baby Boy Cahill, summer 1946."

Three snapshots on the last page were dated summer of 1946. The first was of a building that looked like a hotel, located somewhere on a narrow brick street. The second was of Ruth Cahill, wearing an apron, standing on the front steps of the same building. The final snapshot was an indoor picture of a woman, apparently Ruth, again wearing an apron and standing next to a bar. There was a long mirror behind the bar, and customers could be seen. Ruth was apparently a barmaid in that summer of 1946.

Brian put the album on the glass coffee table, leaned back on the couch, and looked up at the ceiling.

The photographs stunned him. Brian could not imagine why someone would contact him in such a strange way. He guessed that the woman in the picture was his mother. He looked at the unidentified man and wondered if that was his father. Mackenzie Cahill might be his grandmother. He wondered if the missing photograph could be a picture of himself with his real mother and father.

Brian was filled with sadness. He thought of the parents he had never known and all that he had missed and wiped his eyes. If these people were his relatives, what did it all mean? What did he feel, after all these years? It was so painful, there was nothing, honestly nothing he could write down or express to another person.

To make matters worse, Brian and Charmon had argued earlier in the week. Charmon was terribly upset and had gone to visit her parents in Wisconsin. Brian could not understand his anger toward her. He wanted to tell her about the album tonight. Brian called her in Lake Geneva. There was no answer; he was suddenly angry with her again. Brian went to the kitchen, fixed a drink, and doubled his Amitriptyline dosage. He walked back to the couch, looked at the pictures again, and fell asleep.

Tomorrow was the first day of vacation, and Brian planned to leave for Stamford Bridge in the morning. The Parsonage Bed & Breakfast brochure had fallen to the floor.

Chapter 7

Brian was up early and ran through his Chicago neighborhood. He went back to his apartment, took a shower, dressed and packed bags and sports gear in the trunk of his red Camaro. The photo album was on the back seat.

Charmon was not there. *Maybe it was all over,* he thought. All he was certain of this morning was that he had once been close with Charmon, and that he had probably lost her for good. He had sent her away to Wisconsin. That much was certain. He might never see her again, and it was his fault. It was probably over, finished. He would go to Michigan alone.

Brian made his way through Chicago traffic to highway I-94 and drove north where evergreens lined the highway and he could see Lake Michigan.

As Brian approached Benton Harbor, he saw a boy slowly riding a bicycle on a side road. Brian slowed almost to a stop and looked at the boy, and their eyes met. The boy was Asian, and something happened quickly. Brian's grip on the world disjoined in a blinding flash of artillery and the sound of helicopter gunships and screaming. Second Platoon, Bravo Company—a rifle company with six officers and under strength with 29 enlisted men, 1st Battalion, 7th Cavalry—was part of the first American battle group shuttled in by Huey into Landing Zone X-Ray, in the Ia Drang Valley on November 16th, 1965. X-Ray was a red dirt area about the size of a football field. It was next to a clump of trees, within eyesight of tall, thick elephant grass, anthills, and the jungle. Bravo Company was to secure X-Ray and establish a protective zone for a battalion command post in the Ia Drang. The commanding officer's instructions were simple—"Body count, gentlemen."

The nightmare of mayhem and killing for the outnumbered Americans began. Corporal Cahill, attached to 2nd Platoon, carried an M-16 rifle, two hand grenades and as much ammunition as he could handle. Others soldiers carried M-16s, M-79 grenade launchers, rocket launchers, 81mm mortars and M-60 machine guns. 2nd Platoon, one of four Bravo Company platoons, was commanded by 2nd Lieutenant Harry G. Williams–2nd Platoon was ordered to make immediate contact with the enemy, and they raced through the elephant grass and across a dry creek bed and came under enemy fire right away. First Platoon also came under fire as the battle spread and the Americans took casualties. Major Jack Emerson, company commander, called for artillery and air support. Emerson then directed 2nd Platoon to move to the right of their current position, up a slope, and set up machine guns to relieve pressure on 1st Platoon. The order changed quickly; 2nd Platoon was ordered to move 50 yards farther to the right of 1st Platoon. Williams quickly reported that he was pursuing a sighted group of North Vietnamese Army regulars. Emerson told Williams to not get cut off from the rest of Bravo Company; the major then ordered 3rd Platoon to provide firepower for 1st Platoon, which was pinned down.

Second Platoon searched for the NVA regulars, then in retreat. The rapid pursuit of the enemy at this point was a serious mistake, since the platoon quickly lost physical contact with Bravo Company, but they continued ahead at a fast pace anyway. In a few minutes, the platoon collided with a group of about 50 NVA soldiers, and a savage firefight started, as both sides opened up. Corporal Cahill and others hit the dirt and began firing M-16s; some fired with two magazines taped together. Other elements of 2nd Platoon, led by Sergeant Selby, circled behind the NVA soldiers and wiped them out. That skirmish was over. Then another group of about 25 NVA soldiers came out of the trees, and another firefight erupted. Brian stayed in a prone position and fired his M-16 for full effect, targeting each enemy he saw. Americans pumped grenades into the ranks of the NVA regulars, and it was over in half an hour; both sides had taken heavy casualties.

Brian and the rest of 2nd Platoon reloaded their weapons and helped the remaining medic care for the wounded. The first medic was dead. Many soldiers were injured and screaming in pain. The platoon's supply of morphine, medical dressings, and water was almost exhausted, and they were surrounded.

After a stillness of about ten minutes, all hell broke loose. Screaming NVA regulars charged out of the jungle at 2nd Platoon. A series of wild, confusing, moving firefights followed that cost the platoon its officers, several sergeants, a machine gunner, a weapon assistant gunner, another medic, a radioman, an artillery recon sergeant and a M-79 grenadier. Those still alive and many of the wounded kept firing. It was hard to spot NVA regulars in brown uniforms and hats in the brown grass. Continuous fire support, called in by Sergeant Selby, came from helicopter gunships firing 2.75-inch rockets, fighter bombers dropping 250-pound bombs, napalm, and heavy fire from 105 howitzers. The noise of battle, the confusion, the dust, the screaming, the sounds of weapons, the wild disorder, the artillery fire, and bombing made it impossible to be heard. The Americans could only communicate to each other by hand signals. With all officers killed, the platoon was under the command of Sergeant Selby. Efforts by other elements of Bravo Company to rescue them were met by heavy gunfire and the Americans had to turn back.

By 2:45 p.m., Brian and the rest of 2nd Platoon were exhausted. There was no water or medical supplies. The heat, the battle, the prolonged terror, the volume of noise and screaming had worn them down. The battlefield was quickly silent. Brian and the others collected ammunition, grenades, and weapons from their dead. Another medic, although hit twice, made it to the small American enclave. He worked with what medical supplies he was able to carry.

By the middle of the afternoon, ten of 2nd Platoon's 29 enlisted men had been killed, and nine were wounded. Brian thought they could not possibly hold out much longer. After a lapse of ten minutes, the firestorm started again, with the enemy coming at the tiny group of Americans from three directions. Brian remembered screaming at the enemy as the attack began: "C'mon, you slant-eye bastards. We're still here. You want some of this? Let's get it on, you yellow, chicken-shit bastards. Let's do it, you miserable sons a bitches!"

Then the Americans still able to fight opened up with everything they had. Sergeant Selby called in a tornado of artillery fire on top of the American position, and the noise was deafening. The NVA attack was cut to pieces. Brian, shaking after the attack, was still holding his M-16 and fired into enemy soldiers already dead. He was practically hysterical with rage. Brian's physical courage had almost deserted him, and he fell to his knees in exhaustion.

A trucker's air-horn warned him away from hitting the center median guardrail on Highway I-94. Brian almost hit it, then pulled his fast moving car across the inside lane in front of the oncoming truck. The truck's air brakes screeched as the semi narrowly missed Brian's Camaro. Brian crossed over two more lanes of traffic to his right and missed a collision with a pick-up truck by inches. He made it to the shoulder and skidded to a stop.

His heart was pounding. Both hands, shaking, gripped the steering wheel, and sweat was pouring down his face. Brian looked in the rearview mirror as a highway patrol squad car pulled in behind him. The trooper got out and walked to the Camaro's left front door. Brian put the window down.

"I want to see your driver's license and proof of registration," the officer said.

Brian blinked. He nodded and pulled items from his billfold, and they fell to the ground. The officer reached down and picked them up.

"Step out of the car, please."

Brian got out. He and the officer circled around behind the squad car and stood facing the ravine on an incline down from the shoulder, away from the highway.

"You want to tell me what went on back there?"

"I don't–I don't–I don't think I know. I think–I think it was flashback. Jesus Christ, it was a flashback," Brian replied. His face was ashen.

"All right now," the officer said. "You're upset. Let's take it slow. We're going to talk, and we're going to find out what the hell happened. Can you hear me?"

Brian nodded.

"Okay, now. You're saying flashback. There could have been people killed, including yourself. It was a flashback? Is that what you're telling me?"

'Yes, yes, yes, sir, that's right sir."

"Drinking?"

"No, no, no, sir."

"Drugs?"

"Hell, no!"

"Do I need to call in another officer? Do I have permission to search your car?"

"Whatever."

"Let's not be a smart-ass!"

"No, go ahead. It's okay."

"Okay, let's take it easy. Now, step back. That's it. Thank you. Now, take it easy. I want you to do something for me. Okay, now, step back a little. That's it. Now, keep your eyes on my fingers as they move from left to right. Very good, and now from right to left. Good, thank you."

Brian did as he was told.

"Okay, good. Now, hold both arms out straight on both sides, level with your shoulders. Now, bring your right hand, with your left arm still extended, over and touch your nose with your right index finger. Good, that's fine. Now, bring your left hand over and touch your nose with your left index finger."

Brian did as he was told.

"Thank you. Good. Okay, now, let's keep taking it easy. I'm here to help you. You do realize what almost happened here today?"

Brian nodded. He folded his arms and he paced back and forth. The officer said, "People could have been killed here today. It would've been your fault. Talk to me."

"It's another damn flashback. That son of bitch gook kid did it! That little bastard. I blacked out!"

"Flashbacks, blackouts, gook kid–what gook kid? What are you talking about?" the officer said.

Brian said nothing.

"That's a 1st Cav patch on your jacket. Nam?"

"Yes, sir!"

"When?"

"Sixty-five through, '67."

"Two tours?"

"I was one of those bastards dumb enough to stick around."

"A death wish, hazardous duty pay, or just gung-ho?"

"Don't know."

"Okay."

WHY DID I GROW SO COLD?

"You in Nam?" Brian asked.

"I was there, but I had a job in the rear. I was in the motor pool in Da Nang in '65. I got lucky. One night Charlie hit us with some rockets, and we all freaked. A lot of us were new boots in country. Then a few more times that year, but nothing to write home about. We were quite a way from the bush."

"I was in the Ia Drang Valley in '65," Brian said.

"In the Central Highlands?" the officer asked.

"Right."

"You were in 1st Cav, then! Jesus! I read about that. A guy I knew was there, and he never came back."

Brian nodded.

"Jesus, we heard about it at Da Nang. You guys really wasted Charlie there. I'll be damned, you were in the Ia Drang Valley! I've never known anyone who survived that shit."

"It was more NVA than Charlie. I was there at X-Ray on the first day. They screwed up our platoon. The NVA guys thought they were tough. They shot our wounded. That really pissed me off. We started out in 2nd Platoon with 29 enlisted men, plus officers. God, in a couple of hours, the officers were all dead. Jesus Christ, only eight of us were left. The artillery saved us. It was unbelievable. The noise was deafening. God, the flash was blinding. The death smell was everywhere. The smoke cleared, and somebody yelled, 'We're still here, you slope bastards.'"

"How'd you keep your sanity?"

"I try to hang in there. I lost some hearing on my right side. Shrapnel did a number on one of my legs and on my right side. It's hard keeping my head screwed on right. How'd you adjust when you got back to the world?"

"Easier than you, I'm sure."

"Nam freaked me out, but there was a brighter note to all of this, if you can call it that."

"Really?" the officer asked.

"I made some money from two tours and went to college on Uncle Sam, and hazardous duty pay from two tours came in handy. One of my officers said he thought I could be a college boy. I thought he was blowin' smoke, but I guess he meant it. I had a free ride through college. After all the insane rehab and red tape and all the crap, they finally helped me and they owed it to me. After all, the whole damned war was for nothing. Most of the people on staff at the VA hospital in Chicago hired to deal with us grunts didn't know a thing and couldn't have cared less. I mean, we're talking about people who were supposed to help us. Hell, they didn't know a son of a bitching thing about Nam. Shit, they just kept talking about World War II. It was very different. So, what did they know, anyway? I was pretty well torn up when I got back here. Jesus, God, some sons of bitches were asking us about killing kids! Welcome home, losers. Many guys I knew over there never came back. I have no idea why I wasn't killed. God, if you believe in that stuff, must have had other plans for me."

"What happened today?"

"I told you, a goddamn blackout."

"What the hell happens; what's it like?"

"I was on the highway, and then, bam, I was back in the bush. The other side of the world. I was outside of myself, watching some kind of weird mirror images of what happened over there flash like some screw up photo images in my mind. Those little yellow bastards were all around me. A VA therapist said my system of self-preservation is in a constant maximum alert status, expecting Nam and the terror to return."

Brian seemed like a decent guy who could explode if pushed. Officer Adams knew that he himself could have been in the Ia Drang.

"You understand what happened today?"

"I do," Brian replied.

"You were damn near killed."

"I know."

"You can't let whatever it was that set you off today happen again."

"I'll be okay now."

"There's color back in your face, shaking's gone. What brings you to Michigan from Chicago?"

"I'm on vacation."

"Good for you. Where're you headed?"

"Stamford Bridge."

"A great place, it's only about 15 miles ahead. You have reservations?"

"The Parsonage Bed & Breakfast."

"Looks like a good place. Two things to do. First, have dinner at The

Promontory Inn. It's expensive, but the food is great. Also, go to the Saturday night party. It's at the hotel. You'll probably meet some people and relax. You might look up a couple of friends of mine. Pen Meacham owns The Promontory Inn, and the police chief is Henry Plunkett. Pen and Henry are good friends. I get up there and have lunch with those guys every now and then. Tell them C.J. Adams said hello. I might even be there tonight."

The officer pulled out a scratch pad, wrote down a telephone number, and handed the paper to Brian. "One more thing. I live in Three Oaks, not far from Chicago. You're carrying a lot of grief. I was in Nam also, but I was in the rear, while you were humpin' the boonies. If you need to talk, let me know. Today never happened, but I'm worried about you. Take care of yourself. Get some R&R on vacation. Call me if you think I can help. You might want to talk on the phone, or whatever," the officer said.

Chapter 8

The wind picked up sharply and waves hit the breakwater and sent spray in the air. A row of birch trees ran from the hotel front porch down to the water. Poplars along the water's edge were bending with the wind. From the hotel back door, Pen Meacham saw Charlie Putnam at the breakwater. A small cement mixer was turning, surrounded by bags of cement and a pile of stones and a wheelbarrow turned on it's side.

"How we doin' tuday, Mr. Pen?"

Charlie Putnam, 67, a large, well-built man with short white hair and ruddy face, wore tan coveralls, a t-shirt, work boots, and a baseball cap. He was born in the Deep South and, with a sixth-grade education, spent 45 years working on Great Lakes iron ore shipping barges. Over the years, Charlie had seen Stamford Bridge from a distance off-shore. Four years ago, while docked in Charlevoix, Charlie left for Stamford Bridge. He took a bus to Ludgate Hill and then, with a knapsack, walked the rest of the way to Stamford Bridge.

"I'm doing fine, Charlie. I got the cigars you like. Here's a couple."

"Thanks, Mr. Pen. Them's my favorite, the shorter they git the better they taste."

"How bad's the breakwater?"

"Plannin' to fall apart at some point, I reckon."

"Good Lord, do you really think so?'

"Yessir, I do."

"Why do you say that?"

"Look at them loose stones. Lots of 'em all along the wall."

Pen walked close to the wall and got down on his hands and knees.

"Good God, I see what you're saying. Is the damage just at this spot?"

"No sir. I knowd them stones was loose the whole way. Looked at all of it."

"How long do you think it's been this way?"

"Don't know. Gradual thing, I bet. See where the wall's pullin' out from the earth, like it's fixin' ta fall down, startin' ta crack in places?"

Pen stood up, brushed off his hands, and walked to the end of the breakwater, then walked back. "It looks like it's almost ready to go! How did you notice that?"

"I's cuttin' the grass, an' seen a stone fell loose. Then I seen the wall pullin' away, like it wuz gittin' ready ta fall down in the water or somethin,' cracked in places."

"Jesus H. Christ, I see the damage. So, what do we do now?"

"Been thinkin' about it."

"Okay."

"It's weak. I'm thinkin' it needs lotsa work. More'n I can do. Water's heavy against the wall. Worse'n I thought."

"What've you done today?"

"Jest a band-aid. Cemented some a them stones back. Tried ta fix some a them cracks. Don't know if it'l do any good."

"God, there's always some insane problem or another. It's always something. There's an engineering firm in South Haven that I think does this kind of work. I'll see if they can come up on Monday and take a look at the wall. It'll cost a fortune, but if the breakwater collapses, we'll lose the hotel's front yard. Christ almighty, one damn problem after another."

"Mr. Pen, I wouldn't wait any longer. That's fer sure."

"I'll get on it Monday. Charlie, we've got work to get ready for tonight. Have you done everything you can do here today?"

"Done. I'll git this stuff up to da shack."

"I'll go with you."

"Okey. By the way, Mr. Pen, got a minute?"

"Sure, about the breakwater?"

"Somthin' else."

"Sure, Charlie. What's up?"

"Jest somthin,' none a my business."

"You and I've always been honest with each other, what's up?"

"It's Ida Mae."

"Ida Mae?"

"Workin' too hard."

"She's a very hard worker. Has she said something?"

"No, but a person can tell. Them Saturday night deals are killin' her, ta be honest, Mr. Pen, they're killin' all of us, but especially her. Work durin' the week and then Saturday, 18-hour day for her. Then, come Sunday, all over agin. No time ta rest."

"My God, is she thinking about quitting?"

"She'd never leave you, Mr. Pen."

"Charlie, are you unhappy?"

"I ain't never goin' to leave either, but you're workin' us too hard. Some a them busboys and kitchen help left already."

"Anyone else unhappy?"

"Don't know. Probably. If things don't slow down, might jest have Ida Mae and me workin' here. Them Saturday nights are killin' us. Maybe once a month or somethin' else."

Pen said nothing and lit a cigar. The wheelbarrow was filled with sacks of cement. It was heavy. Some loose stones were left at the wall. Charlie pulled the handles up and pushed the wheelbarrow up the hill to the maintenance shack. Pen walked with Charlie and pulled the mixer up the hill. They put the mixer and the wheelbarrow on the shack's front porch.

"Didn't mean to upset you or nuthin,' Mr. Pen."

"Not a problem, Charlie. God, I'm glad you said something. If you and Ida Mae are unhappy, I want to know. I could not run this place without the both of you. You've been here since day one. I depend on you guys. I guess I've been expecting too much out of everybody. Let's you and me and Ida Mae get together on Monday and make some changes. I can't risk having you guys unhappy."

"Sounds good ta me."

Both men turned and walked toward the hotel, without knowing that tonight's party would be the last.

Chapter 9

Charmon knew that Brian's grip on the real world was tenuous. She recently heard terror in his voice and horrible profanity; it was a voice in the night that was not his. Charmon was now almost certain that he had killed women and children, and she saw him speaking with the dark at the foot of the bed. Brian had apparently killed an American–terribly called friendly fire–but he pretended it didn't happen. There had almost certainly been atrocities. Brian had heard and seen things. He talked in the night about red and green tracer flares and smoke trails in the darkness.

The Blue Arrow Bar & Grill, a small one-story brick building with red shutters, was close to the main highway. Brian turned off at the exit ramp, turned to his left, and went down a narrow gravel side road, and a trail of dust followed him. A driftwood fence was next to the Blue Arrow's red front door and a rose garden was between a small parking lot and the building. From the front steps, Brian looked out across the rows of birch trees near the lake. The wind was coming straight south from Canada.

Inside, the bar was dark and small and there was a scent of Clorox and furniture polish. The floor had been scrubbed, and chairs sat upside down on tabletops. Ashtrays were stacked on a table near the coffee maker, and white trash bags were near the back door. Glasses and mugs, washed and ready to use, were in rows next to bottles of liquor and wine along the back wall. A freezer behind the bar made a humming sound. The empty bandstand and dance floor were almost in darkness, and hangovers from years past were probably long since forgotten. Today, there were no customers. Brian sat at the end of the bar. The first whiskey and water went down quickly. The bartender, a large man with a round bearded face, had a white apron tied around his waist. After the dishes were finished, he wiped his hands dry on the apron. He lit a cigarette.

"Another?" he asked.

Brian nodded, and the bartender filled another tumbler with whiskey, water and ice and set the drink on a white coaster in front of Brian.

"Thanks."

"You bet."

Brian was quiet.

"On vacation?" the bartender asked.

"I think so," Brian replied.

"You don't sound very sure."

"Never had one before."

"That's a hell of a note, always workin'?"

"That's pretty much it, working, Army, working, school, working."

"First time for everything. You're like the rest of us; too damn busy makin' a livin' to have a life."

"I guess so."

"Workin' all the time sucks. Life's too damn short anyway. Here's me, workin' my ass off seven days a week. Workin' all the time. No time for the woman, so she split on me."

"Sorry to hear that."

"It's okay. She's history, screw her. You from around here?"

"I live in Chicago."

"Big city! I have been there a few times. Too big for me. I'll stay up here. We get a lot of Chicago people up here in the summer. Too much money, but boy do they spend it. Keeps me in clover. You work downtown in Chicago?"

"Close to it, on the north side. I work for an accounting firm."

"Sounds heavy."

"Not really. It's easier than it sounds. I push numbers around all day."

"Where you goin' on vacation?"

"Stamford Bridge."

"Good choice."

"That's what I hear."

"You got reservations?"

"Yep."

"Good, you'll need 'em this time of year. It is a popular place in the summer. Where you gonna stay?"

Brian took a reservation slip from his pocket and read it, "Parsonage Bed & Breakfast."

"Expensive?"

"Not really."

"They tell me that a big shot ad man from Detroit has redone that big hotel up there. I guess it's really nice. I'll get up there one of these days and see it. Guy's name is Meacham."

"I heard about him earlier today."

"For a guy on vacation, you sure seem worried. Gotta lighten up."

"I'm looking for R&R."

"Woman problems?"

"Among other things."

"Vietnam?"

"Yeah."

"Saw action?"

"Plenty."

"Jesus! I'll bet you're glad that shit's over with."

"I sure as hell am and I don't like some bastards talking about me, you know, loser, wacko, baby killer. Christ, sometimes I could just..."

"Don't stress on me."

"Comes and goes."

"Time to put it behind you."

"That's cool."

"My cousin was there, but he never..."

"KIA?"

"Don't know."

"MIA?"

"Who in hell knows? That was nine years ago. Nobody knows squat. If you want my opinion, they don't know shit, and the bastards in the Army couldn't give a damn and never did. Back then they gave us some garbage that he was missin' in action. Last word we got was that he was on patrol, and his unit was overrun. There was a firefight. After the smoke cleared, he was declared MIA. Family kept checkin' on him year after year, but always got the run around. Checked everywhere–the Army, Red Cross, VFW, vet groups, and whatever. Nine years and nothin.'"

"I'm sorry."

"We weren't really all that close. He grew up in the UP."

"UP?"

"You know, the Upper Peninsula, up north."

"Oh, okay."

"But still, he was my cousin. We went up there a few years ago for a memorial service. No casket, no cemetery. Just a picture of him in the church with some flowers. People from his hometown, Cold Harbor, came to the service. The minister said that Jack–that was my cousin's name–had the Lord lookin' after him. If the Lord was lookin' after him, he wouldn't be gone, now would he? That was pure crap. The whole thing was sad. Some people started to cry, others just shook their heads. There was nothing there. Only a picture. He was a good guy. Then he was gone, vanished, bingo, gone. Just plain gone to nowhere. No grave site, no nothing. See what I'm sayin'? It's like he never existed. Zero. It tore my aunt and uncle to pieces. Ruined their lives. For a long time, they held out hope. But they woke up one day and figured it was all over. It was too much for 'em. Jack wasn't coming home, not even to get buried. They got a divorce. Jeez, God, and nobody gives a shit."

The door opened and a large man in coveralls came in and sat at the other end of the bar.

"Hold on a minute. I'll be right back," the bartender said. "He's a regular, draft and pretzels."

The bartender walked to the other end of the bar and put a large glass of beer and a bowl of pretzels on the counter in front of the large man. The man thanked him, sipped the beer, and then put a pretzel in his mouth. Brian walked to the back hall to a pay phone and called Charmon in Lake Geneva. He called twice, but there was no answer. He went back to the bar and sat down again. The bartender came back. He was carrying a glass of ice water and holding a cigarette.

"Another?" the bartender asked

"No thanks."

"Here's a menu, if you're hungry."

"No thanks, I've got to get on my way, but I was thinking about your cousin. I know what you're talking about. Nobody gives a damn! You hear all kinds of stuff that's supposed to make you feel better. It doesn't. As you said, if the Lord was looking out for your cousin, your cousin would be home, all in one piece."

"That's right. Nobody was lookin' out for him. The Lord musta' been watchin' a football game, because He sure as hell wasn't lookin' out for my cousin or anyone. The minister made it all up. Hell, I knew it was absolute garbage. The guy just made it up to try to make us feel better," the bartender said as he wiped the counter clean with a small white towel.

"The guy was trying to cover up for whoever or whatever he thought God is or was," Brian said.

"He was in a hell of a fix. Tryin' to make us feel good. He had no idea why in hell God didn't protect my cousin or why He doesn't protect anybody like He's supposed to," the bartender said.

"The minister's a phoney," Brian said

"Probably so," the bartender replied.

"So, he didn't cover up for God at all did he?" Brian asked

"I guess not," the bartender answered

"So who's phoney, the minister or God?" Brian asked and he sipped his drink

"Half the time it seems like nobody's in charge," the bartender said.

"That's because nobody's in charge."

"Is that what you think? Nobody?"

"The idea that God exists is a phoney idea, just like the minister's a phoney himself. Nobody's looking out for any of us. Period."

"You're an atheist?"

"That's right, but you've got doubts yourself about the whole idea or you wouldn't have said the Lord was watching a football game when your cousin was in Nam."

"Oh, hell yes! I've got a lot of doubts. Everybody does, but I think somebody's got to be in charge. Don't you think so?"

"No."

"Who made the world?"

"Whoever or whatever made the world left for good. It's just us here. That's all."

"You're really an atheist?"

"Yes."

"How do you, you know, have a philosophy of life or somethin'?"

"We're all here alone in the universe. You, me, and all of us are all responsible only to ourselves for what we do. God's not there to judge us. He's never been there. There's no standard of right and wrong or good and bad. Life's totally absurd, and one life's as good as another. The whole thing's absurd, without meaning."

The bartender said nothing.

"It's life. If there's a God out there, He can strike me dead right now. I've killed people in my life, because my government told me to do it. I could kill again if I had to. There is nothing except society to say it's right or wrong. Your life, my life and everybody's lives are totally senseless."

The bartender was still quiet.

"Say you've got two guys sitting in foxholes next to each other," Brian said.

"Okay."

"Say one guy prays all the time and reads the Bible. The other guy tells dirty jokes and has never prayed or read the Bible in his life. Now I ask you, who's going to get zapped?"

"Don't know."

"Right, you don't know. The guy praying all the time is wasting his time, because nobody's listening. This is it. Take it or leave it, there's nothing more. We make our own hell. I've seen good guys killed and bastards skate by. Children starve while the worst sons of bitches have full stomachs. Your cousin did nothing to deserve whatever happened to him. Life's not fair. There's no reason to it."

A group came through the door and sat down at a table near the front door. The bartender picked up menus from the counter.

"I'd like to keep talkin' with you, but, I've got the lunch crowd. Want coffee or somethin'?"

"No thanks."

"Okay, play it cool."

"Thanks."

Brian left the bar and continued toward Stamford Bridge. The Blue Arrow vanished in his rearview mirror. The highway passed by South Haven and curved west near the shoreline. Cottages were set back far from the water. Brian saw fishermen with lines in the water sitting on an old wooden pier. At a point north of South Haven, several docks jutted out into the water; sailboats were moored there. A small marina was nearby, and a workman was out front, sanding a hull. The sailmaker's shop was across a narrow street.

The war had no end. The picture album with no explanation unsettled him. He slept badly; Ruth Cahill was in and out of focus. Where has she been all these years, he wondered. Brian saw a figure in shadow–a man, a blurred image.

Brian thought there might be something he was looking for in Stamford Bridge.

Chapter 10

Shannon stopped in Maple Hill at the Cookie Jar Café, a small, cream-colored, one-story building, round and shaped like a cookie jar. The brown round roof looked like the lid of a cookie jar and the shutters and front door were also brown.

Shannon was the only customer, and she picked a table across from the front door. The restaurant was old. Tables with white Formica tops and metal chairs with red plastic cushions were relics from the fifties. The menu had a worn plastic cover. Cream-colored walls were covered with soft drink posters. An old jukebox in the corner near the unused bar, had probably not been used in years. Shannon heard a door open and shut and a waitress dressed in light blue approached her table.

"Hi there! Decided what you'd like? "The kindly, older waitress asked Shannon.

"I saw your billboard a few miles back, and it says to stop at the Cookie Jar Café in Maple Hill. So here I am," Shannon said.

"Well good, glad you stopped by. What can I get for you today?"

"Your billboard says you have the best cherry pie a la mode in the world. Is that true?"

The waitress smiled. "Yes, ma'am, you bet. What's more, we've got the best apple, blueberry and peach pie a la mode in the world. We make 'em from scratch."

"Wow! Sounds delicious! How can I choose what to order?" Shannon smiled and scanned the menu.

"I can come back if you'd like more time."

WHY DID I GROW SO COLD?

"No, I think I'm set. Well, okay," she said to the waitress. "I'm on vacation, so I'll have the works. A plain cheeseburger, fries, a cherry Coke and cherry pie a la mode."

The waitress filled out the ticket, turned and walked back to the kitchen and gave the order to her husband, the cook. She returned with a cherry Coke and set it on the table in front of Shannon.

"So, you're starting on a vacation?" the waitress asked.

"That's right," Shannon replied. "It's been a couple of long years. I'm ready to unwind."

"Going someplace in the state, or are you just passing through?"

"I'm going to Stamford Bridge for a week. I've lived in Michigan for ten years, but I've never been there."

"Really! Oh, that's a wonderful place. Ralph and I spent a week in Stamford Bridge last month. We love it there."

"Really, how exciting. What's it like?"

"It's a little town that overlooks Lake Michigan. It's about as close to the big lake as you can get, without being in the water."

"Yes."

"It's kinda, I guess you'd say, a charming, sleepy little town with huge old trees and narrow brick streets. There's a lot of what I think you'd call, you know, traditional type older homes, mainly big ones, but some smaller ones too, usually clapboard type with wood shutters. Real attractive and well-preserved. Lawns look very nice. Flower boxes seem to be everywhere. There's a lot of shopping and lots of places to eat. There aren't billboards or fast food restaurants in the town. Aren't allowed. Signs on restaurants and stores are pretty much all the same. Nothing loud or splashy. More like shingle signs. The stores up and down Campbell Street, that's the main street, are all painted in light colors."

"Sounds attractive," Shannon said.

"It is. The whole town's kinda spit and polish. Great places to relax go for walks and have a good time. Lot of artists live there in the summer."

"That's what I heard."

"A lot of 'em have little studios tucked away in nooks and crannies, you might say; most live in their studios. A lot of what you'd call finished works or pictures are displayed for sale evenings right there on Campbell Street.

We bought a couple of watercolor pictures. Prices seemed reasonable. There's one of the pictures we bought," the waitress said, pointing to the south wall of the restaurant, "right there on the wall."

"I noticed it earlier. It's very attractive. Was it terribly expensive?" Shannon asked.

"It ran us $45, which we thought was a good price."

"Oh, I'd say you made a great buy. It's very attractive and very unusual. I like it!"

"You might want to look the guy up, his name's Errol, just Errol. Don't really know if he has a last name. You'll find him down on Campbell Street in the evenings. Do you like music?"

"All kinds."

"I thought so. Classical?"

"Yes, classical."

"Most evenings, when the weather's good, you'll find a few musicians playing outside on Campbell Street, down near the hotel. Most are students from the Amesbury Summer Music Camp."

"I've heard about Amesbury. It's one of the places I want to see. The best musicians and scholars. They have concerts by the water. Isn't that right?"

"You're right. Sunday evenings, right on the beach. I almost forgot to ask, where are you going to be staying?"

"The Chestnut Brook Bed & Breakfast"

"Oh, good choice! A wonderful place! On Canterbury Lane! Reminds me of older homes Ralph and I saw in Massachusetts."

"I am looking forward to it. Tell me something else. What about the main hotel? I understand it overlooks the lake?" Shannon asked.

"That's The Promontory Inn, at the end of Campbell Street. You'll see it when you're driving in. My husband and I went there for dinner. The owners, Penfield and Geraldine Meacham, live in the hotel and they seem like grand people."

"I take it that you and your husband have not stayed at The Promontory Inn?" Shannon asked.

"That's right. The hotel's pretty expensive. But, as I said, we had dinner there. Ralph and I stayed at The Parsonage Bed & Breakfast on Runnymede

Court. We like it there. Well, there's the bell, your lunch is ready. I'll get it for you."

The waitress walked back to the kitchen and returned with Shannon's lunch. "I'm going to shut up and let you eat your lunch."

"Thanks, you've been very helpful," Shannon replied, "and lunch looks delicious. Thanks for telling me about the town."

"That's fine. Enjoy your lunch. You seem like a nice person. I want you to have a good time on your vacation."

"Thanks."

Shannon ate lunch slowly. The cherry Coke was followed by a second. She placed a bookmark in *The Stranger*. When finished, Shannon got up from the table, left a tip, paid the bill, and thanked the waitress.

"Well, you're welcome. Say, you might want to know," the waitress said, "about the Saturday night parties at the hotel. They're a lot of fun."

"Yes, tell me, I'd like to know. What goes on, anyhow?"

"Saturday nights the town sort of lets its hair down, you might say. The parties start at the hotel at about eight and last until, well, whenever, I guess. You don't want to miss the big party. I'll bet you're a hard worker, so I think it's time you had a good vacation. Your name is?"

"Shannon Fitsimmons."

"What a nice name, Shannon. Well my name is Edna and my husband is Ralph. Why don't you stop by and see us on your way back home? Pie and coffee on us. Maybe you'll try peach next time."

"Well, how very nice of you, I'd love to."

"Who knows? We might even see you at the party on Saturday if I can get Ralph to go."

Chapter 11

Brian approached Stamford Bridge in late afternoon. Large trees along the road made changing shades of light and dark. There was little traffic. Three men were working along the road, replacing broken curbs, and laying cement.

The road curved to his right, and Brian came to the crest of a hill and saw the lake and Stamford Bridge unfold before him like a color illustration–the beach, downtown, the hotel, brick streets, cottages and houses were set among evergreens and shade trees. There were high beige-colored sand dunes off to the north, and he continued down the hill to a sand-covered street next to the beach. Brian stopped, got out of his car, and sat down at a picnic table. He looked at the water, clear and shallow near the beach and blue like the sky. The sun felt good on his face. A boat was anchored off shore, and a few people on board were having drinks. On the north shore a party barge, loaded with people, left White Hall Marina.

Brian soon left the picnic table, got back into his car and continued on down the sandy road past the White Sands Boarding House, almost hidden from view by trees.

He stopped near the top of a large breakwater, saw a group of small, white, square wooden buildings near the water–each about three times the size of a double-car garage, and all recently painted. A narrow stone walkway led to a sign near a larger building identified as the Amesbury Summer Music Camp administration building.

Brian continued on the sandy road until he came to Runnymede Street. He turned east and came to a single-lane brick street with older brick homes on both sides, adjoined, without side or front yards. He saw The Parsonage Bed & Breakfast at the end of the block.

The Parsonage looked like a New England Federal style house. It was a large, white, two-story place with clapboard front and rear façades, brick sides and shutters, and black doors. The grass was green and trimmed, and there were no evergreens or plantings.

Brian parked his car in front of a brick wall, went through a wooden gate, up a brick sidewalk and through the front door. The Parsonage lobby opened to the living room, library, and dining room. A French chair stood next to the entryway.

"You are my guest from Chicago?" the tall, thin, suntanned man said as he stood up and walked to the front desk.

"Yes, and I think I'm right on time," Brian replied.

"Yes you are right on time. It's Mr. Cahill isn't it?" the man said.

"Yes, I'm Brian Cahill."

"Welcome to Stamford Bridge and The Parsonage."

"Thank you; I'm glad to be here."

"My name is Michael Carter. I'm the owner of The Parsonage. I'm sure you will have a pleasant stay with us. Is this your first visit to our town?"

"Yes it is."

"How did you learn about Stamford Bridge?"

"I saw a Stamford Bridge ad in a travel guide somewhere. Also, a couple of my friends have been here. They went on and on about your town. As I remember, my friends walked by The Parsonage. They said it looked impressive. They were right."

"Thank you."

"Are you a native?" Brian asked.

"Actually, I am not. My wife and I grew up in St. Louis. I was a labor lawyer with a large firm in the city. I came to a point, after 30 years, where I simply got sick of the rat race. I wanted to do something different. Fortunately, I worked for several large clients and was able to put some money away. My wife was an RN, and she had been able to save. So, one day, we decided to figure out what we wanted to do with the rest of our lives. I was 60 and my wife was 62. We had no children. We had always enjoyed traveling near the Great Lakes. We came, sort of by accident, to Stamford

Bridge on one of our travels and stayed at The Promontory Inn."

"That's the hotel on Campbell Street, near the water?" Brian asked.

"Yes, that's right," Michael said. "Well, anyway, to make a long story short, we had dinner with Pen Meacham and his wife, Geraldine, at The Promontory Inn. They had done, we found out, what my wife and I wanted to do. They told us about The Parsonage, this building, which was really a big family home and Pen told us it was for sale. Interestingly enough, it was empty. My wife and I went through the building the next day and we decided to make the move. We sold our house in St. Louis. I retired from the law firm and my wife ended her employment at Pediatric Hospital. It took us two years to get the place into the shape that you see today."

"That was a gutsy move. I'm sure the effort's been rewarding. This is a fabulous place. Do I understand that you and your wife manage and run The Parsonage?" Brian asked.

"My wife, Lauren, died from cancer three years ago," Michael said.

"I'm sorry," Brian said.

"Thank you. I've decided to stay on here, at least for the next few years, and run the place myself. It's been lonely, and sometimes the nights are long. The winters are cold and difficult, but I keep busy. I like the town better than I like the weather. I have friends here, including the Meachams, who keep me out of trouble," Michael said. "I have my off days and I've thought about going back to St. Louis, but I'm not sure anyone can ever go back. But, you never know. I'll see how things work out. That's enough about me. Lawyers talk too much, anyway. Let's talk about your vacation and your stay here. First, you need to register."

Brian filled out the registration form and handed it back to Mike.

"Thank you, Brian. Here is the key to your room. It's my largest room, on the ground floor. Just go back through the front door and follow the brick sidewalk to your left. Your room is the first one on the left, at the north side of the house. Also, here is our menu. Breakfast is from 6:30 to 9:30. Okay, I think we're all set. You've paid for a week in advance. Thank you for choosing The Parsonage. I'm here almost all the time, so let me know if you need anything to make your stay more comfortable. Can I help you with luggage or anything?"

"No, I can take care of it, thank you," Brian replied.

Chapter 12

There were evergreens along the parkway and small white cottages on the shore. A road came through the forest from the lake to the highway, and an old logging trail led to the hills. There were mailboxes and birch trees along the road. A line of birch trees ran from the road back to a shallow cove where the fishing was good. Shannon saw the tops of sand dunes, and the lake was just beyond them.

Since her mother's death five years ago, Shannon had been alone in a way she had never been alone before. The telephone call long ago from her cousin, Whitney, came through at night. Shannon was asleep.

"Shanny, this's Whitney," her cousin said.

"Hey, Whitney! Hey, what time is it? This's a surprise. What's going on?"

"I wish this was a fun call, but it's not. Shanny, your mom's gotten sick, but we think she's going to be okay."

"Good heavens! What's the matter? I just talked to her on Saturday, the day before Easter. She seemed fine. Whits, tell me, what's the matter? Is she all right?

"She's all right now, but we had a bad scare."

"Whits, tell me exactly what happened."

"Okay, but let me say again, Shanny, we've been told she's going to be okay."

Shannon took the first available flight to Kansas City, where she rented a car and drove on to Wheatstone. She came to the hospital after visiting hours, and the halls were quiet. Shannon stopped at the nurse's station and asked about her mother, Ardith Fitsimmons. The floor nurse told Shannon that her mother seemed to be doing fine. Surgery had taken an hour and a half and there had been no complications. Family members had been in to see Mrs. Fitsimmons, and Father Hanrahan had looked in on her. The nurse told Shannon that the priest had left his card, and she could call him anytime. Shannon took the card, put it in her purse, and told the nurse that she wanted to stay through the night in her mother's room. The nurse said okay. There was a small couch in the room. The nurse gave her a blanket and a pillow.

There was a small light in her mother's hospital room and curtains were closed. Shannon saw her mother in bed asleep. Ardith looked at peace. She was sleeping on her side, with her back to the door, and blankets pulled up to her waist. Ardith's prayer book was on a table next to the lamp. There was a vase of flowers on the table. Shannon walked around the bed and put her hand on the side of Ardith's face. Her mother's eyes blinked open and Shannon saw a faint smile, then her mother went back to sleep. Shannon sat down on the couch and then remembered what Whitney had told her.

"Shanny, your mother came over to Garden City for Easter Sunday, went to Mass and then came over to Neva's for dinner. She seemed happy and was laughing a lot. She left at about 2:30 and was driving back to Wheatstone. She apparently had an attack of severe pain in her stomach and almost lost control on the highway. Thank God, a sheriff's deputy spotted her car weaving. He evidently flashed his red lights and pulled up behind her. She doesn't remember all of what happened, but she must have seen the red lights and stopped. By the time the deputy got to the car, she had collapsed in the front seat. The deputy told us she was incoherent. He knew she was in serious trouble and he radioed for assistance right away. I guess within a few minutes another patrol car, already in the area, was there. The deputy thought she was going into shock. He didn't think she could last until an ambulance got there. He radioed the emergency room at Wheatstone Memorial and told them he was with a woman who was in extreme distress and seemed to be going into shock. The deputy thought it was a heart problem. The emergency room physician said to bring her in as fast as possible. Then, the two deputies moved your mother to the back seat of the patrol car and wrapped her in a blanket. With one patrol car leading the way, they made it to the hospital in about 20 minutes. I don't know how they did it. It wasn't a heart problem. It was colon cancer. The emergency surgery lasted about an hour and a half.

By that time, we had made it to the hospital. The surgeon said he thought he had removed all of the cancer."

The surgeon at Wheatstone Memorial gave her mother another year of life. Medical science had no idea what to do when the cancer came back. At the end of that year, it was all over.

Shannon passed the city limits sign and came down Falmouth Lane where a lawn party was in progress at a corner house. Some people were playing lawn tennis; others were standing next to a portable bar, not far from the house. There were tables and chairs in place on the lawn. On Cotswold, a block away, she found a street facing Lake Michigan. There were Cape Cod style homes, with white clapboard siding and black or dark green shutters. A workman was on a ladder at the top floor of a large corner house painting shutters. There were youngsters on bicycles, and they waved as Shannon drove by. Some homes had white picket fences, gates, and white wooden lawn furniture. People were outside painting, repairing or working in gardens. An old man, on his hands and knees, looked up from his flower garden and waved as Shannon passed by. Shannon waved back.

At the intersection of Campbell Street and Canterbury Lane, Lake Michigan looked hazy in the distance. She turned south and came to The Chestnut Brook Bed & Breakfast–a New England saltbox. Grounds were simple, and white flowers bloomed next to the front porch. A stone sidewalk led across the yard to the front door.

Shannon stopped in front of the main building and went inside.

"I'm Shannon Fitsimmons from Saginaw, reservations for today at four?"

"Yes, Shannon, welcome to Chestnut Brook," the older, slightly overweight, woman said from behind the front desk. "I'm Polly Brooks. My husband and I are the owners. Is this your first visit to Stamford Bridge?"

"Yes, it is."

"Thank you so much for selecting Chestnut Brook. I hope you have a pleasant stay with us."

"I'm sure I will. Your place is so attractive. I feel as if I have walked into the past," Shannon said.

"People say that. This is a saltbox-type structure similar to a farmhouse in Massachusetts, south of Boston. That house was built in 1703. We've been there and saw the original Chestnut Brook on our first trip to New

England. It was love at first sight! We've looked at that original farmhouse and we have tried to replicate it as much as possible here in Michigan."

"Really? How very interesting," Shannon said

"You will be staying in the John and Abigail Adams room. My husband and I've tried to capture a different colonial ambiance for each room. I hope you will be comfortable in the Adams room."

"I'm sure I will," Shannon said.

"This place has sort of developed into the central focus of our lives. We love it. Enough of that. Most of our other guests have already gone to their rooms. Let me see one other thing. Oh yes, you've already paid for your week here in advance. So, let's see…oh, yes, I gave you your key, didn't I? To get to your room just go out the front door and turn to you right. It's the second door on the right. Do you need help with your bags?"

"No, I'll be fine. Thank you," Shannon replied.

Shannon went back to her car, took out her luggage, walked past a low stone wall, through a small gate, and came to her room.

Chapter 13

It was now after three. Pen Meacham and Dave Chester, a salesman for *Great Lakes Travel Companion,* were meeting in the hotel dining room. Ida Mae brought coffee from the kitchen, and Pen put two lumps of sugar in his. Dave Chester drank black coffee. There was no one else in the dining room, and they sat at a table near the large window. Chester watched as Pen signed a new contract for an increased advertising schedule in *Great Lakes Travel.*

"I appreciate this additional business, Pen. It's an excellent decision to reserve our back cover for the year. Your ads will reach our 60,000 subscribers every month. We'll waive color and special position costs," Chester said.

"Thanks, Dave, our ads look good. They've brought Detroit and Chicago people to town. The other merchants are happy. The hotel's business is up almost a third over last year and business is up all over town. If business was down, I'd sure as hell hear about it." Pen laughed.

"You and the association are promoting Stamford Bridge to the whole Great Lakes area. A smart move."

"We've spent the bucks, and it's been worth it so far, I'd say."

"You know what the rumor is about you around town?" Chester asked.

"God, I'd be afraid to know."

"If you want something done, tell Pen Meacham."

"I'm not sure that's at all true."

"There wouldn't be an association without you."

"I guess that's true. It took a long time getting them to advertise."

The salesman, a tall man with a full head of hair, had just made the biggest sale of his career. Pen Meacham and the Stamford Bridge merchants' association made it possible. Pen knew how to negotiate a contract.

"Pen, how long has it been since you left Detroit?" Chester asked

"A little over four years. God, it doesn't seem possible," Pen said.

"Do you miss Detroit?"

"Not at all, we haven't been back since '71."

"Do you miss the agency business?"

"Hell no! I wouldn't go through that nightmare again."

"Obviously, the hotel business agrees with you."

"It's been good, but there've been rough spots. When we bought the hotel and moved over here, we didn't have the faintest idea what we were doing. We made every mistake in the book. Managing a hotel turned out to be a hell of a lot more difficult than we imagined. We paid too damn much for the building. It was in far worse shape than we originally thought, and our lawyer said there was no way to back out. We were royally screwed, but we should have known better. The first year we lost money. The building was a tinderbox. We had to replace the roof, the wiring, and the plumbing right away. The kitchen hadn't been used in years. We had to remodel it from top to bottom and put in new appliances. All the guestrooms were empty. So, we had to replace all the upstairs furniture, plus every room and bathroom had to be refinished. The lawn had been abandoned years ago, so you now see all new landscaping. We added the pool a couple of years ago. The dining room, living room, bar and the other main floor rooms were all in good shape, and we just refinished the floors. There was a huge storage room off the first floor's long hallway that we've converted to an art gallery. The outside was painted the first summer we were here."

"You've had your hands full," Chester said.

"During that first year it was touch-and-go, but we're finally making some money. It's a full-time job, but I've got good help. Ida Mae Murphy handles food service, cooking, and hiring and firing of cooks, waiters, and busboys. Our food business has been fantastic, and most of the credit goes to her. Charlie Putnam takes care of maintenance. My wife handles the books and works with housekeeping. My son Cooper's in high school. He and his girlfriend tend bar for us when they can on the weekends. Cooper also works at the front desk a few nights each week. My other son, Graham, is in college in California, and I hope that he and Cooper will own and manage this place some day when I'm old and gray. If something happens to me, I know this place would be in good hands."

"Pen, you're still a young man. You won't be old and gray for a long time."

"I've got a lot to be thankful for. I think Stamford Bridge and The Promontory Inn have a great future. Business is going to grow for all of us."

"I saw people moving furniture?"

"They're getting ready for tonight's party. Saturday nights in the summer, from 9 to 1. Last Saturday we had 300 or so people. Stick around and enjoy the fun."

Chester stood up and put the contract and media file in his briefcase. He had an appointment in Kalamazoo scheduled for 4:30, and it was time to go.

"Pen, thanks again. I'll take a rain check. Your business is important to us. We'll do everything possible to make your campaign a success. I'll be back in a couple of weeks with some new layouts. Send any news items about Stamford Bridge and the hotel to me, so that I can make sure they are published. Send me pictures of Ida Mae, Charlie, and Cooper, his girlfriend, and some copy teiling us what they do at The Promontory Inn. I'll check with my editor and see if we can do a story in our September issue."

"That's a great idea!"

"We need photos and copy by the end of next week."

"I'll do it. An article would be terrific. Dave, I appreciate your hard work. We look forward to seeing your new layouts."

Chapter 14

The room at Chestnut Brook was large. A single bed was built into the south wall near the bottom of a sloping ceiling and the furniture was rustic. Books lined a shelf by the headboard, and Shannon put the Camus book there. The wooden chest of drawers stood next to the bed, and a small white pitcher on top of the chest held a bouquet of fresh red carnations. The high sloped ceiling had exposed posts, beams, and the walls and floors were of dark wood. A rocking chair next to the fireplace evoked an image, she thought, of Massachusetts Bay.

Shannon folded some of her clothes and put them in the chest of drawers and others on hangers in the closet. Make-up, hairbrush, bath soap, and toothpaste were put on a shelf in the bathroom. Shannon slept for an hour and then took a shower and changed clothes. She put on a long-sleeved blue blouse, a white knee-length skirt and penny loafers. Shannon tied her hair in back with a white bow and put her mother's pendant around her neck.

She left the room and walked downtown to Campbell Street. She saw The Promontory Inn at the crest of a hill overlooking the water. White Hall Marina lay beyond the hotel on the north shore of the lake. The downtown, surrounded by evergreens and shade trees, looked small silhouetted against the lake.

In the next block, Shannon came to the Chapel of The Holy Cross, a small, ivy-covered church at Campbell and Cadbury. The church had white siding and a tall steeple topped with a Celtic cross. A vaulted roof angled sharply downward to eye level. There were red clay pots, filled with red and white impatiens, next to double doors. An old brick sidewalk led to the sanctuary entrance. Shannon stopped to read the sign by the front door: Mass 4:30.

It was cool and dark inside. Shannon found an old liturgical atmosphere The sanctuary was small, with room for 40 communicants. Light filtered through a latticed window at the rear of the church. A dozen older persons were seated. Most did not notice or seem to care that Shannon, a stranger, had entered. The communion rail was narrow, the pews old and worn. Kneeling pads, not far from the small altar, were threadbare.

Shannon was early. She found a pew, genuflected, crossed herself, sat down and opened her purse. She took out her Prayer Book and opened it. The pages of the Eucharist were creased and worn. The chapel was quiet. She looked at the altar candles and thought about her mom and dad. Both took the sacraments all their lives, both died within the Church, and both suffered before death. *Where was God's mercy then?* she asked. She did not know, and the Church did not know. The Church had all kinds of answers, but none came to terms with the fact that two people suffered for no reason–the prolonged agony served no purpose. *If God was all-powerful, why did He sit by and let John and Ardith Fitsimmons suffer until death itself ended their suffering?* she asked. *If it was His will, what purpose could there be? Since cancer is an evil, why is it in the world at all? If God made all things, then He must have made cancer. But why? Why did God, if He loves us, as the Church tells us about every 15 minutes, make cancer? Did God not have the power to kill cancer before it killed my parents?* she asked.

She thought of her own ineptitude, her own irrelevance, and her frail processes of thought. It was in the silent moments between simply sitting and thinking and the start of the Mass that the darkest fears surrounded her: *What if He wasn't who He said He was?* she asked.

She doubted God's kindness, but she knew, or thought she knew, that without belief in the sanctity of Christ, darkness would follow. If a person accepted the Church as God's instrument on Earth, then a person must take the sacraments. *Maybe,* she thought, *we only live for a moment or two anyway. Maybe it's all just a pipe dream or a brush fire.*

The sacristy door opened and the priest entered slowly. He was a small, thin man with a lined face, who seemed in pain as he moved toward the altar.

The priest's hair was gray, and he wore heavy, thick glasses. Shannon found it hard to believe that he had ever been a young man. He looked tired and knelt with difficulty. The Mass he knew by heart, and he waited until everyone had knelt and the sanctuary was silent. His speech was not clear, and he chanted the liturgy and stumbled over a few words. He administered the sacraments with faint solemnity. At the end, he managed a smile, "The Mass has ended, go in Peace."

The priest disappeared through the sacristy door. His work for the day was over. Shannon put the Prayer Book back in her purse. It was 5 o'clock when she left the church. Then she saw a man jogging on Cadbury Street. She turned toward Lake Michigan and walked down the south side of Campbell Street until she reached downtown. There were crowds of people on both sides of the street, some were in groups, and others were ambling and looking in store windows. Many carried cocktails and a few were smoking cigarettes. Some had the emaciated appearance of long-time drinkers, and others were probably long-term smokers. Some had children with them, and others had grandparents with them, and some were grandparents. Teenagers in the crowd had the same arrogance and dressed in the same expensive manner as their parents.

The women were tanned. Most wore tan or white knee-length shorts, white blouses and topsiders or penny loafers. Others wore white or blue denim skirts and long-sleeved white or powder blue blouses. Most men wore tan or white khaki slacks or knee-length shorts. They also wore topsiders or penny loafers, without socks. Many wore golf shirts or long-sleeved dress shirts.

Shannon soon heard Mozart, Telemann, or Vivaldi coming from the north side of Campbell Street. A group had gathered on the sidewalk around four violinists. The musicians were seated on folding chairs, with their sheet music on portable stands. Their violin cases were placed on a wooden table. They were smoking, and there were beer bottles on the sidewalk.

A spectator asked to hear "Four Seasons."

"'Four Seasons,' it is," a musician said with slurred speech and a gesture of his hand. He pushed hair out of his eyes, and the group began to play again. An old man wearing a white shirt and red tie sat on a chair nearby and listened to Vivaldi with eyes closed. Shannon listened for a while and continued on her way.

It was late afternoon, and Shannon crossed Campbell Street. The sidewalk curved south down an incline to an outdoor gallery where artwork was for sale. Paintings and illustrations were mounted on displays. The aisles were crowded with people, and a man was serving hot coffee at a nearby sidewalk stand. Artists displayed their artwork in small booths and talked with customers. Shannon looked at watercolors.

"I've seen your work before," she said to an artist with red hair. The man was holding a beer, and his face was round. He was wearing a paint-spattered shirt, shorts, and sandals. A small cocker spaniel was sleeping on a table next to his artwork.

"Really? Where?" he asked.

"I came from Saginaw today and stopped at the Cookie Jar Restaurant in Maple Hill. Your watercolor, 'Windscape' I think it is, is in the dining room."

"Yes, that's my work all right," he replied.

"I like contemporary watercolors. I noticed yours in the restaurant in Maple Hill, while I was having lunch. I saw your one word signature–Errol. I thought it was a good piece of work, and I asked the waitress where she bought it."

"Well, I'll be damned, it's a small world. Okay, yeah, right, I remember, about a month ago. And their names…"

"Edna and Ralph."

"That's right! Edna and Ralph," he replied. "Yes, Edna and Ralph from Maple Hill. Nice people. I thought I'd lost the sale, but they came back late on Sunday and paid cash. Well, I'll be damned, you remembered my work. Well, that's nice. I'll be damned. Made my day. Everything here's looking for a good home."

"This looks like 'Windscape,'" Shannon said, as she pointed to a mounted piece. "It may be too big for my apartment, but how much is it?"

"Today, framed and all, and since you're probably my last possible sale of the day, how about $60?" he said.

"Not a problem. It's nice work. I like it. I'll think about it."

"How about $55?" he asked. "Just for you."

"Your price is fine, I need to decide if it will fit in my apartment," Shannon replied.

"Could be gone tomorrow, $50?" he asked.

"Hey, c'mon," Shannon said as she looked at her watch.

"On vacation?" he asked.

"Yes," she said.

"Where're you staying?" he asked.

"Chestnut Brook," she replied.

"Oh, that's cool. Looks like a nice place. Are the rooms nice?" he asked.

"They're big and roomy. It's nice. Anyway, I'll let you know about the picture. That's the best I can do. I've got to run," Shannon said.

"Do you want me to put it back for you, you know, save it?" he asked.

"You can if you want to," Shannon replied.

"Okay, I'll put it back. You going to the shindig up at the hotel tonight?" he asked.

"That's my plan. Sounds like a blast. I've never been there," Shannon replied.

"Every Saturday night. I've heard people say they heard music from way off shore, but I guess nobody's complained. When you get there, look in the big hallway between the lobby and the dining room. The best things I've ever done are right there. They're pretty good size. Right there in the hallway. I hope you'll take a look. Pen and Geraldine Meacham, owners of the hotel, bought them from me a couple of years ago. It was a big sale for me. Made my season that year. The Meachams are very decent people. There's a room next to the lobby. It's a tea room with high ceilings. It's a big room. The Meachams let each of us display one piece there, with name and price. With so many artists in town, the room's full of art all the time. Some stuff gets sold. That's important, since none of us can make a living doing what we enjoy. I make some money selling my work, but I have to do other stuff to make ends meet. The Meachams are popular. You might make a point to meet them. Maybe I'll see you there?"

"Maybe so."

"Hey, what's your name?"

WHY DID I GROW SO COLD?

"Shannon Fitsimmons. I'll look for your stuff in the hotel. I'm not much of a drinker or party person. I probably won't stay late, but I might see you there."

Chapter 15

Brian's room at The Parsonage was small; sunlight came in through the window and shone on an early map of Stamford Bridge. Woodwork and floors had been left to their natural colors. There was a four-poster bed in the center of the room and an oval-shaped coffee table next to the fireplace. Antique linens and a carpenter's rule pattern quilt, created by an Appalachian craftswoman, covered the bed.

Brian put bags, sports equipment, travel brochures, books and the photo album on a couch next to the bed. He unpacked. Some items went on hangers, others went in the chest of drawers and the bathroom medicine chest. He sat down on the couch, put his feet up on the bed and closed his eyes. There was no one to tell how nervous he was. But more than being nervous, he felt cold fear in his stomach. He thought about the album and the war. It was all with him, he was very frightened. Brian stood up and changed to a t-shirt, shorts, socks, red bandana and running shoes, and left the room.

It felt good to be outside, and Brian ran down Runnymede Court to Cadbury. He turned and ran east on Cadbury through a neighborhood of small, one-story cottages. Many had flower gardens, and children were playing in the streets. He ran north on Berkswell Mill, picking up speed and then downs to Guildford Lane. Brian was running fast as he turned onto Marston Moor. After four miles, he slowed to a walk.

Brian's clothes were soaked. He took off his bandana, tied it around his belt, and rubbed his face. The breeze felt good, and the day was very quiet. He walked to the corner of Cadbury and Campbell Streets, and from there, he could see the blue water of Lake Michigan. There were whitecaps, and he saw barges far off shore, going toward the Straits of Mackinaw. Brian turned and saw the Chapel of The Holy Cross across the street. Mass was over. A tall woman was leaving the church, dressed in blue and white, her blond hair tied with a white bow. She looked at Brian and smiled, turning toward downtown.

Brian jogged across Campbell Street to Tristram Lane and turned south down a narrow winding street past a picnic ground, a botanical garden and baseball diamond to the sandy street by the beach. He saw the White Sands Boarding House, partially hidden by trees.

He crossed the sandy street and looked again at the White Sands. The building seemed familiar. Brian shrugged his shoulders and walked to the water's edge. There were other people at the beach, and some were swimming. A c-boat was anchored offshore, facing the wind with the main sail down. The skipper was polishing brightwork. Brian took off his running shoes and socks and walked into the water. The sand crunched under his feet and the cool water felt good.

I've seen that building before, Brian thought. *There's a picture of the White Sands in the photo album. How in hell is that possible?* he wondered. Brian left the water, put on his shoes and socks, and left for The Parsonage.

Chapter 16

It was quiet in the large white kitchen with the high ceiling. Stainless steel cabinet doors were closed and work areas were cluttered with bottles, steaks, chops, fruit, vegetables, and open food cases and cartons. Filled saucepans and cauldrons steamed on the large stove. There were small benches along the back wall of the kitchen, and two cooks on break sat there smoking cigarettes. Three busboys took off white jackets and sat on a bench near the freezer. A waitress stood in the doorway and watched the approaching clouds. Charlie Putnam came in and put cases of red and white wine on a table near the freezer. Ida Mae thanked Charlie, and he left through a side door.

Ida Mae sat down in the kitchen office and lit a cigarette. A large gin and tonic with a bright green lime tucked in with the ice was on her desk next to the telephone. She pulled a clipboard full of invoices and papers from the desk drawer; then she laid it down on the desk and sipped of her drink. Ida Mae leaned forward on the desk to read, and she smoked. Then she put the clipboard back in the desk drawer. There was too much paperwork to go though tonight. She would review the bills tomorrow when it was quiet. On Monday, she would give the invoices to Pen.

Ida Mae bought the food for the hotel, planned the menus, and managed the kitchen and dining room help. It had been a hard day, and she had not been happy. Ida Mae had been in the kitchen since 7; she would work past midnight. She was tired. Much of the day's work was done. Soon they would feed guests at tonight's party.

From the time Ida Mae had gotten up today until now, things had been different. *Something,* she thought, *was going to happen soon, maybe today, for the first and last time–as a person at tonight's party seeing people never seen before, never to be seen again.* Something forced itself to her attention, and she sensed danger for someone.

Chapter 17

Ida Mae needed to talk to Pen Meacham before people started arriving. She walked toward the south terrace and passed the Tea Room Gallery. She heard something and stopped. The gallery was dark. Ida Mae saw the light of a cigarette in the darkness. She heard someone crying. Ida Mae walked into the gallery and looked in the darkness. Geraldine Meacham was sitting on a bench in the center of the room.

"Oh, God! Ida Mae, I don't want anyone to see me like this," Geraldine said and wiped her eyes.

"Miz M, whatever is the matter?" Ida Mae asked and sat down beside her.

"I get so far down."

"Miz M, what do you mean?"

"Oh God, Ida Mae, the bottom falls out. Everything seems to go to hell inside of me."

"I hate to see you so sad, you of all people."

"It comes quickly."

"Does this happen often?"

"A few times a month or so, I guess. I never know. I think I've always been able to hide it."

"Miz M, you've so much to be thankful for. You're the most popular person in town. Everybody likes you and respects you. You, Mr. Pen, the boys, and the hotel are the best thing that has ever happened to me. You have this wonderful place. Everybody wants to come to town and stay at The Promontory, you know that. The hotel's always sold out, dining room's filled every night. You have all this, and I can't stand to see you suffering. Everybody likes you."

Geraldine wiped her eyes again and said nothing.

"You're so outgoing. You're so friendly to everyone!"

"Thank you, Ida Mae. I'm not sure what you say is true, but it's not me they see. It's what I want people to see."

Ida Mae said nothing.

Geraldine, still crying, buried her face in her hands and then looked up. "If anyone saw the real me, they would see a frightened little girl in a dark bedroom in Sutton's Bay, crying herself to sleep."

"I'm so sorry. That's so sad, but surely you and Mr. Pen…"

"Pen and I just had an argument at lunch, a bad one."

"I'm sorry, I didn't know. I've never seen you two disagree about anything."

"Oh, it happens. I was on him today about money. He spends to damn much money. That new plaything in the carport is way out of line. We don't have that kind of money. He's been drinking too much this summer."

"Well yes, he's been drinking, I've noticed that."

"When he drinks that makes me drink, and I don't like that, and I feel terrible and depressed the next day. I didn't like the way he danced with one of the college girls last Saturday. I went on and on, and finally he left the table. I shouldn't be telling you all this."

"Not a problem with me, Miz M. I know how hard you two work. Graham will be home in a week, and he'll brighten your spirits won't he?"

"Oh, yes and no. The visit will be short, and all the time he's here I'll be trying to grab hold of time so that it doesn't pass so fast. I'll be thinking that the visit will be over, and then he'll leave again. I can't enjoy the moments. Life goes by so fast, and we can't slow it down. It just goes faster–so fast and I have no control. Then I worry if Graham will come back here after college. His childhood is gone and I can't have that back. I think he wants to marry Darby Staltonstall some day. He's never said, but I think he does. I hope they will live here. But what if they live somewhere else, what then? Do you see what I'm saying?"

Ida Mae nodded and said nothing. She handed the handkerchief from her pocket to Geraldine.

"Thank you. Then, I think about Detroit and I wonder what those years were for. Pen, the boys, and I were lost for so long. So much of our life passed in that dreadful place, and I can find no reason for it," Geraldine said.

"I think of my life before becoming a part of this hotel. What were those years for? I have not a clue. But Miz M, what about Cooper? He must bring happiness to your life," Ida Mae said.

"Oh, again, yes and no. He's having wonderful years in high school and he's doing so well in everything, but it's all passing so fast and then he will be gone, too. I can't slow it down or stop it. He'll probably go to college wherever Mary Meade goes or she'll go wherever he goes, and I hope it's not far away. I've already lost him. Cooper and I argued recently. Cooper is so aggressive. He's always been that way, and Pen simply will not discipline him. Sometimes, I feel caught in the middle. I don't know, maybe it's all my fault."

"Miz M, you're being so hard on yourself. It's unfair. You do like it here I hope. You're not thinking about leaving or something are you?"

"No, probably not, Ida Mae. I have to tell you that I don't know how you do all that you do and do all of it so well."

"Thank you."

"The parties exhaust me, and I think they are a terrible strain on everyone. I see people having a good time, I wonder why they're having a good time, and I'm not. Then I think this will all pass and it will be over and what could it all mean. Pen drinks at the parties, and then I drink, and I still wonder why everyone is having such a good time. Then when I do drink, I'm so depressed on Sunday morning I can hardly move. Sometimes I'm able to make it to Mass, but once I'm there, my depression gets worse, and then I think everyone in the church knows I have a hangover. Cooper and Mary Meade are always there as acolytes. I've stopped going whenever I've been drinking. Pen hasn't gone for a long time, and I think that's really wrong. I see time passing me by, and that scares me."

"Should you stop drinking? Is that part of the problem today?"

"I'm sure it is. I had a couple of drinks last night. I wonder if I'm even supposed to be here in this town. Is this what it's all about? Is this home, and should I be thankful for what we have? It is hard for me to be thankful, and I always want more and I don't know what more is. That's a terrible attitude."

WHY DID I GROW SO COLD?

"Miz M, I shouldn't say this, but should you get professional help? It sounds that way, doesn't it?"

The light clicked on in the gallery.

"Sorry Miz M, didn't know you wuz both here. Ida Mae, Mr. Pen's in the kitchen, sez he needs to talk to ya. Somethin' about the wine I picked up today. Sez he needs to talk to ya right away," Charlie Putnam said.

"Thanks, Charlie, I almost forgot. I'll get over there right away," Ida Mae said. She stood up and looked at Geraldine, "I'm sorry Miz M, I should check on this right away. You okay?"

"I'll be okay."

Ida Mae stood up and left the room with Charlie.

Geraldine, on the final day of her life, felt better and left the gallery. She put her fingers on the Saint Anthony locket around her neck. She walked to the apartment on the third floor. She thought about leaving a note for Pen and driving to Grand Haven and taking a motel room and spending the night alone. Geraldine knew doing that would create more problems than it would solve.

Chapter 18

Brian ran back to his room at The Parsonage. The album was still on the wooden coffee table. The curtains were closed and the room silent. Brian picked up a towel from the bathroom, wiped his face and hands, and had a drink of water. He sat down on the couch. Someone had information about his parents. It was strange how he so hated them without knowing them.

He was stunned by what he saw from the beach. Brian opened the album and turned pages until he came to the picture of Ruth Cahill sitting on the lap of the unidentified man. The picture was taken thirty years ago in front of the building with "WS" over the front door– the White Sands Boarding House.

Why, after all of these years, was the album sent and by whom? Why did it come last night, just before leaving for Stamford Bridge? Brian had no idea.

Brian took a shower and changed clothes. He left the room, got into his car and drove to the boarding house. It was the same building. The sign was still over the front door. Brian got out of his car and walked to the front of the White Sands. His footsteps made a crunching sound as he walked across the parking lot's broken concrete. The building needed paint and window shutters were missing. Windows had not been cleaned, and roofing tiles had fallen to the parking lot. Brian saw the bench where the two people in the photograph had been sitting. Brian went to the front screen door and knocked. There was no answer.

He opened the door, went inside, and found a small lobby with gray walls. A small electric fan in the corner was running. A flight of stairs evidently led to dorm rooms upstairs. Concrete floors had once been painted red and were faded and partially covered with rubber mats. An old couch in the corner was dirty. Almost-empty mailboxes covered part of the right wall. Brian heard a washing machine in operation somewhere.

He peered down a long, dimly lit hallway, where a door was standing open. A hallway to the right led to a large yellow-colored room with windows and a vaulted ceiling. Brian saw a bulletin board covered with faded snapshots, held in place with thumbtacks. They were pictures of students who had worked summers in Stamford Bridge and lived at the White Sands, beginning with 1945. Brian focused on a snapshot of a woman sitting on the same bench in front of the White Sands. It was Ruth Cahill. She was sitting alone. Her face was larger in this photo, her features more sharply defined. She was more attractive than he originally thought. There was no mistaking the curious wistful smile. He may have seen hope in her deep-set eyes, but that was long ago. "Ruthie C., midsummer '45," was the caption. Brian heard footsteps behind him and turned around.

"Do you know someone on the photo board?" the young man asked.

The person, maybe 18, was muscular, tanned and wearing a Charing Cross t-shirt, running shorts and sneakers. He had a friendly smile. His hair was short, blond, and brushed like a crew cut. Brian liked his friendly manner. The young man looked strangely familiar to Brian.

"I'm sorry," Brian said, after looking at him, "I thought for a moment you looked like…"

"Like who?"

"Oh, it was just a thought that crossed my mind."

"What's going on?" the young man asked.

"I'm looking for someone who, I think, lived in this building 30 years ago," Brian said.

"Here?"

"Yeah."

"Wow! Thirty years ago, that's before I was born. Let's see, that would be the 1940s. Did you live here?"

"No, I've never been here."

"You've never been here?"

"Never."

"But, the person you're looking for lived here?"

"Everything points in that direction," Brian replied.

"Really? Well, that's cool. Check this out," Cooper said, as he pointed to the wall. "I've heard these are shots of people who've worked in town and lived here. Maybe the person you're looking for has a picture on the bulletin board somewhere."

"I already found a picture of one of the persons I'm trying to find. There's the picture," Brian said, as he pointed toward a snapshot held in place with a thumbtack.

"Really, that's cool. You found the person's picture? You're sure it's the same person? That's pretty incredible, don't you think? Thirty years ago, wow!"

"I'm sure. Her picture's right there," Brian replied, as he again pointed to it.

Brian heard more footsteps. He turned and saw a woman of about 18, with blond hair. Freckles covered the bridge of her nose. Her elegantly shaped mouth turned easily into a broad, beautiful smile, which revealed straight white teeth. Her green eyes seemed larger when smiling. She was wearing a Charing Cross swim team shirt, tan shorts, and topsiders.

"What's happening, Coopy?" she said, as she put her arm around Cooper Meacham's waist.

"He just recognized someone on the board," Cooper said.

"Hi, I'm Brian Cahill."

"I'm Cooper Meachan," Cooper said. "This's Mary Meade Saltonstall."

"Nice to meet you guys. I'm from Chicago, and I came here for a vacation. However, after getting here, my vacation's changed."

"For the better, I hope," Mary Meade said.

"I don't know. I've been looking for a person that I haven't had contact with for 30 years. She lived or spent some time in Stamford Bridge. She probably lived in this building. I found a picture of her here. Have you ever heard of Ruth Cahill?"

Cooper and Mary Meade said no.

"Relative?" Mary Meade asked.

"Could be," Brian replied. "I think she's my mother."

"Your mother. This person's your mother," Cooper said, as he handed it to Brian. "How could you not have seen her for 30 years? Divorced or something?"

"That's right," Brian said, looking at the picture. "I have no memory of her, just a photo. I always thought I was an orphan. My father is a... I have no idea how he fits into the picture. I lived in different orphanages over the years. I've never had the time or money to look for my mom and dad. I have no idea why I was left," Brian said.

"I can't imagine," Mary Meade said, "all the years... That's so sad."

"That's all in the past," Brian lied. "I'd like to keep the picture, if that's okay?"

"Susan wouldn't care," Cooper said, as he looked at Mary Meade.

"Susan?" Brian asked.

"Susan Worcester," Mary Meade said. "She owns this place. Cooper and I clean up for her on Saturdays."

"Okay."

"What brought you here to look for your parents?" Mary Meade asked

"Interesting question," Brian replied with an empty stare. "I decided to come up here this summer, and I'm staying at The Parsonage."

"Okay," Cooper said.

"My plans were to leave Chicago on Friday."

"Last Friday, yesterday?" Mary Meade asked.

"Yes."

"Okay."

"Anyway, I got home from work on Friday night, and there was a package from Seattle at the front door of my apartment. The mailing label was addressed to me, but I didn't recognize the handwriting. There was no return address."

"Have you ever been to Seattle? " Cooper asked

"Never."

"You know anyone from Seattle? " Mary Meade asked.

"Not a soul."

"Okay."

"There was an album of old photographs inside. There were pictures of people with my last name, but they were people I had never heard of. Some had captions. I decided that a person in the album identified as Ruth Cahill might be my mother. One picture really caught my attention. It was a snapshot of the Ruth Cahill person sitting on the lap of a man. It was taken in front of an older building. Here's the really weird part. On my first day here, today, I went down to the beach. As I was looking up from the beach, I noticed this building, the one we are in right now. Then it came to me. The WS sign was over the front door of this building, exactly where it was in the picture in the old album. This is the same building where the photograph of the two people sitting on the bench had been taken 30 years ago."

"The same building, exactly the same building?" Cooper asked.

"Right, nothing's changed, the bench where the two people were sitting 30 years ago is still in the same place. It's the same building, the White Sands Boarding House." Brian said.

"That's weird, man," Cooper said.

"God, that's what I was thinking," Mary Meade said.

"So, Brian," Cooper said, "let me see if we've got this right. This album thing came to you last night with no explanation. It's got pictures of people you've never seen before?"

"Right."

"You think you found pictures of your real mom?"

"I think so."

"Then, today, by accident, you found the place where that picture was taken."

"Right."

"Then, again by accident, here today, in this building, you found another photograph of the person you believe, or I guess you know, to be your mother?"

"Right again."

"Damn, how do you make sense of all this?"

"Beats the hell out of me."

"Any more shots of your mother?" Cooper asked.

"Two more," Brian replied. "In one, Ruth Cahill is standing in front of what looks like a hotel, on a narrow brick street. It looks like she's standing on a sidewalk, next to a narrow street."

"A hotel on a narrow brick street here in town? I don't think it's in this town. The Inn, the only hotel in town, is on Campbell Street. It is a brick street, but it is not narrow. What do you think, Mary Meade?" Cooper asked.

"We have lots of narrow streets, but not downtown," Mary Meade replied.

"The other photo," Brian said, "was taken in a bar with a long mirror. She must have been a barmaid or something at one time, at least in this photo she is wearing an apron and standing in front of a bar somewhere."

"Have you got the album with you?" Mary Meade asked.

"No, it's back in my room," Brian replied.

"We might be more help if we saw the pictures," Mary Meade said.

"Mary Meade's probably right," Cooper said, "but, we've got our work here, and the function tonight. Let's talk tomorrow. What the hell, we'll take a look."

"Great."

"Tonight's party night at the hotel, everyone's invited." Cooper said.

"I'll look forward to it. You guys help with the party?" Brian asked.

"Cooper's parents own The Promontory and he lives in the hotel. It's a family project I'm glad to be a part of," Mary Meade said.

"I might run into you guys tonight."

"Cool."

They walked outside to the parking lot.

"This's where they were sitting. The bench hasn't moved in 30 years. There's the White Sands logo, too," Brian said.

Cooper and Mary Meade said nothing and turned to go back inside. Suddenly, Mary Meade turned and asked Brian, "Who's the man in the picture?"

"I don't know, it might be my father. I don't know, that son of a..."

Brian got into his car and watched Cooper and Mary Meade as they walked back into the boarding house. He could not help staring at Cooper, as if he had seen him before.

Chapter 19

    The walkway led to a garden overlooking the beach. Flowers were in bloom, and the air was still, as if waiting for a storm. Clouds gathered in the west, and thunder sounded from great distance. The water, like slate, was calm. The sunset would soon be lost in darkness. A few powerboats were slowly motoring toward White Hall Marina, leaving white bubbly wakes behind. A fisherman and his son carried a tackle box and fly rods up the wooden stairs from the beach below. They looked tired.
    At the edge of the garden, before she turned to go, Shannon looked west. She so wanted to visualize in the real world the mystical images her soul imagined but could not see. Her mind brought up things about her parents from the past, and she thought of them both standing with her on this shore and then asleep in Wheatstone, as the leaves there turned in the fall. Beyond incantations of the Mass, contact with her parents was gone, and she could no longer reconstruct either of their voices in her mind. She soon sensed something out of focus coming her way soon–something beyond her depth. There had been strangeness all day, something arcane. Apprehension settled in a distant part of her mind. She shivered and walked to the hotel.
    She reached the hotel front steps at 8:15. The Promontory Inn was larger than she had imagined. Green shutters, against white clapboard siding, looked freshly painted. The lawn, trimmed short, was laid out in a broad sweep toward the breakwater. There were wooden flower boxes along the sidewalks filled with white petunias. A small lighted sign on the west lawn, identified "Gerry and Charlie's Garden." Three white Kennedy roses were at the center of the garden.

WHY DID I GROW SO COLD?

The front porch was filled with people; most were drinking and talking. Many were smoking cigarettes. A few men were smoking cigars. Some people were standing in groups and others were sitting on white wicker furniture. One couple was sitting on the front porch swing moving back and forth. People were across the lawn and one group stood next to wooden lawn chairs. Someone said something about Watergate or White House tapes, and a group exploded in laughter. The east lawn was also covered with wicker furniture and several people were milling about. None were sitting.

Shannon saw a man and woman walking toward the breakwater, and they were yelling at each other. Shannon could not hear all of what was being said, but apparently, the man or the woman had been dancing with the wrong person in the wrong way. It was evidently a serious matter. Both were waving their arms, and it looked as if they were ready to come to blows.

Shannon walked into the lobby. A large man with a reddish weatherbeaten face and crewcut white hair was standing behind the check-in desk. His nametag said Charlie Putnam. He was wearing a white long-sleeved shirt and a wide blue tie. His bright eyes crinkled shut when he smiled. Charlie was holding red brochures in his large hands and was giving them to guests as they arrived.

Shannon walked to the desk, and Charlie handed her a brochure.

"Howdy, ma'am. Welcome to The Promontory Inn. This here's a list of art and pitchers fer sale in the Tea Room. Yer welcome ta look around as much as ya want and have a good time at the party. Go to the Tea Room any time ya like. It's open till one. If ya want, jest go beyond the lobby here, and you'll see a little sign sayin' Tea Room Gallery. Lots of purdy pitchers fer sale in thur. Them's all done by local people. Mr. and Ms. Pen try to help the local people. Have all ya want to eat and drink and maybe dance a spell and then, if you're fixin' to do so, go to the Tea Room."

Shannon looked at the brochure. Errol had told her about the gallery. She folded the brochure and kept it with her purse.

"Thank you, Charlie, that's very kind of you. I have a question for you."

"Yes, ma'am."

"Is that your name on the little sign by that beautiful garden?"

"Yes, ma'am, it is. I thought Ms. Pen's name should go thur by 'self. Mr. Pen said my name had ta been there too. Mr. Pen's a kind man."

"You did a fabulous job!"

"Thank ya, kindly, ma'am. Have yerself a dandy time."

"Thank you, Charlie. I'm so glad that I met you."

"Yes, ma'am, same to ya."

High ceilings with arched moldings, dark hardwood floors in the lobby and dining room, tall chairs, and large mahogany coffee tables suggested an old London men's club, perhaps past its prime. In the far corner of the living room, a few older people were sitting close to the fireplace, reading magazines and newspapers.

Shannon saw some of the people she had seen earlier on Campbell Street and noticed the same nonchalant manner. Several were still drinking, and conversation was more animated than earlier. Most seemed at home, as if they went to parties every night. Others were more wide-eyed and less at ease; drinking would blur the differences. The band was playing in the dining room. The bar next to the dining room was crowded. People were talking, laughing, smoking, and ordering drinks. A young couple was filling drink orders.

"Hi, Shannon," a voice behind her said.

She turned and saw Edna from Maple Hill and a tall man.

Edna gave Shannon a hug.

"Ralph, this's the nice person who had lunch at the Jar today and talked about Stamford Bridge. She's on vacation and was on her way over here."

"Nice to meet ya," Ralph, a man in his sixties, shook hands with Shannon.

"It's great to see you, Edna, and to meet you, Ralph. I didn't realize that you were going on vacation this weekend," Shannon said.

"We hadn't planned to come over here this weekend at all," Edna said. "I had such a good time talking with you that I got all excited about getting away. Shannon, after you left, I talked to Ralph about coming over here. I didn't have to talk very hard. We closed up The Cookie Jar and packed our bags. There'd been a cancellation, and we got a room at The Parsonage, and here we are."

Edna took her husband's hand and asked, "Ralph, would you get me a white wine?"

"Sure."

"White wine, I always like a glass or two on a night like this. Shannon, how about you?" Edna asked.

Shannon nodded.

"Drinks for all, back in a minute," Ralph said, as he left for the bar.

"Your husband has a friendly face," Shannon said.

"Thank you. After 34 years," Edna said, "I guess we'll stick it out for a few more. Bless his heart, treats me like a queen. We could not have children, so we've had only each other all these years. We have just about no family at all. Been together through thick and thin." Edna paused and pushed her mouth tightly together.

"I've had a lot to see since I got here," Shannon said.

"You're here by yourself?" Edna asked.

"Yes," Shannon said.

Ralph returned from the bar, handed a glass of wine to Shannon, one to his wife, and kept a draft for himself.

"Well, thank you so much," Shannon said.

"It's our pleasure," Ralph said.

The three touched glasses and each had a drink.

"Good wine, Ralph," Edna said.

"Glad you like it, "Ralph said.

"Yes! I'll say!" Shannon said.

"Glad you like it, too," Ralph said.

"You have the best apple pie and cheeseburgers in the world," Shannon said.

Ralph nodded. "Thank you. Edna tells me that you live in Saginaw, and you're a newspaper reporter?"

"Yes," Shannon replied, "I was a journalism major in college."

"That's interesting. Edna and I talked about college a couple of times but we just never got around to it. I sometimes wish that we had. Do you like your job?"

"I enjoy it well enough for now."

"You like what you're doing, that's the important thing."

"I give it my best."

"Is it difficult work?"

"It's hard work, but it's what I am trained to do."

"Shannon, the way you talk, you don't sound like you're from around here."

"I'm from western Kansas," Shannon said

"What brought you to this part of the world?" Ralph asked.

"I went to school on a sports scholarship," Shannon replied.

"You're a long way from home," Ralph said. "Still have folks in Kansas?"

"No, they're both gone," Shannon said.

"I'm sorry," Ralph said.

"Oh, Shannon, I'm so sorry. You're such a young person to have both parents gone," Edna said.

"Thank you," Shannon replied.

There was a pause.

"Aren't you glad I told you about this shindig?" Edna asked.

"Yes! I am. It's a great party," Shannon said.

"We're glad we met up with you. Are you starting to enjoy yourself?" Edna asked.

"I've been working hard for so long, it's hard to slow down."

"I had that feeling when you were having lunch," Edna said. "I told Ralph, after you left, that I'd bet money you're a hard worker. You're young, but you've got to take time to enjoy life. That's what Ralph and I always say."

"This town's so nice," Shannon said. "I so like the cute little brick streets and shade trees and the old houses. Everything is kind of sleepy and relaxed. It's so neat for a town to be this way."

"So, you're glad you came?"

"Oh, heavens, yes!"

Edna and Ralph finished their drinks. Ralph left and returned with two more glasses of wine.

"Now tell us, Shannon, what have you been up to?"

"I've walked around some. I went to Mass at a tiny little chapel, Holy Cross on Cadbury Street."

"You're a Catholic?" Edna asked.

"Yes," Shannon replied.

"We're both kind of non-denominational you might say. We don't go to church very often. Ralph says it doesn't make any difference where you go," Edna said.

"I think, as long as you feel like going to church sometimes," Ralph said, "you should go. Doesn't matter if you go to church once a week or once a year. I can't see God up there saying this person's a Baptist, this one over here's a Lutheran, this person's a Catholic, and this person hasn't followed church rules, and this one hasn't been going to church every week, boy is he in trouble and what-have-you. See what I mean?"

"I know some people think that way," Shannon said.

"Shannon, I'm sorry I got you off track. You were going to tell us about your day," Edna said.

"Okay, I found the artists' booths you told me about. I saw some things that were out of this world. There were tons of people. A couple of women, sitting on wooden lawn chairs along Campbell Street, with a big St. Bernard sitting at their feet, were playing guitars."

"We see those two every time we're here," Edna said. "They're sisters."

"They are attractive and they sounded nice. They added to the ambience of the day."

"Ambience?" Ralph asked.

"They added to the mood or the atmosphere of the day," Shannon replied.

"Okay," Ralph said.

"Well, as I was saying, I liked the music and put a few dollars in the till. I came to a booth that had what I was looking for–a watercolor for my apartment. The artist was sitting on a lawn chair, smoking and drinking beer. His booth was a total mess. He didn't seem to be paying attention to what was going on. He has a round face and red hair, and his clothes were covered with paint. I saw a couple of his things I liked. I told him I had seen his work before and that I liked his work. He thought I was putting him on."

"That was Errol," Ralph said.

"That's right," Shannon replied. "I told him I'd been to your restaurant in Maple Hill earlier in the day and that I liked the work he sold to you guys. He remembered both of you. I got there late in the afternoon. He seemed discouraged and bored. Apparently, he hadn't sold a thing all day. Anyway, as I said, I saw a painting that's a lot like the one you guys bought. I think I am going to buy it. The price is about the same as yours."

"He seems like a lost soul," Ralph said. "There's a sadness about him."

Edna and Ralph, on their second drinks, were relaxed. Shannon and Ralph talked, and Edna listened.

"I see why you say that. I think he has a lot of talent. I'm sure he would prefer to make his living by selling his work, or having someone, like an agent, selling it for him. To him, the actual selling, whether he admits it or not, is probably demeaning."

"Demeaning?" Ralph asked.

"Yes, he probably feels that he is lowering himself by having to sell his own work. He wants to be an artist, not a salesman. He probably can't imagine Shakespeare or Michelangelo selling their work in a booth or going door to door."

"I'd never thought about it like that, but I'll bet you're right," Ralph said.

Shannon nodded. Ralph was drinking fast.

"When you think about it," she continued, "very few artists or musicians or performers can make a living doing what they do best—creating art or performing. They all pay a price. That probably applies to all of the students and instructors in this town every summer. Errol is like the girl who goes to New York and waits tables for years before getting her big break on Broadway, if it ever comes. She practices, trains, auditions year after year, and gets small parts while waiting tables and living in a tiny room somewhere in New York. She'll endure almost anything to be on stage."

"It's her life," Ralph said. "Her big break may never come, but when you think about it, maybe that's okay because maybe she's been on stage, maybe many times, and she loves to perform."

"Errol's like that. He wants to be recognized for the work he creates. He wants to be only an artist," Shannon said. "But like the girl waiting tables, he will go to almost any length to follow his creative impulses and to be recognized as a serious artist. The sad part is that after a lifetime of hard work, he may never be recognized."

Ralph left and got another drink and came back from the bar. Edna was quiet.

"Errol is the quintessential artist," Shannon said. "He's always in the process of creating and always in the process of searching for acceptance..."

"Quintessential?" Ralph interrupted.

"Yes, something in its purest form, the real thing, the best possible example," Shannon replied and set her drink down on a nearby table.

They stood there, Shannon talking to Ralph, Edna smiling and Ralph drinking rapidly. Shannon wanted to move on.

"Ralph, since you and Edna have been here several times, I'll bet you guys probably know other people here tonight?"

"Well, yes," Ralph's speech was fuzzy. "We know people here. We saw people from Maple Hill on the lawn. We thought we might see if you wanted to meet them and maybe we could all have dinner together."

"This's such a great party," Shannon said. "I'll bet you'd like to see your friends. This's such an interesting place. I want to see what's going on, maybe even dance, Then, later on, I'll catch up with you guys, and we can all get together on the front porch and have dessert? Okay?"

Ralph managed a half smile. "You know that sounds like a..."

"Ralphy, Ralphy," Edna said. "What did ya put in that wine? Ralphy, you're a bad boy! I need fresh air. Ralphy, I think we better go." She took hold of Ralph's arm and stumbled slightly. Ralph put his arm around her and they made their way to the front door. Ralph looked over his shoulder and said, "Shannon, sorry, we'll catch you later?"

Shannon waved.

It was 10 p.m.

Buffet tables with white linen were set up on the back patio and the front terrace. Each table had a centerpiece of red and white carnations. Tubs filled with ice and champagne bottles were next to each table. Ida Mae and her crew had finished their work.

Shannon walked past a buffet table to the dance floor and saw the Calder print on the dining room wall. The music was loud. People were dancing, and couples walked on and off the dance floor. Some smoked while they danced. Most set their drinks down at the edge of the dance floor. The couple Shannon had seen arguing earlier were face-to-face in the middle of the floor. They each held a drink and glared at each other. The woman threw her drink in the man's face and stormed off the dance floor. The man shrugged his shoulders, went to the bar, picked up a towel and a new drink, and headed for the lobby.

At 10:15, the band went on break.

Shannon noticed two young bartenders behind the bar. They were holding hands.

"Looks like you two are taking a breather," Shannon said.

"I'll say, and it's about time," Mary Meade laughed.

"Did you talk to that man? The person who had the drink thrown in his face?" Shannon asked. "Those same people were yelling at each other on the lawn a couple of hours ago. What's with that?"

"Our tag team match," Cooper said with a laugh. "They're here almost every weekend. They don't live here. His name's Carl. We do not know her name. Someone said they are engaged and have been for years. God, if they got married, they'd probably kill each other or something."

"They stayed with Polly Brooks once or twice. It was a disaster. They started yelling and woke up other guests. One tossed the other one's clothes in the parking lot and took off. I guess the other one took a bus or taxi to get home. They liven things up around here," Mary Meade said.

"What can I get for you?" Cooper Meacham asked.

"Chablis, please."

"This wine's popular. We ran out last Saturday night, and that was not a happy situation," Cooper said. "We don't want that to happen again."

"Things have quieted down," Shannon said.

"Calm before the storm. The band's on break, people are eating. That will slow things down for a while, and then a stampede. This'll go full blast until one o'clock," Cooper said.

"Yes! "Mary Meade said.

"Do both of you work here for the summer? It looks like fun, but could be hard work. I'll bet the pay's good," Shannon said.

"The pay could be a whole lot better," Cooper said with a laugh. "I live here at the hotel with my parents. They own The Promontory. My name's Cooper Meacham," Cooper said.

"Your father is Pen Meacham?"

"Yes, and my mother's name is Geraldine," Cooper said.

"My name's Shannon Fitsimmons. I've heard nice things about your parents and this hotel and what your folks have done for Stamford Bridge."

"Thank you. It's Shannon, right?" Cooper asked.

Shannon nodded.

"Shannon, this's Mary Meade Saltonstall," Cooper said.

"Hello Shannon, here on vacation?" Mary Meade asked.

Shannon nodded.

"You came to Stamford Bridge from where?" Mary Meade asked

"Saginaw," Shannon replied.

"I hope you're having a good time," Mary Meade said.

"Thank you, I am. It is nice to meet you guys. When I went by here a while back, people were standing three-deep around the bar. It looked like a madhouse," Shannon said.

"It usually is," Mary Meade said, as she and Cooper broke out laughing.

"Shannon, I don't believe you're staying here?" Cooper said.

"I'm staying at Chestnut Brook," Shannon replied.

"Chestnut Brook's a nice place," Mary Meade said. "Polly Brooks and her husband will probably be here sometime tonight."

"Good, I'll look for them," Shannon said. "It was nice to meet both of you."

Shannon left the bar and walked to a wide hallway between the dining room and lobby. Error's murals were on display.

"Well, what do you think?" Errol, standing behind her, asked.

Shannon jumped and spilled part of her drink.

"I thought I might see you sometime tonight," she said. "You look different."

"You mean I look more presentable," Errol said.

"I didn't mean that," Shannon replied.

"I know. Anyway, I'm glad I caught up with you. So, what do you think of my two big pieces? Wait, before you answer, do you want me to fix your drink?" Errol asked.

"My drink's fine," Shannon said.

"Okay, so?"

"I'm glad that you're so interested in my opinion, but I only had one quarter of art history. I'm not an expert by any means."

"Doesn't matter; you know what you're looking for, so I value your opinion."

"Motherwell," she said.

"Motherwell?"

"Yes, Motherwell," she said. "The abstract imagery is there, implicit and explicit in your work, like it is in his. Even a casual student like me can see that. Isn't that really what abstract expressionism is all about, abstract imagery, particularly American expressionism?"

"Yes, you've hit it pretty well," Errol said. "I'm impressed."

"That's nice of you to say, but don't be all that impressed. I covered a few Detroit gallery openings for my paper. I picked up a book somewhere along the way that talked about American modernism. Motherwell was one of the people that caught my attention. I like Calder and Rothko, too, but I don't think your work is like theirs. You've seen the Calder litho in the dining room?" Shannon asked.

"Yes, I like it, it's a signed litho. Pretty expensive," Errol said.

"Oh, I would think so. In any case, I'll take the drink you offered," Shannon said with a smile.

Errol returned with two white wines.

"Thank you for what you said about my work," Errol said.

"Fishing for more compliments?" Shannon joked.

"Could be. C'mon, let's take a look at the Tea Room. It's just down the hall."

The gallery was large. The ceiling was high, and walls were off-white. Pieces of art were mounted in vertical rows, each identified with a red tag. There were wooden benches in the center of the room. It was quiet.

Shannon noticed a tanned woman in her early fifties. She was sitting on one of the benches. Geraldine Meacham was wearing a yellow summer dress, matching earrings, necklace and sandals. Her black hair was tied with a yellow scarf. She was smoking a cigarette.

"Hi, Gerry," Errol said. "You look a thousand miles away."

She turned and stood up.

"Oh, hi, Errol. Actually, I was thinking about Graham. He will be home from California in a few days. Also, I was taking a breather. It's been a busy day. Everybody's tired," Geraldine said.

"Gerry, this's Shannon Fitsimmons. She's on her first visit to Stamford Bridge and this's her first party at your hotel," Errol said.

"Hi, Shannon. I'm sorry for ignoring you," Geraldine said.

"Not a problem," Shannon said.

Shannon looked at Geraldine while she was talking with Errol. She had a beautifully proportioned face, but there were deep lines around the sides of her mouth and at the corner of her eyes. She had an annoying nervous laugh and a smoker's voice. Sadness seemed to lie just behind the laugh.

"Welcome to The Promontory Inn and Stamford Bridge. I'm delighted you came to see us. I hope you are having a good time and that you like our town," Geraldine said.

"I'm having a great time. I'm going to be here for a week. This's a wonderful party, and I love your town," Shannon said.

"Thank you. Did you notice Errol's paintings in the hallway? Aren't they fabulous?" Geraldine asked.

"We've just been looking at them. They are so dramatic, hanging in the large hallway by themselves. I've been telling Errol how much I like them," Shannon said.

"I'm sure he enjoys hearing that," Geraldine laughed.

"He sure seems to," Shannon replied. "But, I think both paintings are marvelous."

"Pen, my husband, and I thought so, too. That is why we bought them." Geraldine said. "You must realize, Shannon, that we can't spend all of our time talking about Errol, although he would like us to do so."

"Praise could go to his head," Shannon said. "Boys are like that."

"Don't let me stop you," Errol laughed.

"Enough about Errol. Cooper and Mary Meade make a cute couple," Shannon said.

"I don't know what we would do without them. They're such a help," Geraldine said.

"Mary Meade looks terrific, particularly when she's with Cooper," Shannon said.

"Thank you," Geraldine replied.

"Gerry, I've heard so many nice things about you and your husband and what you've done for the town and for this hotel and I've only been in town for a day," Shannon said.

Geraldine said nothing.

"You guys seem to be the most popular people in town," Shannon said.

"I'll second that," Errol said.

"You're both being kind. Pen and I try very hard. We wonder if we upset people," Geraldine said.

"Everything about you guys is always so positive!" Errol said. "People in town say you're the best thing that's happened here in a long time."

"Errol always says the nicest things. Shannon, it's nice meeting you and thank you for your nice words. With Errol bending your ear this evening, you'll be in good company. You might even get a word in edgewise. I have to check on the kitchen. Shannon, thanks for coming. I'm sure we'll see you again in the next few days," Geraldine said.

"Gerry, we'll see you later," Errol said.

"Nice person," Shannon said.

"This gallery wouldn't be here if they hadn't come up with the idea," Errol said.

"I see a lot of things I like," Shannon said.

"I see some of my goofy friends at a table over there by the dance floor. Why don't you eat with us? C'mon, we'll have a blast!"

"Errol, thanks. I'm going to look around here and then go out to the pool. I'll catch up with you guys later," Shannon said.

"That's fine. If we miss connections tonight, maybe we could have lunch tomorrow or something?" Errol asked.

"Good idea; buzz me at Chestnut Brooke," Shannon said.

"It's a deal."

"Good, Talk to you later."

Shannon turned to go. She saw, at the end of the hall, the man she had seen earlier today jogging along Cadbury Street after Mass.

Chapter 20

Brian returned to The Parsonage at 6:30. The room was quiet and dark. He turned on the light and sat down in a wicker chair next to the bed. Brian now knew that Ruth Cahill had lived in the White Sands sometime during the summer of 1945 and in 1946.

He put the photo album in the center of the bed and turned to the 1945 photograph of Ruth Cahill–the picture of Ruth Cahill sitting on the lap of the unidentified man. He removed the picture and placed it on the white linen bedspread, next to the Ruth Cahill photograph found today. Ruth was probably 18 years old when both photos were taken. The man in the first photograph was about the same age. The photograph found today was left at the White Sands some 30 years ago, the other found its way to Seattle and to the old album. In the second picture, Ruth was wearing casual clothes. She was sitting on the same bench in front of the boarding house. There was a melancholy look in this second photograph. Her features were in sharper focus. Ruth's smile in this picture looked quizzical–if she was going to ask a question. Brian studied both photographs, looking for any message from that summer of 1945.

Thoughts turned over in Brian's mind. Cooper Meacham was probably 18 and he looked familiar to Brian when they met. Cooper, probably the same age as the man in 1945 picture, was that person's double– Cooper could pass for the man's twin brother. Brian sat in silence as his eyes focused first on one photo and then on the other and then back again. Brian shut his eyes and ran his fingers through his hair. Something was coming to surface that seemed inconceivable.

With the two photographs side by side on the bed, Brian stood up, turned, and looked into the mirror on the wall. A familial resemblance was there, and it seemed impossible to imagine. Could Cooper be, he wondered, his half-brother or even his brother? Probably 12 years separated them. *If Cooper is my brother or half-brother, why did he seem to have had everything in life, while I, after barely escaping death in the jungle, have known damn near nothing except loneliness and despair,* Brian asked.

Since the unknown man in the picture looked like Cooper Meacham and since Ruth Cahill was in the picture with that man, did that mean that Ruth Cahill was the mother of both himself and Cooper? If so, what about Ruth Cahill? If she was his mother and Cooper's, why was her name Cahill instead of Meacham? If Ruth Cahill was his mother, where was she? Did she live here? Had she lived here all these years? If not, who was married to Cooper Meacham's father? If Ruth Cahill was in this town, why did neither Cooper nor Mary Meade recognize her from the photo at the White Sands? Why, he wondered, was the album sent to him from Seattle? Why was there no return address on the album package?

How, after 30 years, could this be happening, he thought. Why here, in a place he had never been? Ruth Cahill was emerging as a presence from another lifetime–a presence that filled him with a strange dread. *Cooper was the linchpin,* he thought. It was Cooper who sharpened his focus on Ruth Cahill and the unidentified man and now himself. How did Cooper and Ruth Cahill and he fit into this picture?

Brian went to the telephone and called Charmon in Lake Geneva. The line was busy. Brian called five minutes later; no answer. He tried again, still no answer. He called information in Lake Geneva. The number was correct. He tried again; still no answer.

He thought about the evening ahead at the hotel. Cooper Meacham's parents owned the hotel and they would be there. Cooper and Mary Meade would be there. Would he see the man from the 1945 photograph? That had to be Cooper's father. Could that same person be his own father? If he was there and he looked like Cooper, which almost certainly he would, Brian believed all doubts would be removed–Cooper's father was also his own father. This was the night he would see at least one of his parents for the first time, he thought. At least part of his search was probably ending, and events might be spinning out of control.

Brian took another shower and put on khakis, loafers, a powder-blue shirt, and a yellow tie. He left the room and walked to Campbell Street. After turning west on Campbell, he walked toward The Promontory Inn. In the next block, he passed a large flower garden–a sprinkler was slowly watering a bed of perennials. Across the street, couples were having drinks on a patio. They looked over and smiled at Brian, and he waved back. An outside family gathering was in force at a house with a white picket fence. Next door, several young girls were running in circles and laughing as a parent sprayed them with water from a garden hose. A car went by and Brian heard the nubby sound of tires on the brick street. After two blocks, Brian came to a stop. He looked down a long tree lined sidewalk and saw the steps where Ruth Cahill had stood in the 1946 photograph.

Brian went back to his room, picked up one of the 1946 pictures of Ruth Cahill, and returned. Little had changed in 29 years. The trees were larger, but that was all. He determined that the building in the 1946 picture must have been The Promontory Inn. It was not located on a narrow brick street. The camera angle in the 1946 photo depicted the brick street as narrow. That was why Cooper and Mary Meade could not identify it. The hotel's front sign was beyond the focus of the 1946 photograph.

He reached the steps where Ruth had stood 29 years earlier. Brian looked at the front of the hotel for the first time. It was a larger building than he had imagined, and from the front sidewalk he could look out across the tree line that ran down to the lake and across the bay to the marina on the north shore. Ruth had apparently been a barmaid in this hotel at some time in 1945 or 1946. The bar with the long mirror would surely be inside. It seemed impossible that Ruth Cahill would still be there.

People were talking in groups on the lawn; dozens had gathered on the front porch. Brian made his way up the brick front steps, across the front porch with the gray wooden floor and inside the hotel. He met Charlie Putnam, standing behind the front desk in the lobby and asked for directions to the bar.

"Yessir, I'm Charlie, welcome ta ya suh. Yer fixin' ta go to da bar, okey, jest go around this wall, jest to the right. Yessir, jest ta the right. Thurs a big crowd, thur always is. They've got whatever ya want ta drink. Lots ta eat, too. Here's a bersure fer ya. Be shur ta look in the Tea Room, lots a purdy pitchers in thur. Welcome suh, have yerself a dandy time," Charlie said.

"Thanks," Brian said.

"Yessir, have yerself a jolly time," Charlie said

"Thanks, Charlie."

"Yuh sir."

Brian walked through the crowded lobby to the dining room and then made his way down a long crowded hallway to the bar's entrance. Brian went through double doors. The room was filled with people. Some were sitting at tables, and others had gathered around the bar. This was the bar in the photograph and Brian saw where Ruth Cahill had stood. Tables and chairs were new. Other than that, nothing had changed. Brian went to the end of the bar and saw Cooper Meacham and Mary Meade.

"Brian, you made it!" Cooper said, as he looked up from the sink.

"Wouldn't miss it," Brian said.

"What can I get for you?" Cooper asked.

Brian did not answer.

"Brian, what can I get for you?"

"Oh, sorry, a draft, a big one, whatever you've got on tap, as long as it's cold."

"A big draft it is," Cooper said as he handed a stein to Brian.

"Thanks."

"First one's on the house."

"Thanks, a cold draft on a hot summer night. What could be better than that?"

"We'll have a couple of cold ones later," Mary Meade said, as she moved next to Cooper.

"Mary Meade and I talked about you. We've never known anyone who was raised in an orphanage," Cooper said.

Brian said nothing.

"It's wild that your search led you to Stamford Bridge."

"Cooper, my search didn't lead me here. It's an accident that the photo album I received and Stamford Bridge are connected," Brian replied.

"Remember, Coopy," Mary Meade, said as she tapped him on his head to jog his memory, "he planned the trip up here before he received the album."

"Got it."

"Okay," Mary Meade said. "Once again, you hadn't made a connection with the parents you've never seen and Stamford Bridge until you saw the White Sands."

"No connection until I saw that boarding house. I've got something more about all of this that I found out on the way over here from The Parsonage, about 20 minutes ago."

"Shoot."

"Remember that I asked you about one of the photos of my mother, Ruth Cahill? She is standing in front of what looked like a hotel of some sort, on a narrow brick street, on steps at the end of a sidewalk. I wondered if you guys might have had any idea where that photograph might have been taken, you know, on a narrow brick street?"

"Sure," Mary Meade replied. "We haven't seen the picture, why?"

"I found out where that picture was taken. The camera angle in that 1946 photograph made the brick street in the picture look narrow. It isn't a narrow street at all. The picture must have been taken from the east, facing Campbell Street, near the front of The Promontory Inn, probably late in the afternoon, on the sidewalk facing the steps leading up here," Brian said, as he pointed to the front of the hotel.

"How in hell did you figure that out?" Cooper asked, raising his eyebrows.

"I left The Parsonage 20 minutes ago. I walked south about three blocks to the corner of Campbell Street."

"Down Runnymede?"

"Right, down Runnymede to Campbell."

"Okay, we know where that is, go ahead."

"Then I turned west and headed this way."

"Okay, you were about three blocks away from here."

"Okay, I walked west about two blocks down the sidewalk on the south side of Campbell Street. When I was about halfway down that third block, something looked familiar, like I'd seen it before. It came to me that I'd seen this same sidewalk next to a pond in one of the photos of Ruth Cahill. I looked ahead of me and I saw the sidewalk leading up to the small flight of steps. Just to make sure that I wasn't losing my mind, I went back to The Parsonage, picked up the photo and brought it back here with me. Here, take a look."

Mary Meade and Cooper looked at the photo. "Look, Coopy, there's Miller's Pond, just to the right of the steps, across the street."

"I'll be damned. This is right down our front steps and across the street. That is where the picture was taken. It's the same woman. Someone wrote '1946' on the back. Any idea who might have written that?"

"None whatever."

"That old camera angle made Campbell Street look narrow. I'll be damned. God, that's amazing," Cooper said.

"Sounds like you're getting closer to something," Mary Meade said.

"There's more. In one of the other pictures, Ruth looks like a barmaid. Part of the bar where she must've worked is in the picture." Brian said, as he pointed to the mirror behind the bar. "It's this bar right here, and she was standing about where I'm standing now, "Brian said. "I recognized the strange shape of the mirror."

"Good Lord, you're sure that Ruth Cahill, the person you think is your mother, worked as a barmaid in this hotel, in this bar?" Mary Meade asked.

"Yes, all those years ago, where I'm standing now. I left that picture back at my room," Brian said as he stared into the mirror.

"This gets more fascinating by the minute. Maybe we can get together tomorrow," Cooper said, hoping to end the conversation.

"There's more," Brian said. "Mary Meade, remember asking me about the man in the photograph sitting on the bench with Ruth Cahill? Did I know who it was?"

"I wasn't sure you heard me."

"I heard you. I went back to my room and took another look at that photo. I want you guys to see it," Brian said.

"Okay, that's cool, maybe we can see it tomorrow," Mary Meade said. "You seem upset about something. Is it something we said?"

"No, it's nothing either of you said, but I think you should see the photograph of the man in the album, the one sitting with Ruth Cahill."

"Okay, well sure, now we're curious," Cooper said. "You didn't bring it with you tonight?"

"It's also back in my room."

Cooper and Mary Meade looked at each other and then back at Brian. "We're extra curious now. Can you tell us anything more about that picture before tomorrow?" Cooper asked.

"I'd rather you see it first."

"Can you at least tell us something more about it?" Cooper asked.

"Trust me, you both need to see it," Brian said, raising his voice.

"Two people are in the photo, and one is Ruth Cahill?"

"Right."

"It's the man you want us to see."

"Right, it's the man," Brian said.

"Something about the man in the photo?" Mary Meade asked.

"It's the man in the photo I want you to see, taken in front of the White Sands."

"Can you tell us any more?" Cooper asked

"Trust me. You need to see the picture. It's unlike anything you could imagine."

Mary Meade and Cooper looked at each other. Both laughed nervously. Brian said, "Cool!"

Mary Meade sensed Brian's anger. Something was wrong. She looked at Cooper then back at Brian, "Well, okay, we'll die of curiosity first, but let's get together tomorrow. As long as you're here, have a good time."

Cooper turned and glanced into the mirror and saw Brian staring at him. Cooper was on edge.

"Cooper, Mary Meade, we'll talk to you later," Brian said as he left the bar.

Mary Meade looked at Cooper and punched him on the shoulder. "Do we have any idea what he's talking about? He's upset. Is it something we said? What's going on? This's too weird for words. He makes me very uncomfortable."

"I don't know what the hell's going on. I don't know what that secret photo crap is all about. Why didn't he just tell us who or what is in that stupid photo or whatever it is? I guess his story or whatever is interesting, if any of it's true. It is starting to freak me out. Son of a bitch, we don't know what's true and what isn't. I mean Jesus, God, why did he come here anyway? What are we supposed to tell the bastard about that damn photo? Where does he get off? We're here to have fun, and this clown from nowhere comes across like a downer. I'm about ready to tell that son of a bitch what he can do with that stupid photograph. We were having a good time until he strolled in. I mean where does he get off?"

Mary Meade punched Cooper in the shoulder, "You know I don't like your cussing, Coopy, but I feel the same damn way."

"Mary Meade, this guy's a time bomb. I don't know what in hell's under the fancy clothes and slick manners. He's wacko. We got to be careful about what we say and do around this goofball."

"Coopy, he frightens me. Do we want to see him tomorrow?"

"He's too psycho for me," Cooper said. There was a pause as Cooper looked in the mirror and said nothing.

"Coopy, you're not talking."

"It's something I didn't see at first, but now I think I do or at least I'm starting to. I'm not making sense, am I?"

"Perfect sense."

"You know what I'm thinking?"

"I saw it this afternoon at the Sands. It hit me. I looked at him and then you and back again. Then I looked in the mirror and turned away. I think you saw it, too, didn't you? I could not believe what I was seeing. You two are so alike. You could be brothers. Oh God, Coopy, we have to be careful. What does this mean?"

Cooper put his arms around Mary Meade as he watched Brian walk away.

***

Brian went through the double doors and down the hallway to the Tea Room Gallery.

"Hey, Brian; I thought I might see you tonight."

Brian turned.

"C.J. Adams, the highway patrol guy, glad you made it," the man said.

"Well sure. C.J., didn't recognize you out of uniform."

"Most people don't."

WHY DID I GROW SO COLD?

"Just get here?"

"About 15 minutes ago."

"You've been to these functions before?"

"A few times."

"You said you know the owners?"

"The Meachams, yes, they've done a lot for this town."

"I met Cooper."

"Oh, okay, Cooper, yeah, great kid. It's interesting that you mentioned him. They say everyone has a double somewhere in the world, and it looks like Cooper is yours, and Cooper looks like his dad. I did a double-take the first time I saw you. Well, anyway, Cooper's here tending bar with his girlfriend."

Brian, wishing he were back in Chicago with Charmon, said nothing.

"Cooper's one hell of a football player. He will play college ball somewhere. His brother, Graham, is in college in California. I met him once. Also a nice kid. I'm sure you've heard that the Meachams rebuilt this hotel from ground up?"

"Right; I've heard how wonderful they are."

"I remember the old Promontory Inn. It was a wreck. Sat empty for 20 years or so. I need a drink and you need a beer. There is another bar by the pool behind the hotel. Let's head that way; maybe we'll run into the Meachams."

C.J. and Brian went to the back patio. The lake was still visible. The bar was near the swimming pool's deep end, and the pool, blue in reflection, was lighted from beneath the water. Clouds were gathering, and guests seemed not to notice. Tables and chairs were near the shallow end, and a large group had gathered near the diving board.

C.J. ordered a scotch and Brian switched to bourbon.

"You're in better shape than earlier," C.J. said.

"You could've thrown the book at me."

"Forget it."

"That's cool. I appreciate what you did."

"Not a problem. I was hoping I'd catch up with you tonight. You are like my cousin was years ago. He was injured in Nam."

Brian said nothing.

"That was years ago. He's gotten on with his life, like I think I have, after Nam and the death of my wife."

"God, man, I'm sorry, I didn't know"

"It's okay, but we're not talking about me. After seeing the shape you were in today, we need to talk about you. If that's a problem, you can walk off."

"Not a problem," Brian said.

"My cousin, after Nam, was like you this morning, out of control."

Brian said nothing.

"He needed physical therapy and lost part of his hearing and his right foot. Our family gave him support. He talked about Nam a lot. I think it helped him distance himself from what happened. He has bad days. Hell, we all do. He seems okay. He went to law school, has a family, an understanding wife, but he was in deep distress when he got back."

Brian nodded.

"Question?"

"Shoot."

"You said you've been to vet centers?"

"Right, on and off. They seem like zoos."

"That's what I want to know. How so?"

"They start out by telling you that you've got a disorder. Hell, I already knew something was wrong. After that, nothing goes anywhere. You are convinced at that point, if you didn't think so already, that you've got a screw loose. They don't give a damn about Nam vets. They are geared to World War II and Korea vets, vets from conventional wars, whatever that means. Few, if any, had been to Nam, so what the hell did they know? All of us were screwed by the system, and nobody cared when we got back. Hell, even the VFW avoided us. Those of us who did a lot of killing were probably more messed up than anyone else. Nobody wanted us back. Nobody cared. There weren't parades or anything. Most people gave us the finger, not high fives, the finger, you know, screw you, up yours. I asked myself, why did we go over there anyway? I mean what the hell for? Nobody gave a damn. Screw you, that's what the system and everybody said to us. You know what I'm talking about, don't you?"

C.J. Adams nodded.

WHY DID I GROW SO COLD?

"The vet centers may help some guys. I don't know. I've drifted in and out. You were in Nam; you know what it's all about. You've got your act together."

"Yeah, but I wasn't in the boonies. I was in the rear drinking beer. We went out a couple of times on convoy near Da Nang. One time, we got in a real firefight. Son of a bitch, it scared the hell out of me. A lot of dirty bastards shooting at us! Air strikes came in, and it was over in a couple of hours. When I came back here, I did not have many problems, but I joined up with the Vietnam Vets Association anyway. Then, I lost my wife to cancer, and that was pretty sobering. Losing her seemed to say we are all here for a short time, and we had better make the most of it. After that, I guess, I've been able to put things in some kind of perspective, at least it seems so. My priest said that for everything, there is a season and a purpose under heaven, and maybe that is so. Why I had an easy time of it over there, I don't know. I sometimes lose sleep over it. Maybe everything evens out in the end. I don't know. Let's get back to you."

"Okay."

"Okay, you were talking about vet centers."

"I've tried different things–drugs, analysis and whatever. The only thing that helps is exercise."

"Exercise."

"Right, lots of it. All that stuff about endorphins and runner's high is right. Seems stupid, but it helps with anger. The centers that I went to are big on group therapy, which told me there are other people like me. I still have very great anger, very great rage. I think about violence everyday. Jesus God, I never stop thinking about violence. Sometimes I can't deal with it. One of these days..."

C.J. and Brian stopped for drinks. Brian looked out at the water and was suddenly quiet. He wished he had never come to this town.

"You've got family to fall back on?" C.J. asked.

"None."

"None, at all?"

Brian did not answer.

"No parents, aunts, uncles, grandparents, brothers, sisters, cousins?"

"None! Nobody gives a rat's ass anyway," Brian raised his voice.

"I'm sorry."
Brian nodded and said nothing.
"How about friends?"
"I have some friends."
"Close friends?"
"Social friends."
"Are they a help?"
"Not in the way you're asking."
"Okay."

"I've been lonely most of my life and I need friends. I work at being a good friend. I'd lose the few I have if they knew everything about me. They know I was in Nam, and that is all. We are all about the same age, we have all been to college, we all work and live near downtown Chicago. A few of us get together sometimes on the weekends. We drink a fair amount, but I always feel detached, like I'm removed, watching what's happening from a distance, like watching myself in an old movie. Still, it's about the only fun I've ever had. I cannot lose that. I'm afraid of what I'd do," Brian said, knowing his pursuit of Ruth Cahill and his father would cost everything.

"You're not married?"
"No."
"Never married?"
"Never."
"Girlfriend?"
"Yes, Charmon, couple of years."
"Serious?"

"I think so. She is a good person. We talk about things. We like our time together, but it all seems artificial. Like we are faking everything; like watching ourselves in a movie. There is sadness between us, we haven't been able to overcome. I guess I'm a cold person. I don't think she is. I bring the sadness to our relationship. She want's to help, but, well, whatever. We may get married at some point…" Brian stopped.

"You've told her about your PTS problems?"

"She knows something. She's seen me in a bad way a couple of times, but beyond that we've talked around it."

"Is she with you here?"

"No, she went to see her folks in Wisconsin," Brian said, looking away.

"Wouldn't it be better if she was here?"

"Probably. I don't know. I don't know why I didn't ask her to come with me."

"By not coming to terms with Nam and the other pain in your life, you are living with a lighted fuse. You know that don't you?"

Brian nodded as he sipped his drink.

"I see in you the same thing I've seen in other guys. It's the same far-away look, the same 'I've been there' look, the same 'I can't forget' look, the same 'I've seen and done things' look, the same emptiness. I know what I saw today. You're not fair to the other people you might have killed today."

Brian shuddered, as he saw lightening offshore.

"Brian, I've heard it all before. Rage, self-pity, uncontrollable anger, sobbing, depression, hallucinations, nightmares, and an obsession with killing and death and even suicide. There are people who can help you."

Brian said nothing.

"Anger and thoughts of violence are with you every day?"

"Most days and most nights. Sometime's near the surface, sometimes barely under control…"

"Is Nam the only reason?"

"Violence has always been with me. It's the only way I had, or thought I had, to deal with any problem. I was an orphan and didn't know my parents. I have always hated my father in particular for abandoning me when I needed him most. I beat the hell out of a couple of kids at the orphanage. Then I was sent to a detention center. After that, I was transferred to another place, and I had more fights. One time I was put in one of those children's center places run by the Salvation Army. They decided my salvation wasn't worth it. They hated me. My anger was usually all out of proportion to what might have happened. Football was great. I liked to hurt people, and I was good at it. I guess I would still like to hurt people, badly."

"So, facing any problem with violence started early?"

"I joined the Army when I was 18 to get away from where I was living. By going infantry, I knew I could kill people and get paid for it. When I landed in country, I was with 1st Cav. I knew there'd be action."

"You signed up for infantry, 1st Cav, because you thought there would be fighting?"

"That's about it. A couple of months after the Ia Drang, somebody wrote that Americans went looking for a fight with NVA regulars in the Ia Drang, and, by God, we sure as hell found one. I got what I was looking for."

"Those NVA bastards weren't afraid to fight?"

"Those bastards were tough, but, Jesus Christ, were they stupid. They'd stand in the face of our artillery fire until it just blew the sons of bitches to pieces. Every firefight was a slaughter. It's hard to imagine what we did to those gook bastards. The Ia Drang made us killers. We were like animals. Jesus God, there were leeches and snakes and stench and body parts and booby traps. At night, we heard our guys, captured and wounded, and begging for life. We'd hear this insane laughter and a shot. Those dirty bastards! I enjoyed killing them. It was like stepping on a bug; you just wanted to grind them into the ground. If we shot a gook once, then right between the eyes. It got to be a game. We would shoot body parts and make the bastards suffer and scream and then kill them. It's always freaked me out, that out of millions of rounds fired, none hit me."

"Go on," C.J. said.

"When the Ia Drang was over, our unit was shot to pieces. I was sent to another unit."

"To the rear?"

"Short time."

"Go ahead."

"After the Ia Drang, we went on patrol about half the time. We'd have boredom and terror. When I had the M-60, I learned to fire in short bursts, otherwise the gooks would figure out who had it and they'd try to blow you away right away."

"What did you guys carry?"

"Probably the same stuff you guys carried on convoy: grenades, M-16s, mortars, M-79s, flack jackets, jungle boots, radios, and I guess that's about it. I remember the damnedest things. Like hitting LZ. Chopper touches down and we would go. Like jumping into ice water, with no place to hide. Adrenaline is off the chart. You could beat a cheetah at top speed."

C.J., listening, said nothing.

WHY DID I GROW SO COLD?

"On the first day in the Ia Drang, we touched down at X-Ray and took off running for cover. Stuff was coming from everywhere. Jesus Christ, you wanted to fit in a matchbox! Then, an insane silence as we started to move through the elephant grass. We were scared shitless. God, it was eerie. Then bam bam, I heard, 'Medic up here, medic up here on the double.' I ran up there with the medics. A Chicano kid, looked about 16, had been hit in the chest. It looked awful. God, the guy was on the ground. He was trying to pull air into his lungs. It was a terrible, scraping sound. The first medic scrambled around on the ground and started mouth-to-mouth. The other medic tried heart massage. Nothing was working. Then all hell broke loose. We could not hear anything. The medic guys kept working on the guy. One put a tube down the kid's throat. They started breathing through the tube. But nothing worked. After about five minutes, the kid died. By then, we were surrounded, and other guys were getting hit."

"First time you'd seen anybody get killed?"

"Jesus, God, yeah! We started to get used to it. I remember one time, after the Ia Drang, one of our guys was shot up. We got him to a field hospital. He was in a bad way. We found a bed and put him down. There was an unconscious NVA guy several beds away. They were trying to fix the gook up so they could interrogate him or something. He had IVs in him. The only doctor there was trying to save a Special Forces guy, who looked like he was going to die. A couple of nurses rushed over to our guy's bed. One started cutting off his shirt and the other started an incision for a tracheotomy. A few minutes later, the NVA gook woke up, looked around, pulled out his needles, and lunged for one of the nurses. He had his hands around her neck and was grabbing for her scissors. They both crashed to the floor. The doctor looked up, saw what was happening, grabbed a .45 and rushed over. He freaked. The doctor slammed a bedpan hard on the NVA soldier's head with his left hand. With his right, he jammed the barrel of the .45 into the gook's mouth so hard he broke off the guy's front teeth. You could hear the NVA guy choking on his own teeth. The doctor pulled the gun out and then put the gun to the guy's forehead and pulled the trigger. It literally blew the top of the gook's head off."

"You saw it all?"

"About two feet away."

"What about your guy, did he live?"

"He did."

"The Special Forces guy?"

"He didn't make it."

"The doctor went off the deep end?"

"He was more concerned about the patients and nurses. The nurse was roughed up, but okay. The doctor seemed to take the thing in stride, like it was part of the job."

"The doctor probably thought he had seen everything."

"Probably so. Most GIs, you know, when they were first in country anyway, felt sorry for kids. Orphans and mixed kids, whatever they're called, were all over the place."

"We'd see them all the time around Da Nang," C.J. said. "They were on the streets. We learned to look out for those little bastards."

"A bunch of guys from our unit were in Saigon for a few days of R&R. They were hanging out at a bar somewhere. This kid walked in, and I guess one of our guys walked over to him to see if he had a sister or something. Bam, right there the kid exploded, seven of our guys killed and three wounded. The bar was blown to bits. Jesus, God, can you imagine that? The little bastard had a bomb and was blown in a thousand pieces."

"You were in a bad part of the world. It was insane. The country's a rotten septic tank."

"God, I'll say. Welcome to Nam, the cesspool of the world. I remember when we landed in country from the States, our plane stopped just long enough for us to jump off with our gear, and then it was off down the runway and out of there. A trip to the Asian outhouse! Then we were in the bus going from the airport to wherever and, I'll be damned, we got stuck in Da Nang traffic. The driver knew we were sitting ducks, a target full of American GIs. He got nervous and, God, it's amazing what happened. He pulled that huge bus off the street and drove up over the curb on to the main downtown sidewalk, filled with people and bikes and scooters. It was a really big bus going 20 miles an hour or so, and off we went right down the damn sidewalk, running over everything, tearing down awnings, street posts, right over the top of bikes–I mean, everything. It was wild. Every son of a bitch in our way was running for cover. God, it was wild. People were yelling, throwing stuff at us, calling us everything. It didn't matter, we couldn't understand it anyway. Then the driver started to laugh, and then we started to laugh and cheer the driver on. Everybody hated us anyway, so to hell with them. We must've laughed for 20 minutes."

C.J. Adams laughed aloud. "I'd never heard that one before."

"Anything could happen," Brian continued. "They always said don't get close to your buddy."

"Heard it all the time. Do not get close to anybody. The other guy's going to get blown away."

"With 1st Cav, we had to be close. We'd trained together forever. We knew what each of us could do and couldn't do. We were loyal to Colonel Moore and to each other. After I was transferred out, attitudes toward other guys were different. We were with units, still infantry, from all over the place. Didn't seem to have a hell of a lot in common any more. After I re-upped, I got to know a lifer. Riley was the guy's name. He seemed to be looking out for me. Since nobody had ever done that before, we got to be friends. Riley was from Omaha. Talked about Omaha a lot, said he was going back there when all this was over. I promised him I would look him up in Omaha after we got out. He said he might be able to find a job for me there someday. Since I'd never had a hometown, that seemed like a good idea. One day we were coming back from patrol, a bad one. Our wounded and what was left of our unit was up ahead of us. Jesus, we were tired, we had helmets on and were carrying flak jackets. Something made Riley and me and a couple of other guys drop back. As we moved out of the jungle, we came to some rice paddies, and then zing, zing, zing, Riley was hit in the gut. The other two guys were each hit in the chest and died instantly. We all went down. I thought I knew where the shots came from. I fired a whole magazine into a clump of rubber trees. Then I ran over there to blow the son of a bitch's head off, and there was a boy, probably 16, on the ground near a bicycle. He must have seen us coming, saw the ambush coming and hid behind the rubber trees. He didn't have a weapon. I'd hit him five or six times. Must have been sitting on his bike when I hit him. He was face up, next to his bike. His chest was full of holes. One hit his neck.

"I ran back to Riley, who was screaming. His insides were falling out. The other guys were dead. I tried to push Riley's guts back inside, using his flak jacket, strap from his M-79, anything I could find. We had no morphine. I can still hear him screaming, 'Dammit, Cahill, Let me die. Let me die, you bastard. You dirty bastard, let me die." I ran ahead for help. Another guy and I half carried him back to the LZ. When we got there, he was dead. I went out of my mind. C.O. took me off patrol for a month. I still see the kid with the bicycle in my sleep. I saw him this morning. Riley is still screaming."

Adams knew this could go on all night.

"I know where you're coming from."

Brian nodded.

"A lot of grunts had it as rough as you. You re-upped, thought you were fighting for something and money. We can't change what's happened. You can't, I can't. It is over. It is done. This Nam thing and other bad things that've happened can ruin your life if you let them."

Brian said nothing.

"You've got to come to terms with what's happened and move on. I see in you what I've seen in others. If you don't move on, you're going to do something stupid that'll ruin the rest of your life. I see it coming. Others can help. As bad as it's been, you're taking all of this too hard. From some of the things you've said–college, some friends, good job, Charmon–you got some things to be thankful for."

C.J. knew that Brian was truly disturbed and violence or suicide seemed possible, even imminent. He handed Brian a piece of notepaper. "Write your phone number down for me. I'll go over to my room right now, call a person at the vets group in Chicago and leave a message for him to contact you when you get back from vacation."

Brian said nothing. He wrote his number on the piece of paper and handed the note to C.J.

"Thanks!" C.J. said, as he punched Brian in the shoulder. "I'll be back in 20 minutes. While I'm gone, brighten up your evening by introducing yourself to the hotel owner, Pen Meacham, just about the happiest guy I know. He's standing right over there talking with one of the waiters."

Chapter 21

It was past eleven. Shannon stood on the hotel terrace. She looked out at the lake and saw the marina across the bay on the north shore. There were no running lights, and the slips were full. Shannon turned and looked at the crowded dance floor and could stand the noise and smoke no longer. She made her way across the terrace and the dance floor and through crowds of people to the front door, and she said goodbye to Charlie Putnam.

Mist was starting and a rainstorm was moving across the water toward shore. The night air and mist felt good on her face. She walked around Gerry and Charlie's Garden on the west side of the hotel and followed the walkway leading back to the garden above the beach. The marigolds looked like glowing candles in the darkness. Someone had left a coffee cup and newspaper on a wooden table next to the flowerbed. A chair stood next to the table. A foghorn sounded in the distance. Shannon stood at the edge of the garden and looked at the lake below for a long time. A small boat had been left on the beach; a bilge bag was tucked under the bow.

She walked back to her room at Chestnut Brook, put on a raincoat and hat, and left for the beach. It was raining hard by the time she reached the breakwater. Shannon held on to a hand railing and followed two flights of wooden stairs down to the beach. Her footsteps on the sand-covered stairs made a scratching sound as she made her way down. The rain was steady. Shannon took her shoes off and walked north along the water's edge. It was cool and the wet sand felt good under her feet.

Shannon had been happy all day, but she knew it would not last. From the moment she had gotten to town and checked into her room, something had been different. She thought she had left everything behind–the need to somehow find meaning and purpose was still with her. The trip to this town had been important, and now she was here. Breaking away from work had been hard. She envied those at the party with friends or groups and suddenly wished she had never come to Stamford Bridge. Her reflections defied solution. Nothing was behind her.

Shannon saw a person standing far away on the beach, and she stopped to look. The figure did not move. Shannon turned around and walked away. After a few steps, she turned and looked down the beach again and saw the figure walking in the other direction and then disappeared in mist. There was a presence moving in her direction, and she kept walking. Ahead of her, for as far as she could see, was the beach. There were patches of beach grass and a few old trees back from the water. Far off to the left was the lake, and Shannon saw the choppy waves when lightening flashed.

It was the suffering she had seen that destroyed her faith in the goodness of life. She sometimes wondered if God was out of His mind. How else could one explain her parents suffering before death? She asked herself if God Himself had ever suffered as He has made others suffer. She assumed, if God really was merciful, there would be an end to suffering. Did God feel grief at the death of Jesus Christ and the descent into hell? Shannon wondered.

By now, she knew there would never be answers, and she was tired, wet, and cold. She made her way down a steep bank, across a small inlet, and to a narrow pathway that led through tall beach grass. The rain was coming in sheets, and she found the wooden stairs leading up to the garden. She climbed the stairs to the small garden and sat down on the chair. A squad car filled with people from the party went slowly by and Shannon heard laughter. She now saw a heavier squall just off shore, and she could hear the wind blowing from Wisconsin.

Shannon walked barefooted to her room. It was warm inside, and she took off her wet clothes and put them on a hook in the bathroom to dry. Shannon took a shower and put on her bathrobe. She sat down on the bed. Her legs ached, her face felt hot and she was dizzy. The wine had left her exhausted and she was alone.

Chapter 22

Brian knew this moment was coming and he dreaded it. He walked by the bar, sat down at a small wooden table near the long hallway, and ordered a glass of beer. Brian was very nervous. He turned slowly to his left and saw Penfield Meacham for the first time–early 50s, smaller than Cooper, graying, blazer, white shirt, khaki slacks, handkerchief, red tie and loafers. The resemblance between Pen, Cooper, himself, and the man in the 1945 photograph was obvious. Pen Meacham's identity seemed certain–he had to be the man in the 1945 photograph with Ruth Cahill. Cooper Meacham, at 18, looked almost exactly like the man in the photo. Brian's emotions came in a rush; not only hatred; but also a sudden overpowering sadness. He thought of Charmon and the war and he was cold.

Brian could not stop staring; he could scarcely breathe. Pen was holding a drink and talking to a waiter in the hallway and both laughed. Several people spoke to Pen, and he looked happy. A couple came down the long hallway and talked with Pen. The waiter smiled and left. Pen and the couple talked, and they passed by Brian's table on the way to the bar. Pen ordered drinks and shook hands with the bartender.

Pen Meacham was better looking than Brian had imagined, and it bothered Brian that Pen was enjoying himself. Pen walked down the hallway to the pool with another couple and said something to the lifeguard. Pen then met Brian's gaze from a distance. He quickly frowned and looked away. Cooper Meacham came down the long hallway and asked his dad something. Pen nodded, and Cooper left. A woman in a yellow dress approached Pen from a different direction. She hugged the man and woman talking with Pen and then took Pen's hand. *That must be Pen's wife,* Brian thought. *What about Ruth Cahill? That woman in the yellow dress is not my mother.*

Pen Meacham and the woman in the yellow dress and the other couple walked across the tennis court to the carport. They stopped to look at a white Corvette. The top was down, and the interior was red. Pen opened the car door, sat down behind the wheel, and looked up with a grin. The right side window came up, and the new car sticker was still there. Pen got out of the car and invited the other man to sit behind the wheel. The other man shook his head, laughed, and pointed at the window sticker. The woman in the yellow dress rolled her eyes and shook her head. The group walked back from the carport and across the tennis court to the bar. They picked up new drinks. Pen turned from the bar and looked again at Brian, then blinked and looked away.

Charlie Putnam approached Pen with a clipboard. Pen signed something and gave the clipboard back to Charlie, who nodded and left. Charlie waved at Brian as he passed by Brian's table. Brian waved back. Pen and the small group passed by Brian's table on their way to the long hallway. Brian stared at Pen as he came close. Pen, with a questioning glance, frowned and walked on. The group made their way down the long hallway to the Tea Room Gallery. Michael Carter joined them. Pen and Michael shook hands. They talked and looked toward Brian and then looked away. Pen turned again and looked at Brian for the fourth time, as if were about to approach and ask a question. He shook his head and turned toward the Tea Room.

Brian watched as Penfield, the woman in the yellow dress and friends disappeared into the Tea Room Gallery. Brian did not follow them. He picked up another glass of beer from the bar and went back to the table near the long hallway. Brian was angry with himself about not confronting Pen Meacham. *Why*, thought Brian, *should that son of a bitch have had everything, and he left me at an orphanage. He left me with nothing and he's had all this! I thought about him in Nam and I knew I'd find him somewhere. Then I'm going to find Ruth Cahill, and who knows what'll happen.*

It annoyed Brian to see people having fun at The Promontory Inn. It angered him to finally see Pen Meacham at all; Brian wished he had never left

WHY DID I GROW SO COLD?

Chicago, and he longed to get away as fast as he could. Brian got up from the table and made his way through crowds to the bar. He picked up another beer and walked by the swimming pool, the tennis court, the carport, and the patio. It was now raining hard.

Brian left the patio and followed a cobblestone walkway to the far edge of the lawn. Waves splashed against the breakwater. Brian stopped short, as if he did not know what to do. A foghorn sounded, and he moved to the edge of the lawn and saw the beach below. He spotted an opening to a narrow trail between two large rocks. The narrow, winding trail ahead vanished into darkness. It was lined with rocks and shrubbery. Further down, larger trees grew, rising like pillars out of the dark, stone-covered earth. Brian made his way slowly around trees and down winding crossbacks. Sharp slippery rocks jutted into the trail, and walking was difficult. Leaves and branches felt wet in his hands as he reached out to steady himself. After falling down on the muddy trail, Brian stopped at a small plateau. His clothes were wet and dirty. He followed a curve in the pathway and came to a tree stump, where the path split in two directions. Brian was unsure which way to go and stood motionless in the rain. A foghorn again jogged his senses. He moved carefully down the trail to his right, holding onto branches and tree limbs to keep from falling again. Soon, the trail abruptly circled around an old shed, close by a stack of decaying logs. Then, the pathway jutted deeply into the ground. Brian could only make his way by placing one foot directly in front of the other. The rain was pelting his face, and the top of the cliff behind him was hidden from view. Around a sharp bend, a small stream crossed the path. Brian slipped on smooth stones under water and fell on the far bank. He got up and continued on his way through long grass, up and down small ravines into darkness, until the path brought him to the beach. In the gray light of the storm, he saw the whiteness of waves rolling into the beach.

He stopped near the water's edge and saw a person walking in the other direction. The rain was falling heavily toward him and Brian now felt like a man trapped at the bottom of a canyon, where there will never be light. He felt a terrible sense of isolation, knowing his father and mother had discarded him. Horror gripped his spine. Brian now knew what he was going to do, and he was powerless to stop it, as if he was watching himself from a distance.

Chapter 23

When the rain started, guests came inside the hotel. Ida Mae and a busboy were tending the main bar. Cooper and Mary Meade left before midnight and walked down the long hallway to the front closet where they picked up raincoats and left the hotel through a side door. The lawn was lighted. It was green and wet in the rain. The white roses in Gerry and Charlie's flower garden were spotlighted. Cooper and Mary Meade walked together through the rain, past rows of outdoor furniture and then along a white wooden fence next to a jogging path. They crossed the shuffleboard court. On their left was a cabana. The awnings were down, and the walkway to Charlie Putnam's shack was just ahead.

"Nice of Ida Mae to take over for us," Mary Meade said.

"They were done in the kitchen, and she stays late anyway. But, you're right," Cooper said.

"Will she tell your folks we left early?"

"No, she's cool. My folks are drinking with their friends. They'll be wasted. They won't care anyway."

"Do you think anyone knows where we're going?"

"It's nobody else's business but ours. It's you and me. That's what matters."

"I love you, Coopy."

Mary Meade pulled the rain hat down tight over her head. She took hold of Cooper's hand. Cooper put his arm around her, and she put her head on his shoulder.

"Jeez, it's coming down in buckets!" Cooper said.

"I don't think it's ever letting up," Mary Meade said.

They walked around the cabana and across a small driveway to Charlie's shack. They stood under an awning, and looked back at the hotel. It looked like a large, bright light against the dark sky.

"Let's go on down to the cabin," Cooper said.

"Okay, but can we find it in the dark?" Mary Meade asked.

"Trust me. Ready to get rained on again?"

"Okay. I was tired when we left the hotel, but I'm a lot better now, since we've been walking."

"How about it? The rain and alone together in the cabin? Are you good to go?"

"Oh! I'm good to go."

Cooper put his arms around Mary Meade for a long time. They leaned back against the wall and listened to the rain and thunder, and the air smelled clean.

"Ready?" Mary Meade asked.

"Good, let's do it."

They walked across the short grass until they reached the woods. Rain was coming from the west, and trees were bending with the wind. Thunder above them was loud.

"Let's hurry," Mary Meade said.

"It's okay," Cooper replied.

"Okay, but hang on to me. I'm scared."

"I'd never let go of you," Cooper said.

The trailhead was overgrown, and they felt wet leaves brush across their faces as they moved into the forest. A tree had fallen across the trail in front of them. They stopped. Cooper climbed over the trunk and fell to the ground on the other side. Cooper stood up, reached back, and pulled Mary Meade over the top.

"All in one piece?" Cooper asked.

"I'm okay."

The trail narrowed as they moved in single-file through tall trees. They made their way around a winding curve, then the trail split in two directions. The undergrowth was heavy, and they crossed a fast moving stream on a slippery wooden bridge. They stopped and looked west.

"Mary Meade, there's the beach down there. The cabin's not far from here," Cooper said.

"Coopy, look! There's a person down there standing on the beach, almost in the water!"

"Who in hell could that be?"

"I don't know, but I'm glad that person's down there and we're up here."

"Look, Mary Meade. He's walking away."

"I'm glad. Seeing somebody down there in the middle of the night in the rain gives me the creeps."

The wind picked up. Rain was coming off the lake, and the waves were large and white. The path before them was muddy, with piles of wet leaves on both sides. Up ahead, the trail came to a wide creek. They stopped and looked across. The small cabin was between two large trees. Cooper took Mary Meade's hand, and they walked across the creek on large rocks. Leaves and branches had fallen onto the roof of the cabin and it was dark inside. There was a pile of firewood by the front door.

Cooper opened the door, and they went inside. The cabin was small. Mary Meade shut the door behind them. Cooper turned on the gas lantern in the corner, which made a yellow light. The walls were paneled with plain dark wood, and there was a single bed in the corner. They saw two wooden chairs and a table for magazines and books next to the window. Cooper and Mary Meade took off wet coats and put them on small hooks on the back of the door. Cooper started a fire in the small porcelain stove. The wood sparked and crackled and the room smelled like hickory and cedar. They could hear wind outside and rain falling on the roof. They sat down on the edge of the bed. Cooper put his arm around Mary Meade and held her for a long time.

"Madhouse tonight, wasn't it?" Mary Meade asked.

"But everybody seemed to be having a good time," Cooper said. "My folks are feeling no pain. I didn't see your folks tonight."

"They went to something in South Haven."

Cooper walked to the front door and locked it. He sat down and looked at the light from the stove.

"Thinking about that Brian character?" Mary Meade asked.

Cooper nodded.

"What do you think?"

"I saw him staring at me. I don't know him, and I don't want to. The guy's too weird."

"He scares me, Coopy. Freaks me out really bad. We don't know anything anyway and could care less."

Cooper nodded.

"I want to say screw him."

"There's no way he has anything to do with us."

"A day ago, we'd never heard of this guy. It's like he came from outer space and landed here."

"The guy walks in and says he's looking for somebody we never heard of, Ruth something. Says she is his mother, and he has never seen her. Then, he tells us his mother or whoever worked in The Promontory bar, for God's sake. But, for Christ's sake, he's got a picture of her taken across the street."

"The scary part is that he looks like your dad and... you!"

"I know it! Does that mean my dad was screwing around before he met Mom?"

"I doubt that."

"Well then, how else can he look like my dad and me? What does that mean about my mother? I mean, Jesus, what goes on here? What about my folks? Is there something to hide somewhere? Something they haven't told me? Something I've sure as hell never known? Think about it, how else could he look like me and like Dad?"

"Coopy, who do you think's in the picture? What'd the guy say, 'unlike anything you could imagine' or something?"

"I guess the scariest thing would be if it's a picture of my dad. But, I don't see how that's possible. This Brian character says the picture is a big deal. God, if it's a picture of my dad, what then? Would I go up to my dad and say, you know, like, 'Dad, I've been meaning to talk to you about something. Were you messing around before I was born?' On the other hand, 'Dad, do you want to tell me about Ruth Cahill?' Or, 'Dad, where does Mom fit into all this?'"

Mary Meade laughed. "Forget it tonight. Otherwise, we'll just get upset. Tonight is our night."

Cooper put more logs in the stove, and the room was warm. He went to the small window and looked out. It was raining hard and Cooper turned off the lantern. The light from the fire was yellow orange.

"I love it here with you. I wish we were married and this was, you know our retreat from the world. Just you and me," Mary Meade said.

"This's our time. Sometimes I feel like there will never be another time, another place. There's only this time, this place, this moment and you."

"We're going to have a wonderful life together. I don't ever want us to be apart."

"Ditto."

"Our life here's so wonderful, I don't ever want to leave it."

"I don't like to think about leaving even for a minute."

"We'll leave to go to college. You and me together and then take it from there."

"I love our life here. I don't see how it could be any better, We're so lucky. I'm so lucky."

"This rain scares me."

"Why?"

"Never mind."

"No, why?"

"It's stupid and scary."

"Tell me."

"It's a dumb thought I had today."

"You don't have dumb thoughts."

"I did today. I'd be really afraid, if I wasn't with you."

"Okay, shoot."

"This morning, when I was getting dressed, I looked at the lake, you know, from my bedroom window. I saw a bright day without a cloud. But I was thinking about rain. It was strange, I can't explain it. I don't want to think about it any more."

"I had a strange feeling too when I got up this morning, Something out of control coming this way and it can't be stopped. It was a cold feeling."

Mary Meade started to cry. "Let's talk about something else; this scares me."

"It doesn't matter now. We've got each other."

The light from the stove was burning low and the room was almost dark.

Cooper put his arms around Mary Meade, and they lay down on the bed together. They were still and listened to the rain on the roof.

"There's no longer me. There's only us. That's the only way I think any more. I want you more than anything in the world. Let's get under the covers and keep each other warm. Do I talk too much?"

"No."

"I feel like we're already married. We'll have children won't we?"

"Yes."

"What'll they be like?"

"I want them to look like you."

"They'll look like us, and they'll be smart like you."

"No, they'll be smart like you."

"I feel so close to you. I am so happy, so very happy. We'll have to be careful tonight."

"Happy?" Cooper whispered.

"Very happy."

Chapter 24

    The rain was heavy and the person Brian had seen walking on the beach did not return. Brian made his way north across the sand at water's edge, and the wind was blowing in his face. His footsteps on the sand made a crunching sound as he walked; he stopped at the base of a sand cliff and looked in all directions. The beach was deserted. Boats were not out in this storm. He saw a few tied down in slips on the north shore. Above him, it was dark at the top of the cliff. He found the wooden stairs that led up from the beach, and he climbed to the first landing and stopped. The Inn was to the south and The Parsonage was directly above him.

    Brian climbed the next flight and followed a wet pathway to The Parsonage. Sidewalks and streets were deserted, and guestrooms were dark. Brian went into his room and sat down on the edge of the bed. The only light came from a small table lamp by the coffee table. It was ten minutes past three.

Chapter 25

The air was soggy Sunday morning, as the sun was coming up. Boats, moored at Whitehall, were almost motionless in the water, the horizon still covered by early fog. A sloop, looking no larger than a thimble from the shore, moved westward toward the horizon and disappeared. Waves slowly moving to shore made quiet splashing sounds. An artist stood on the beach working at an easel, silhouetted against the sky. She was wearing a straw hat, tan clothes, and a bright red scarf.

At 7:30, Ida Mae Murphy in her blue work uniform and black shoes walked down Campbell Street from her home to The Promontory Inn. All the damp streets were deserted, stores and restaurants were closed, and there was no traffic. Ida Mae tossed her cigarette, crossed over from Campbell Street, and made her way across the parking lot and up the sidewalk to the hotel's front porch.

"When I reached the front door," Ida Mae told Deputy Martin, "I remember how quiet it was. Maybe Sundays were always quiet and I never noticed before. Hell, I don't know. The only noise I remember was the sound of my own footsteps on the wood floor, you know, the front porch, and they sounded kind of spooky to me, but I didn't know why. There was no traffic, I'm sure of that. Most people had been to the party and they didn't get up early on Sunday. I did notice that both of the Meachams' cars and Cooper's Jeep were in the carport."

"Did you see anyone around the hotel or anywhere?" Freddie asked.

"I saw an artist wearing a straw hat, a woman, painting at an easel on the beach, near the picnic tables. I remember that I waved to her and she waved back. I don't know who it was, but I remember wondering what she was painting. Anyway, I also remember seeing sailboats way out, you know way out there; and then they were gone, out of sight. Why am I saying dumb stuff like this? Jesus Christ, Freddie, why am I saying all this? It's so damned stupid to remember idiotic things like that at a time like this isn't it? Oh, my God! What's happened? Oh God! Freddie, how could this happen? I'm going insane! My God, there was blood on the wall and the floor. I was standing in it, it squished under my shoes, and I must've tracked it down the hallway. God how awful! Mr. Pen's eye was wide open, like staring. The whole side of his face was just a mass of red. He only had one eye left. Freddie, I can't stand it…"

"You're doin' okay, Ida Mae. Let's get through this. This's hell, it's hell for all of us. Jesus, Henry is on his way back from Lansing. He'll be floored, he doesn't know. God almighty, what'll I say to him?" Martin said and he reached for a cigarette.

"My eye hurts, but I'll keep going," Ida Mae said.

"Okay, anything more you remember is important, anything at all," Martin said. "Just for the record, did you see anyone inside the hotel, you know, in the lobby or anywhere at all?"

"No, the Meachams would sometimes get up early on Sunday," Ida Mae continued, "but not always. Getting to work early on Sunday morning wasn't unusual for me. I had been at the Inn early on Sundays before. We'd cleaned up last night so the place was a neat as a pin. Jesus Christ, I don't know what that has to do with anything."

Ida Mae cleared her throat and closed her eyes. She used index fingers to wipe away the tears from her eyes. Her left eyelid was inflamed.

"Oh, my God! Oh God, how awful! Oh, God, why did this happen? God, why did you let this happen?" Ida Mae said. She buried her face in her hands.

"Try to stay calm. I know this's hard. Jesus Christ, it's hard for all of us."

"Okay, Freddie. Good Jesus, please help me," Ida Mae said. "Saturday was different."

"Don't you mean Sunday, you know, today?"

"No, I'm talking about yesterday, Saturday. It was the strangest Saturday of my life and I don't know why. I had a feeling of something odd, very odd, I guess you'd say, when I was walking to work on Saturday morning, yesterday morning. The feeling, or whatever it was, wouldn't go away. It lasted all day and last night. The damnedest thing. Like something had happened, or was going to happen or whatever. I felt the same way this morning when I got up to go to the hotel. I can't explain it."

Ida Mae's fall down the hotel's front steps had broken her nose. Dr. Oliver stopped the bleeding, examined her nose, and stitched the gash over her left eye. She was sitting in the police department lunchroom and gripped the blood stained towel around her neck.

"You saw nobody but the one person painting?"

"Nobody, that's right, nobody. The Inn has four entrances. On Sundays, I always use the main one, you know, in the front, by the porch. So, I went to the front door and let myself in, as I said, like I do every Sunday. Nobody was awake, but that wasn't unusual after party night. Good Christ almighty, I'm repeating myself again. I can't focus on what I'm saying."

"Ida Mae, take it easy, we're all upset. We'll get through this. Just take it slow and we'll be done."

"Okay Freddie. Well, I walked through the lobby, through the dining room to the kitchen and everything seemed in order. As I said before, we'd cleaned up after the party. I planned to do some work in the kitchen for a couple of hours and then go home. It was after I got to the kitchen that it dawned on me that I'd seen something peculiar and I went back to the lobby. The cash register drawer was open. Cooper Meacham, working at the night desk, wouldn't have left it open. Then I saw something else that was odd. The Meachams' apartment is on the third floor, in the west wing of the hotel. I'd never been up there, but I knew which door led up there to it. I'd never seen it left open."

"Ida Mae, did you hear anything like a shower going or a door open and shut or someone walking or something?"

"No, nothing."

"Okay, nothing at all, go ahead."

"I walked over and looked up the stairs. As I said, I'd seen both cars and the Jeep in the carport, so I knew the Meachams had to be upstairs. Oh God, I'm repeating myself. I know it. I know it. But God almighty, I knew that none of them would have been down at the beach at that hour. So I asked myself, where could they be? I called up the stairs several times. No answer. I got very damn nervous. I just knew something had to be wrong, just really wrong! At that point, I decided to call my folks and ask them what I should do. I picked up the telephone in the lobby to call home and the telephone was dead. That really startled me and I thought maybe I should go to my home right away and talk to my folks and then I would call you or Henry. Then for some reason I went over and looked out through the front door window. I don't know what I was expecting to see or why I did that. I guess I was hoping to see somebody, anybody. I guess I did it to get up my courage to go upstairs or something. Then, I started up the stairs."

"Still, no sound or anything, you're absolutely sure?"

"Freddie, dammit, I'm trying to tell you. I heard nothing."

"Okay, I just wanted to make sure."

"Well I'm damn sure!"

"Okay"

"Anyway, it scared me a lot, the phone being dead and the strange feeling and then hearing the sound of my footsteps on the stairs really scared me. I'd never been up there before. So I went up the first flight of stairs just one step at a time and turned on the landing to go up to the next floor. Then, I must've lost my head. All that blood on the wall, the floor, and everywhere. Mr. Pen's eye was wide open, staring at me. His mouth was wide open and his tongue. Oh God! Oh God, how horrible! The side of his face was totally gone. There was nothing there. He only had one eye left! It was horrible. The next thing I remember is running out the door. I tripped over a flower box and fell down the stairs. I got up and ran down here screaming."

Ida Mae's eyes filled with tears. She asked for a glass of water and a cigarette. Her uniform was covered with blood. Her father put his arm around her as Mrs. Murphy took her hand. Nothing like this had ever happened in Stamford Bridge.

Chapter 26

By 9:45 a.m., Sunday, Deputy Freddie Martin, Frank Scott, Dick Schroeder, and officers from St. John's Woods, Cornwall Bay, and Ludgate Hill had cordoned off The Promontory Inn. Official vehicles arrived in slow procession down the center of Campbell Street. Ambulances were the last to arrive. Paramedics, the county coroner, a state police photographer, the sheriff, and a deputy went up the hotel's front steps, across the front porch and into the hotel. A few minutes later, a state trooper, homicide detectives and Father Cudahy, returning from the Saltonstalls' home, went inside. Many came directly from church.

Frightened hotel guests, awakened by police, came down from their rooms, made their way though a hotel side door and across the lawn to Campbell Street. Some were dressed, others were in bathrobes. A quiet crowd was gathering in the street in front of the hotel. There was little conversation. By mid-morning, the crowd had grown to more than 200. Rumors began to spread and friends of the Meachams and people from all over Barry County began to gather outside the hotel, but none were allowed into the hotel.

Soon, Father Cudahy and an officer from St. John's Woods emerged from the hotel front door and stopped on the front steps in front of the street crowd.

The crowd was silent.

"In my life as a priest, this is the saddest announcement I've ever been forced to make," Father Cuddly said, as his eyes filled with tears. He stopped, looked toward the lake and continued. "I must tell you that three of our favorite citizens, Geraldine Meacham, Penfield Meacham and Cooper Meacham are dead. They were slain in the hotel sometime in the early morning hours by an individual or individuals unknown at this time."

The crowd gasped in disbelief, some began to cry, and none could believe their ears. Soon, the police barricade around the hotel was lifted to allow the exit of three ambulances from the back of the hotel. A police squad car pulled in front of the three vehicles and another followed. Brian Cahill watched from his room as the white cortege passed slowly through town on the way to Grand Haven.

Chapter 27

Deputy F.G. Martin lived alone in a small second-floor apartment off Campbell Street. He could see from his front window the police department and The Promontory Inn. Freddie, a retired railroad worker, had been police chief Henry Plunkett's deputy for three years.

The chief had been out of town from Friday evening until late Sunday afternoon.

It was midnight. The sparingly furnished apartment was quiet; streets and sidewalks below were empty. Moonlight coming through the front window provided the only light. The deputy, having a beer and a cigarette, was worn out and closed his eyes and the horror came back. He remembered telling Henry how the day unfolded.

"The first thing I remember was somebody screaming. Until then, it'd been a normal Sunday morning. Screaming came out of the blue, like from nowhere, I mean, bam! Then another scream, louder than the first. Frank Scott, Dick Schroeder, and I were having coffee in the lunchroom at the time. It was about 8. We heard it again. For a second, the three of us just looked at each other. Then we got up and ran out the front door. There was Ida Mae Murphy coming toward us. I swear to Andy-by-God-Jackson that woman was terrified. She was running down Campbell Street as fast as she could go. She was hysterical, out of control. Blood was pouring down the left side of her face and out of her nose. She kept screaming, 'He's dead, he's dead. Oh my God, he's dead! That wonderful man, he's dead. Somebody blew the side of his face off.' She wasn't making sense, we tried to calm her down, and we took her inside to the lunchroom. She was in terrible pain. Dick ran to the back and brought out a couple of towels, and we got her to sit down, but she could not stop crying. It looked like her nose was broken. It looked real bad and swollen, and the crying was probably making it worse. We were afraid to touch it. There was a big gash over her left eye, and we didn't know how to stop the bleeding. Her cheekbone looked smashed. We didn't think it would be a good idea to take her to the hospital in the squad car. I told Frank to call Ludgate Hill Hospital and see if Doc Oliver was on duty. He was, thank God. I asked Frank to call his wife, because she's a nurse. Amanda, bless her heart, made it to the office in ten minutes. I asked Frank to stay with his wife and Ida Mae 'til Doc Oliver got there. I think Amanda got the bleeding stopped before the doctor got there.

"We had no idea what had happened at the hotel. What had Ida Mae actually seen? Who'd she seen? Who'd been shot? Had somebody really been shot? We didn't know, but we knew something must have happened. Dick and I got in the squad car and got over to the hotel right away. We had no idea what to expect. It rained Saturday night and early Sunday morning, and the streets and sidewalks were drying off. There was nobody on the streets. From what we could tell, hotel guests were still sleeping.

"When we got to the hotel, we saw an overturned flower box at the top of the front steps. Must've been the spot where Ida Mae tripped. We made our way up the steps and walked across the front porch to the front door, which was ajar. Charlie Putnam had already made it to the front porch, said he'd heard the screaming and wanted to know what was going on. We told him we didn't know, but we were going inside to check things out. We went inside to the lobby, and Charlie followed us. It was totally quiet, but we thought some guests must have heard something. It was just too damn quiet. It seemed strange, the place was clean as a whistle. You couldn't tell there'd been a party last night. The only noise was our footsteps. We asked Charlie to wait for us in the lobby in case anybody came over from the other part of the hotel. Then, Dick and I went through the dining room, the kitchen, the living room, the bar, the art gallery, the long hallway, and to the pool, the tennis courts, the carport and saw nothing unusual. Then we went back to the lobby, and Charlie was there waiting for us, nervous as hell. He had not seen anyone. Then we saw something strange. The cash drawer at the lobby check-in desk was open. Charlie said he'd never seen it open before. On the west side of the lobby, across from the fireplace, one of the lobby doors was standing open. Charlie told us it was the door leading to the Meachams' apartment. He said that he'd never been up there, and the door was always closed, day and night. We went over there, looked inside, and saw the stairs. We called upstairs to see if anyone was up there. There was no answer. Something seemed wrong. It was so quiet, and the room was warm.

"It was like a ghost town, with only three of us awake in that huge old place. Dick, Charlie, and I just looked at each other. I asked Charlie to wait in the lobby in case any of the guests had heard anything and maybe came down from the main part of the hotel. Then I led the way up the stairs with Dick behind me, and we moved very slowly up the first set of steps and I kept a hand on my revolver. We went up several steps and came to a landing, which we thought might lead to more steps. We turned to look for the next flight of steps and there was Pen Meacham on the floor. Unbelievable. It was very bad. There was a lot of blood on the wall and floor. Pen's left eye and his mouth were wide open. He'd been hit with terrific force on the side of his head, probably point-blank, with what must've have been a shotgun, Everything on the right side of his head and his right eye was gone, blown away. His head was a mangled red mess. We had to turn away. The gunshot must've hit Pen sideways and slammed him against the wall. He was wearing khakis and a t-shirt. No shoes or socks. Dick Schroeder and I looked at each other. Jesus Christ! Pen Meacham had been our friend. Half of his head was blown off. Dick Schroeder whispered, almost to himself, 'Freddie, my God, my God, what's happened?' Dick covered his face with his hands, staggered and fell against the wall. We were stunned out of our minds.

"We knew we had to find the rest of the family, and we were so scared that we were whispering to each other. Were they upstairs, or had they escaped? Was there still somebody in the hotel with a weapon? We turned on the landing to look for the next stairs, and, my God, we found Cooper Meacham. He was saddest of all, because he was so young. It broke our hearts. Dick and I'd seen him play football. What a nice, likeable kid he was. Cooper was sitting on the floor, leaning against the wall. There was a wound across his forehead; his eyes were closed. Like he was asleep. There was a fire axe on the floor, by his right hand. He was wearing a t-shirt, shorts, no shoes or socks. Dick and I couldn't figure out how Cooper could've been killed in that position. Looked like the killer or killers had put him there, maybe after he was dead, to make him more comfortable or something. Jesus, it looked like the blood around the wound on his head had been wiped away, like maybe the attack on him was an accident or something. Dick and I wondered if he could have been alive after the assault and moved to that position. God, what are we dealing with? Looked like a rifle barrel might have made the wound or something like that. Cooper looked like he was asleep. God, it's so sad, almost fell to my knees. Dick just about collapsed.

"Dick and I were scared. Where could Geraldine be? Was she dead or alive? Could she be injured somewhere up above?

"This time Dick led the way. I remember him saying, 'We've got to find Geraldine. She must be here somewhere.' We were both sick, but we pressed on up the stairs. At the top, we saw a door on our right that was ajar. We slowly pushed it open. We went carefully through a living room to a bedroom and pushed that door open. It was awful. There was Geraldine Meacham. She'd been hit point blank on the right side of her face. Her eyes were open, like maybe she'd watched the killer or something. God, how tragic. That beautiful woman looked like maybe she'd tried to get away. She must've known Pen heard something. She must've heard the first shotgun blast. Cooper must've come from his room or somewhere and found his mother scared to death. She probably went to the apartment door and called for Pen and there wasn't any answer. Probably tried to call the police station or anybody, but the line was dead. Cooper and his mother probably called out to Pen again. They may have heard somebody on the stairway. Cooper must've grabbed the only weapon he could find, a fire axe. He broke the glass, but the alarm didn't go off. His mother must've begged Cooper to stay with her. Cooper probably said he had to find out what happened to his dad. Must've gone down the hallway with the hatchet in his right hand. Probably the last his mother saw him. Probably surprised the killer or killers and was hit very hard in the forehead, which killed him. The explosion and the silence must've been terrifying. Geraldine couldn't use the telephone to call for help. Had no place to hide, no way to escape. We checked the back door to the fire escape. Hadn't been used in years. She was trapped. She probably heard footsteps. Probably screaming as the door opened. Must've seen a shotgun was pointed at her. God almighty. Must've begged for her life. The shot must've have thrown her against the chest of drawers and killed her instantly. As I said, her eyes were open. That beautiful woman, by God, she was massacred. The bedcovers were pulled back, so it looked like she and Pen had been asleep at some time during the night. We looked in the other parts of the apartment and found nothing out of place. There were no signs of a struggle and no shell casings that we could see. We looked in what we thought was Cooper Meacham's room. It was filled with boy stuff and the bedcovers were drawn back like he had been asleep.

"As far as we knew, we'd accounted for the Meacham family members in town. We knew the older boy, Graham, was away at school. As I said, we checked out the rest of the apartment. We couldn't look at the victims again."

Freddie opened another beer and a new pack of cigarettes. Sleep, he knew, would be impossible.

Chapter 28

Brian was awake by 9:30. The rain stopped and the curtains were closed. The room was dark and quiet. His wet clothes were on the wood floor. Brian pushed the covers aside, got up and looked for bloodstains on his clothes. There were none. His shoes were muddy and he washed them in the bathroom sink.

I must've been insane, he thought. *Is it over? Which one is the one? Are there two Pen Meachams?*

Brian felt cold and wrapped himself in a blanket. His hands were shaking. The room turned around and he buried his face in his hands. Brian went to the window and pulled back a curtain. It was a sunny day. The grounds were empty, and he closed the curtain. He knew leaving town would be a mistake.

He remembered the beach in the early hours. Brian had remembered things he had done in Vietnam and made his way up from the beach, along the narrow trail. It was still raining and the climb was difficult. The trail was muddy. He saw a faint light in the little cabin by the stream. Brian walked past it, across the stream and up the trail to The Parsonage. He did not see anyone and went to his room. Brian changed clothes and left his muddy shoes in the bathroom. Hunting gear was in his car. Brian brought his weapon inside and put it on the couch.

Brian was watching himself in an old movie. Thunder followed flashes of yellow lightning. Rain was coming straight off the lake and streetlights were out. Some porch lights were on, but most houses were dark. Water was running over sidewalks and curbs to flooded sewers. Lawns were saturated. There was no traffic and few cars were parked in the streets. The wind came in gusts, and leaves and branches were falling to the ground.

Brian put on rain gear and put the weapon under his poncho. A large boonie hat came down over his ears, and he wore gloves. He buttoned his coat and left the room. Brian moved in the rain from street to street. At Campbell and Canterbury Lane, the streets and sidewalks were under water. Brian circled a flower garden, and crossed to a brick sidewalk on Chestnut Brook grounds. From there, he walked down a narrow lane where homes were close to the street. A dog was barking somewhere. He heard thunder again.

Brian was cold and alone and he remembered smoke patterns in the sky and strange hollow sounding voices in the night. Brian could do little except watch himself from a distance. He came to Campbell Street. The Promontory Inn looked strange in the storm's half-light. An awning had blown down from the front porch and shingles had fallen to the grass. Outdoor furniture was in the side yard, gardens and flower boxes were flooded. Water was pouring from downspouts, splashing on the front porch. The hotel grounds were dark. Brian saw a single point of light in the lobby. Wooden front steps were wet and slippery, and Brian held onto the railing. His face and rain gear were wet. The loaded weapon under his coat was dry.

Brian came to the front door and looked through a small window. The lobby was empty. There was small light near the fireplace. Brian opened the door, moved inside, and listened to the storm. The clock above the fireplace said 3:40. Brian could see the living room and dining room on his left. On his right, he saw a door. Brian dropped his poncho and hat on the wood floor. He took off his wet shoes and left them on a throw rug by the door. He slowly opened the door. There was a night light at the top of a small flight of stairs. He stood still for a minute, holding the shotgun and listening. Then, each step made a creaking sound, and he came to a landing. Brian hesitated. It was too late.

Brian heard someone on the stairs and gripped the weapon.

"Someone there?" Pen Meacham asked from somewhere up above. Brian heard more footsteps. Pen Meacham came to the foot of the landing and could not believe his eyes. Brian was standing in front of him, holding a shotgun.

"What the hell is going on?" Pen asked.

"You know what I'm doing here. I've been tracking you for 30 years. Now I'm here. It's payback time!" Brian said.

"What the hell are you talking about? What's going on? Why the gun? You were at the party tonight. I saw you in the long hallway. You were by yourself."

"Shut up!"

"You're staying at Michael Carter's place."

"Shut up!"

"You're very angry about something. You look like my son, Cooper, but who are you? Why are you here? It's the middle of the night. What do you want?"

"You stupid bastard, you know why I'm here. Remember Ruth Cahill?"

"Who?"

"Ruth Cahill, dammit to hell!"

"I don't know anyone named Ruth Cahill!"

"Yes, you do, you lying son of a bitch. You slept with her 30 years ago and ditched her. Well, I'm here, right in front of you. Aren't you glad to see me, Dad? I look like you, don't I? I'm your bastard son. I look just like Cooper, don't I? That's why you noticed me at the hotel. That's why you asked Michael Carter who I was. Aren't you glad to see me, Daddy? I'm here."

Pen started to back up. "I don't know who you are or what you want, but there's a hell of a misunderstanding here. I don't know anyone named Ruth whatever, and I don't know you. I have no idea why you're calling me Dad. I don't know who you think I am. Can you just leave, and we'll forget this ever happened?"

"If you move one inch, I swear I'll blow your head off! I swear I will!"

"Okay, okay. What do you want from me? Is it money you want?"

"I want to know why, you bastard, you did what you did?"

"I don't know what you're talking about. Why I did what? I don't know what you want me to say. What do you think I did? Tell me."

"Where's Ruth, my mother?"

"I don't know anyone named Ruth."

"Yes, you do. You slept with her 30 years ago right in this damn town. Don't lie to me!"

"I lived in Detroit 30 years ago."

"You keep lying, you son of a bitch! I thought you'd be man enough to face the truth. I saw your damn picture at the White Sands with Ruth Cahill. You can't get out of this. It's you! Ruth's my mother and you're my father. You should have kept your pants on!"

"You're out of your mind."

"Watch it Dad, smart ass. You get me mad enough and I swear I'll blow your head off. Why in hell do you think I look like Cooper."

"Jesus Christ, I don't know."

"Figure it out, meathead. It's because Cooper and I have the same father. Is that too hard for you to understand? The same father is you, you son of a bitch."

"I don't know where you're coming from. Tell me what I'm supposed to say. You're talking about stuff I know nothing about. Believe me, I don't know what the hell you're talking about. Please, would you put the gun down?"

"Not on your life. I have been looking for you, Meacham and Ruth Cahill, for 30 years. You're not getting out of this. You want me to tell you what happened? You, with your big ritzy hotel and fancy car and fancy clothes and fancy friends? You won't have a friend left when I'm through with you! You screwed with Ruth Cahill all those years ago. Then you guys left me at a damned orphanage. An orphanage, for God's sake! I had no family, no friends, no nothing. I was pushed from place to place. I had nothing and nobody. You guys never cared enough to see if I was alive or dead. You've had your big fancy life, and I didn't have shit. Well, I thought about you and Ruth all those years. I was going to find the two of you if it took the rest of my life. It took 30 years. You son of a bitch, you ruined my life. After I'm through with you, I'm going to find Ruth Cahill, and I'll deal with her."

Pen's hands were shaking. He reached out. "Can you please put that gun down? I swear to God, I don't know what you're talking about. I don't know what I've ever done to you."

The blinding blast hit Pen in the face and threw him against the wall, and he fell to the floor. Brian did not remember pulling the trigger until the room exploded. He picked up the used cartridge and put it in his pocket. Blood was on the floor and the wall. Brian looked down at Pen's mangled skull and stood up to see if anyone was coming.

Brian heard someone behind him, "Dad! God, Dad! What has…"

Brian turned and the shotgun barrel struck Cooper Meacham across the forehead and killed him instantly. Cooper fell to the floor and dropped a fire axe. Brian put the shotgun on the floor, pulled Cooper over to the wall, and set him there. He wiped blood from Cooper's forehead and closed his eyes.

Brian looked up. It was dark at the top of the stairs, but he saw someone there. A shadow. Then it moved away. He stood still, holding the weapon and listening. The only sound was the storm. Each step made a low creaking sound as he moved up wooden stairs to the third floor. A door at the top of the stairs was open. Brian saw a lighted candle at the end of a narrow hallway. A dim light was coming from a room to the right off the hallway.

"Pen, is that you? Penny, what's going on? What was that loud noise? It sounded like a gun! Penfield? I saw somebody down the stairs! What's going on? I'm scared, please answer me! Coops, are you there? Hello! Who's there? Please answer me! Oh God! Please answer me! Who's there? Who's in the hallway? Answer me please!"

Brian moved down the hallway and through the bedroom door on his right. A candle, on a table next to the bed, was the only light. Geraldine Meacham was standing next to the bed and backed up as Brian entered the room.

"Who are you?" she screamed. "Why are you here? Where's my husband? Who are you? You look like Cooper, where is he? Oh my God, what is the gun for? What do you want? What have you done? Is my husband hurt? Is Cooper hurt? What have you done? God no! Please put it down, oh, no, please no!"

Brian didn't know the trigger was pulled until the room exploded. Geraldine was hit in the face and thrown backwards into the chest of drawers and it fell down on top of her. Brian looked at Geraldine. She was crushed under furniture. The side of her head was destroyed and the floor was covered with blood. He picked up the discharged shell, went to the living room, and listened.

A candle was burning in the living room. Light reflected on a large picture of Pen Meacham and someone else, identified only by 1946. They both looked exactly like PM in the 1946 picture with Ruth Cahill.

"Which son of a bitch is the real one?" Brian said to himself.

He hit the picture hard with his fist. The glass shattered and the picture fell to the floor behind a wooden chest. Brian left the room and made his way slowly down the stairs to the landing and looked at Cooper and then opened the door and listened. Except for the storm, it was quiet. The lobby was almost dark. He went to the front door and looked out. The streets were empty. The fireplace clock said 3:59. Brian put on his poncho and shoes and hid the weapon under his raincoat. He left through the front door. Brian went down the muddy trail to the little cabin by the stream. The cabin was dark. He walked across the stream to underbrush, near a well. Brian threw the shotgun and shells down the well, put branches, leaves, and rocks on top of them. Brian then again climbed the long winding trail to The Parsonage and went to his room. His wet clothes went into a pile on the floor. Other than the victims, he had not seen a person.

Chapter 29

    Shannon was awake by noon.
    She came back from the beach at one o'clock in the morning. By two o'clock, she was sick and afraid to leave the bathroom. Motion made her sick and she threw up. She lay down in her robe on the bathroom floor for the night. In the twilight half-sleep that followed, she saw her home and her mother and her dad, and she cried in her sleep for a long time. Later, she saw leaves turning in the small cemetery and Christmas in tiny Wheatstone and a highway. Her cousin Whitney was there, wondering if Shannon was ever coming home. She saw her Saginaw apartment, the door was open, and the rooms were empty. Shannon remembered that a priest had once told her to take her sadness and put it in a package, and tie the package with a bow, Then go to the altar and put the package on the altar. Slide it across the altar and give it to the Lord. Tell Him you can no longer deal with these problems. She saw the package coming back with the bow still in place.

Chapter 30

The Seattle apartment was empty except for two old chairs, a small table, and a metal bed frame.

Ruth Cahill died on Friday, July 25. The funeral was Monday. Jim Sudbury returned for a last look at the small apartment. Ruth Cahill, he found over the last weeks of her life, was a lonely person, ravaged by guilt and regret. She had not seen her son in 28 years. The photo album had been her only contact with the past before Brian was born and she wanted Brian to have it. Jim wanted to close the final chapter of Ruth's life and he assumed that receiving the album with no explanation would have confused Brian. He wrote to Brian on July 30.

Dear Brian Cahill:

I am with the hospice organization in Seattle and I spent the last several weeks with your mother, Ruth Cahill. Unfortunately, Ruth died last Friday after a long illness. She was buried here in Seattle on Monday.

Your mother was 53 years old. We made Ruth as comfortable as possible during the final stages of her life. She asked me, close to the end of her life, to send you an album of family pictures, which I am sure you have received by now.

I think you should know that she said many times that placing you with a state welfare organization 28 years ago was the most difficult decision of her life. I am sure that wondering about your mother all these years has been terribly painful for you. Ruth told me that she left you because of her love for you. As a young mother with no money, she felt that she could not provide a good home for you. Both of her parents, your maternal grandparents, died a few years before you were born. Ruth felt alone in the world with no one to turn to for help. Placing you with state welfare, she hoped, was a way for you to have a chance for a better life than the life she believed she could provide for you.

As the years went by, Ruth came to believe that you hated her and she was increasingly afraid even to try to find out where you were living. The records, of course, were sealed. She always hoped that you somehow knew that she loved you in her own way. Life for her was difficult and she finally succumbed to problems of alcohol and smoking at a relatively young age. She never married. Ruth lost all contact with your father 30 years ago and said very little about him. She never mentioned his last name, but I did learn that his first name was Paul and he lived somewhere in a large city in the Midwestern part of this country. I have enclosed a card with my name and address, should you wish to contact me. It may be of some comfort for you to know that at the end of her life, her last thoughts were with you.
Sincerely,
Jim Sudbury
Seattle Hospice Chapter

The letter was waiting for Brian when he returned to Chicago from his Stamford Bridge vacation on Saturday, August 2.

Chapter 31

Henry Plunkett sat in the small church, his head bowed. Altar candles were burning low. Father Cudahy, leaving the sacristy, saw Henry sitting alone.

"I know they were your friends, Henry. They were my friends, too, and I will miss them," the priest said, as he sat down near the police chief.

Henry nodded.

"They were friends of all of us," he continued. "We'll all miss them. Neither I, nor you, nor anyone understands the strangeness of God's mercy. Tomorrow is not promised to any of us. God has a plan for us, as he had for our friends. The plan may not be what we want, but there is a plan. It is through the sanctity of Christ that we ask for mercy. It is through the Mass and mystical union with Christ, that we give glory to God through His Son and ask for everlasting life. You must thank God, through Jesus Christ, that you knew your friends as long as you did."

The police chief rubbed his eyes. "Why the cruelty? These were good people, you knew them as long as I did. Why were they killed like animals? What was all of this for? Did they suffer so that God can show He's in charge? If that's what this is about, God's pretty damn mean. Tell me what to think, father. Maybe I'm missing the point."

The priest paused. "This is the day the Lord hath made. The rain falls on the just and the unjust alike. As we've seen, terrible things happen to good people. Christ Himself suffered, but He did so for all of us. We honor Him through the sacraments and good works. Remember, Henry, I'm paraphrasing: Christ said that anything you or I or anyone might do unto them–any person–you also do unto Me. The person who committed these homicides assaulted Christ Himself."

Henry, looking toward the altar, made no comment.

"I know you're thankful for your wife, Paige, and the joy she brought into your life while she lived. I know you have never come to terms with her suffering. In spite of such adversity, we must believe that God loves each of us in a manner beyond understanding. I hate to see you suffering so deeply, but we're all suffering. Fear is spreading. People are afraid of what might happen next. People may become afraid of each other. People want someone brought to justice. They want, with sadness, to get on with their lives. People trust you. I know you're doing everything possible to protect and reassure them. Pray for our friends who have died. Pray for me too, because I am a sinner like everyone else."

Henry went back to his office.

Stillness settled on Stamford Bridge. Tourists were gone and the Inn was closed. The summer ended in mid-season. People were frightened. In the two restaurants still open, customers talked of little else.

"But, Christ almighty," Polly Brooks asked Henry, "who could've hated Pen, or Geraldine or Cooper Meacham? The family was so popular. I mean, my God, they were friends of all of us! It must have been a grudge thing or something like that, but who could have a grudge against the Meachams and for what? If the Meachams weren't safe in their hotel, then who's safe in this town?"

Graham Meacham returned after the funeral and stayed with Frank Scott and family for a few days. Graham, shattered by the loss of his entire family, faced a harrowing ordeal–a trauma that would take years to sort out and, if ever, put in perspective. He also spent time with Henry, Father Cudahy, Freddie Martin, Michael Carter, the Brooks, and other friends of his parents. Mary Meade Saltonstall was in the hospital under sedation. Charlie Putnam and Ida Mae agreed to stay on and close the hotel. The bank in Ludgate Hill, with funds from Graham, would pay them. Graham would return to college in California. He had no home left.

West Michigan broadcast and newspaper media headlined the story of the "shocking multiple homicide in the well-to-do resort town on the big lake…" Coverage reached as far as Chicago and Detroit. Follow-up stories

WHY DID I GROW SO COLD?

would continue for weeks and then fade almost entirely, whatever the outcome. Shannon was the only reporter still in town. The curious would lose interest. State police worked with Henry and detectives from Lansing questioned friends, relatives, teachers, neighbors, merchants, former and current hotel employees, guests, anyone Pen had done business with over the last four years. The Inn and grounds were searched.

On Tuesday, Henry Plunkett and Ralph Skinner of Michigan State Police held a press conference in the police department lunchroom. "I don't have to tell you," Henry told reporters," this case is a heartbreaker for all of us. Ralph, I, and most of you in this room either knew or knew of the Meachams. This is a tragedy for all of us and for our town. We are dealing with three murders. We do not know who the intended victim or victims might have been. It may have been Pen or Geraldine or Cooper Meacham, or it might have been all three. From what we can tell, nothing was stolen. The female victim was not sexually molested. We do not know if we are dealing with one killer or more than one killer, and we have no idea what the motive was. We will deal with this as best we can. On Sunday, July 27, the rainstorm lasted until about 6:30 a.m. It was sometime between 3 a.m. and 5 a.m., according to the coroner, that the homicides occurred. The storm evidently made it impossible for the gunfire to be heard. The band from Benton Harbor left the hotel at 1 a.m. Police from St. John's Woods left at 1:30 a.m. Witnesses say that Pen Meacham, Geraldine Meacham, Charlie Putnam, busboys and Ida Mae Murphy closed kitchen windows and awnings. The same people also moved porch furniture and portable bars back to Charlie Putnam's storage shack. Chairs, coffee tables, and carpet were moved back to the lobby. Dining room chairs and tables were made ready for Sunday guests. Work was apparently finished by 1:45 a.m. Guests had gone to their rooms. R.M. Schroeder and Ida Mae Murphy, apparently the last to leave the hotel, left together before 2 a.m. R.M. walked Ida Mae home, borrowed her umbrella and walked to his house. The cash drawer in the hotel lobby was left open. No footprints have been found. No used cartridges have been found. Two rounds were fired. One hit Penfield Meacham, one hit Geraldine, and a blow to the head struck down Cooper. The crimes were committed by an individual or individuals unknown at this time."

Henry walked to the Inn every day. The chief, not a large man, looked sharp in his blue uniform. His tie was straight, shirt pressed, and shoes were polished. His eyes, at half-mast, were ringed with discolored circles. He may have been handsome at one time. His hair, now gray, was short and brushed to one side. As he became older and lived alone, Henry became increasingly afraid of evil.

As he neared the hotel, Henry looked at the lake. It was calm. There were no boats, and there was not a person at the beach. Some stores were open, with only a few customers. There was almost no traffic on Campbell Street. Two restaurants were open. White Hall Marina's slips were partially filled. Few students were left at Amesbury. Artist's lofts, adjacent to the beach, were quiet. For the first time in days, there were no police vehicles at the Inn parking lot. The Inn was deserted. A group of sparrows landed at the birdbath near the garden splashed in the water and quickly flew away.

Henry made his way up the steps and across the front porch. He turned the lock and opened the front door. He went inside and locked the door behind him. Stillness was complete; windows were shut, and blinds were closed. Henry went to the lobby and stopped near the fireplace. Nothing was out of place. This room, like the front porch, looked inviting, as if nothing had happened. The green ink blotter and luggage bell were both in place at the front desk. The open page of the hotel check-in register was dated July 26, in Cooper Meacham's handwriting. Behind the desk, mailboxes by room number were empty.

The dining room was in order. Tables with ladder back chairs were ready for guests. Henry's eyes stopped on the bright, modern colors of the Calder print on the west wall and smiled. Pen and Geraldine were so proud of the work. The artist signed it for them years ago. The dining room, like the front porch and the lobby, was inviting. Henry looked west and saw the Meacham's table. Geraldine Meacham's coffee cup, saucer, and ashtray were on the table where she had left them. The table was in the corner, by the mirror. Last year, the Meachams and friends gathered there for News Year's Eve.

The good times were over.

Henry walked to the kitchen. It was scrubbed clean and all pots, pans, and utensils put away. The bright Motherwell print high above the sink looked larger than Henry remembered. There were barstools under the worktable, and Pen's clipboard and cigars were on the counter where he had left them.

The police chief left the dining room. His footsteps made a crisp, cracking sound with an echo. Henry crossed the lobby and stopped at the door that led upstairs. He pushed it open and left it ajar. He climbed steps to the landing. After turning left, he saw the spot where Pen and Cooper had been killed. The wall had been repainted and the floor refinished, the hall smelled like varnish. Henry had studied police photographs of the crime scene, looking for anything–Geraldine Meacham, on her side, the left side of her head gone, her mouth and eyes open, her face still intact. Pen Meacham, the left side of his face demolished, mouth and eye open; and the haunting photograph of Cooper Meacham–in a sitting position on the floor, leaning against the wall, eyes closed, as if he was asleep. Cooper looked as if he had been placed in a comfortable position. The blood had been wiped from his forehead, as if the killer was apologizing. The killer, Henry felt, must have had some emotional connection with Cooper.

Henry could not imagine anyone doing this for any reason other than money, and yet there was no robbery. Why, then, were these people killed? Henry dismissed the idea of multiple killers. Two persons at the same level of rage at the same time seemed out of the question. He believed the death of two of the Meacham family members had been the killer's objective. Cooper's death may have been an accident. The homicides occurred in rapid succession. The coroner reported little difference in the body temperatures of the victims. Henry believed the killer came to the hotel on foot and went through the lobby at about 3 a.m. The lobby door was unlocked and the front desk was unattended at that time. The door to the Meacham's apartment was never locked.

The third floor hallway was long. Henry walked to a small table and saw an ashtray. He lit a cigar. There was a small crucifix above the table. Henry looked at it and wondered if Christ will ever take away the sins of the world. *Does Christ even want to take away the sins of the world? Is the liturgy meaningless? If He really can take away the sins of the world, why has He not done so? Why in hell were these people killed?* Henry decided, after 61 years, to leave the Church and no longer take the sacraments.

Henry planned, if it took the rest of his life, to find out what happened and why. He assumed that his own life would last not more than three or four more years, which he hoped would be enough time. He shook his head and put the cigar in his mouth.

He came to the apartment, opened the door, moved inside, and locked the door behind him. The living room seemed larger today than it looked yesterday. Each room, painted off-white, had hardwood flooring. Off-white wooden shutters covered windows throughout. Rooms were sparingly furnished with few, but expensive Shaker pieces.

The police officer went to the master bedroom. There had been more splattered blood, skin, and brain matter in this room than anywhere else. The mattress, blankets, sheets, pillows and pillowcases had been removed and burned. The bed frame was still in place. The chest of drawers was again upright. He looked out the window and saw the empty parking lot, three stories below. White gulls were flying high over the lake. Suddenly, they plunged toward earth at great speed, only to turn upward at the last moment to avoid crashing into the water. Henry watched and marveled at their prowess. He turned from the window and knew it was time to go. There was a sinking feeling. His mood drifted down past depression within sight of the end. Although he had lived in Stamford Bridge for 40 years, it was never home. The Meachams were his final link to town, particularly since Paige had died. Henry was immensely fond of Pen, Geraldine, and Cooper. He stopped by the hotel often. Holidays were spent with the Meachams and Michael Carter. The Cleveland home where he had grown up was sold 30 years ago. Going home was impossible.

He moved to a couch by the window, sat down, and buried his face in his hands as shadows gathered in the room. Then Henry picked up his cigar and put it in the crystal tray on the coffee table. His face was in reflection–no longer the face of a young man with hope. There were lines across his forehead and around his eyes and mouth. Circles under his eyes were deep. The eyes were dull, the skin tone ashen. Henry Plunkett knew he had done his best, beyond that, life had lost all meaning.

Chapter 32

It was evening now, and Brian pulled into the cathedral parking lot in Grand Haven. The sun was almost gone behind the horizon, and there were shadows across the lake and the cathedral and the lawns and gardens. From where he stood, Brian could see that visitors had left. The cathedral was large, with many stained glass windows. Across the lawn, in one of the cathedral archways, a priest stood looking at the sunset, smoking a cigarette.

Brian had watched himself kill three people on Sunday and was not sure he could actually have done it, until he knew that all three were really dead. The funeral was tomorrow. Words like "faith" and "savior" and "Eucharist" were words he could not stand to hear. Brian had walked through the shadow of death and had been violently injured, and the notion of religion simply flew in the face of the facts; the idea of God was plainly out of the question.

The horror of Cooper's death moved close to him, and there was no one he could tell of his grief. Cooper's death was an accident, it came closer, and closer to him, he could not make it to go away, it fell heavily on him, and he could not sleep. Brian thought of how life had always been his main antagonist–a series of small stupid little events, which came together and fell upon him. Cooper's death was there, precisely as it had happened, and it was engraved in memory, and Brian was filled with remorse.

The priest soon left. Brian made his way to the cathedral front door, and it was still open, although visitation was over. He moved inside and saw a large sanctuary, filled with flowers and empty pews. It was cool inside, and candles adjacent to the main altar were still burning. Sanctuary lights were dim. Brian walked to his left through large wooden doors and saw a light at the end of a long carpeted hallway. He passed by the sacristy and came to a separate room. Brian saw the visitation register but did not sign it.

The room was dimly lighted and filled with flowers and three bronze caskets, one was open. Brian was nervous and walked over and saw Cooper Meacham. The injury to his forehead was not visible and he looked asleep. Cooper was wearing a blue coat, white shirt, and tie. A prayer book was in his hands. It seemed to Brian as if Cooper might wake up, and he touched his face.

Cooper died, Brian thought, *probably full of hope and hope is gone.* Brian immediately liked Cooper, and he had hoped that Cooper was his brother. Now he had killed him. Brian's eyes filled with tears and he turned to go, stopped near the doorway, and thought about what might have been.

In a whisper, he said, "I'm so sorry, Cooper."

Chapter 33

The funeral was held on Thursday at the Cathedral in Grand Haven. The church was filled.

For a long time, Shannon, in a pew seated next to the aisle, heard voices chanting in the distance behind her, slowly alternating in cadence, as the procession came closer. As it moved near and then past her, she saw acolytes in white robes: one carried the crucifix, and others carried lighted candles. Next came the cantor, followed by an acolyte carrying the censer, with incense and smoke. Three bronze caskets came in succession, carried by pallbearers, each wearing a dark suit, white shirt, and dark tie. As smoke ascended upward, a deacon, carrying the gospel, and two priests in white, followed in procession. The three caskets were aligned in front of the altar.

Father Cudahy faced the congregation. "Penfield, Geraldine, and Cooper Meacham, three of our most favorite citizens, have been murdered in a senseless crime. We are horrified and grief-stricken and we want to know why. We demand answers and punishment in full measure. Remember, that our Lord said, 'Vengeance is mine.' There can be absolutely no doubt regarding His commandment and what his words mean for us today. Let there be no doubt whatever about the ultimate outcome of this terrible crime. I promise you that justice will be served. The person or persons who committed these criminal acts will face the terrible and eternal punishment of God Himself. Remember also our Lord said, 'I am the resurrection and the life. They that believe in Me, though they were dead, yet they will live; and whomever lives and believes in Me, shall never die.'"

The day was warm. The cortege traveled from Grand Haven to Stamford

Bridge, down residential streets to downtown, where it stopped in front of The Promontory Inn. The hotel flag was at half-mast. Pallbearers carried the caskets up a small grass covered hill to a spot not far from the hotel, overlooking Lake Michigan. Several hundred gathered near the new grave sites. Father Cudahy said, "There could be no finer resting place for our friends than in this town, next to the hotel and lake they so loved. Thus, 'we commend the souls of our friends departed, and we commit their bodies to the ground; earth to earth, ashes to ashes, dust to dust…'"

Shannon closed her prayer book and walked down the hillside to Campbell Street. The crowds left. Many walked home and others left in cars. Shannon again noticed the man she had seen jogging last Friday on Cadbury Street.

Chapter 34

The rain stopped on Friday afternoon, and the sky was dark, with low clouds moving in from the lake. It was hot and humid. The few pedestrians downtown carried umbrellas, and there were puddles of water on streets. The rainwater dripped from large trees, and, when cars went by, tires on the brick streets made a wet, steamy sound. It was the beginning of August, and most tourists had left town. The Promontory Inn was closed. Most stores and restaurants closed for the week. Spirits were low, and there was resentment at the influx of reporters. No works of art were on display or for sale downtown, many artists had left town, and concerts by the lake were cancelled. The Amesbury campus was almost deserted. Few instructors were still in residence. Dark blue vehicles and squad cars were parked in front of the police department. The Promontory Inn was cordoned off with yellow crime scene tape, and the building was dark. Flowers and wreaths had been placed on the hotel's front steps. Awnings, tennis nets and outdoor furniture had been moved to Charlie Putnam's maintenance shack. The pool was drained. Porches, patios, carports, and parking lots were empty. At the crest of the hill, not far from the hotel, there were flowers on the ground and freshly turned earth. Three small white crosses identified new graves. A family in a station wagon parked in front of the hotel, and a young boy got out and took pictures of the building.

Shannon was delighted with Stamford Bridge on the first day. The people were friendly. The murders ruined everything, but she decided to stay on through the end of the week. She traveled to small towns and bought a few watercolors. Shannon, like everyone, did not know if the killer or killers would strike again and she dead-bolted her door at Chestnut Brook every night.

    She drank white wine at the hotel on Saturday night and had not felt well since. Today, it rained until late afternoon. Shannon spent the time in her room reading the papers and Camus. After a few hours, she went to sleep for the afternoon. At 4, she took a shower, changed clothes, and left for a walk to Campbell Street. She saw Polly Brooks on Chestnut Brook's front porch, smoking a cigarette.

"Hi, Polly," Shannon said.

"Hi, Shannon," Polly replied.

"The rain's finally stopped, but I think more is on the way."

"Yes."

"It's been a rough week, hasn't it?"

"God, I'll say. The worst we've ever spent here."

"You know, Polly, this's such a wonderful town. When I came here last weekend, everything seemed perfect. Maybe everything was too good to be true."

"It's interesting you would say that. My husband and I would sometimes pinch ourselves, just to make sure we were not living in a dream. Now, after Sunday, everything is tragic. My husband and I are devastated. We almost lost it at the funeral. We saw Pen's brother there, I don't know his name, and for a moment we had to do a double take. God, he looks exactly like Pen. And Mary Meade, that beautiful girl, poor thing, she's in the hospital. Her older sister, Darby, was at the funeral, and so were her parents. My husband and Michael Carter both said they'd lost their best friend. I know Henry feels that way also, and Geraldine and I were such good friends. Oh, that poor boy, Graham, I don't know what he'll do. That poor soul lost his whole family. Maybe if he had been here he would have been killed too, or maybe it would never have happened. God, I don't know."

"I'm so sorry, Polly."

"I'm so sorry, too. We don't know what we'll do. Everything is so confused. We just don't know anymore. Every one else has left. We don't know. Right now, everything is closed. We think we have guests coming next week, but we do not know for sure. Isn't that crass to be worried about money at a time like this? The graves at the Inn, oh my God, it's awful. It's the perfect place for them to be buried, but my God, it's so sad."

"Have you talked to Chief Plunkett since Sunday?" Shannon asked. "Do they know anything more?"

"We haven't talked to him, but I would guess they do. I understand Henry is not saying much. This's been very hard on him. The rumor, at least from what we've heard, is that police think the killer is still in this area and might kill again. That is terrifying. Also, for some reason, they seem to think that it's one killer, and the person, probably a man, does not live in this town. Everybody is scared, I've never seen the town like this. Something I can't get out of my mind, nobody can: There was no robbery, and we've heard that nobody was molested. That is too horrible to think about, anyway. God, the place has been crawling with police all week. They've been all over town and the hotel. I saw Charlie and Ida Mae going over to the hotel with Henry to look, I would guess, through everything and see if they could find anything that might be a clue or something."

"There must be an answer somewhere in all of this. I've just been here this week, and I'll never be the same," Shannon said.

"I'm sorry, Shannon," Polly said. "You've been in our town during this terrible time. Our lives, for those of us who live here, will never be the same. We'll miss them terribly. My husband is painting the guestrooms to take his mind off everything. He probably wonders what became of me. I had better get back to work. I'll see you tomorrow before you leave. Try to enjoy your evening."

"Thanks, Polly. I'll see you tomorrow."

Shannon left by a side porch, where she could see across the woods that went down to the lake and across the water to the north shore. She followed a steep, single-lane brick street that ran down the hill and through the woods to the beach. The sand looked beige today, and the sky was like a solid gray wall to the horizon. Mist was falling. The lake was calm. Across the bay, a man standing on a pier was casting. Closer to shore, a small fishing boat looked motionless in the water. The man in the boat was wearing yellow rain gear with a hood. Shannon walked to wooden stairs near the cliff. The steps were wet and covered with sand, and she held onto the railing as she climbed the stairs to Campbell Street. An awning-covered cabana next to the flower garden was nearby. There were two white chairs and a small table; Shannon sat down to rest. She had taken aspirin all day, but she still ached and felt hot, and she wanted to be home. Shannon saw the man in the small fishing boat struggling with a splashing line. The empty hotel looked elegant and forlorn. A man wearing a blue raincoat with a hood walked toward her.

"You look like the only person out today," the man said.

Shannon looked at him and said, "Probably so. Didn't I see you jogging on Cadbury Street last Saturday?"

"Right, and you're the person I saw coming out of the church," Brian said. "That's right."

"Is that chair empty?" Brian said, as he pointed to the other chair.

"Sure," Shannon said.

"Thank you. Were you at the hotel party on Saturday?" Brian asked.

"Yes, I went by myself. I drank too much wine and left about eleven. How about you?" Shannon asked.

"Yes, I was there for probably three or so hours. I was drinking gin and tonics, probably too much for my own good. I talked with another Vietnam vet I'd met earlier in the day. The party was fun, many people enjoying themselves. I must've left about the same time you did."

Shannon said nothing.

"So, what brings you out on a day like this?" Brian asked.

"Cabin fever, I guess."

"Me too. You must be a visitor?"

"Yes, I was here for a week, I've been staying at Chestnut Brook. Tomorrow is my last day. I'll leave in the afternoon. How about you?"

"Same thing. Tomorrow is my last day also. I've been at The Parsonage. I'll leave tomorrow, probably about noon."

"Where are you from?" Shannon asked.

"For the last several years, I've lived in Chicago. And you?" Brian asked.

"I've lived in Michigan for the last ten years, and I now live in Saginaw."

"Saginaw, I've never been there. How far away is that?"

"About a 150 miles."

"Where did you live before that?"

"I'm from a little town in western Kansas you've never heard of, Wheatstone, It's out west near the Colorado border."

"You're right, I've never heard of it. You're a long way from home. It doesn't sound like you're from around here."

"What does being from around here sound like?"

"Sorry, just making small talk."

"Sorry too, I'm on edge about everything."

Brian changed the subject. "So what," he asked, "brought you to this part of the country?"

"I went to college in Michigan on a sports scholarship. I majored in journalism and I'm a reporter for the *Saginaw Journal*."

"A reporter! Well, that's interesting. What sort of things do you report on?"

"I'm a general assignment reporter. Which means I cover just about everything."

"It sounds like interesting work."

"Yes and no. A lot depends on the people around you and the editors you're working with. That makes a big difference. Some of it is boring, but at times, a story might be interesting, so then it's fun. What about you?"

"What about me?"

"Yes, what about you? What do you do, and where are you from?"

"I'm from everywhere. I was raised in different orphanages, so I don't have a home town. I was in the Army in Vietnam, and the government paid for college. I went to a small college in Chicago and majored in finance. I work for a large accounting firm in downtown Chicago. My name is Brian Cahill."

"Brian, my name is Shannon Fitsimmons. Well, we've both got Irish names."

"Are you Irish? "Brian asked.

"Yes, I'm afraid so, a true green blood; and you?"

"I have an Irish name, but I don't know if I'm Irish or not."

"You don't know who your parents are or maybe were? Or, have you found them, or have they found you?" Shannon asked.

It's never been a big deal with me. I've been so busy getting on with my life, I've never spent much time thinking about who my mother and father are or were, but if I ever found out…" Brian seemed suddenly irritated and looked at the lake with an empty stare.

Shannon thought Brian's answer was peculiar. "It's been," she said," a traumatic week."

"We couldn't have been here at a worse time," Brian said.

"Of all the places in the world, and these horrible things happened here. God, its incredible," Shannon said.

Brian changed the subject. "Are you hungry?"

"To be honest with you, Brian, I don't feel at all well. I've felt lousy all week."

"That's too bad; what do you think it is?"

"It's probably the flu or something like that. I've taken a million aspirin since I've been here, and I've turned in early every night. I need to get home and see my regular doctor, and she can start me on antibiotics or something. Anyway, I'm probably up for coffee and then I'll turn in. I'm really tired. That's the best I can do."

"That's fine, I'm trying to think where we can go," Brian said.

"I think there are places open in St. John's Woods and Ludgate Hill, but I don't think I'm up for driving anywhere. The only place left in town, I think, is Christie's. I've never been there, but I guess it'll have to do."

"Let's do it," Brian said, as they both stood up.

The rain started again, and the wind was sharp. Raindrops splattered the sidewalk. Water stood in pools on the sidewalks, and they tried to walk around them. Shannon felt cold water seep into her shoes, and she sneezed. Trees above them swayed in the wind, and a branch fell down beside them. They made their way across to the south side of Campbell Street, across from The Promontory Inn. Some flowers and wreaths had blown away from the hotel front steps. The downtown looked empty, the sky was dark at this early hour, and streetlights were still on. They turned the corner and came to Christie's.

It was dark inside, and at the back of the room a waitress was sitting at a table with an old man. Across from them, at another table, sat Freddie Martin. He was smoking a cigarette.

A man and a woman came through the front door, took off their raincoats and hats, and went to the bar. The waiter poured two full glasses of brandy for them.

Further back, a young man in white clothes was reading the papers. He

WHY DID I GROW SO COLD?

looked up and said, "My God, that Meacham funeral must've been something. The paper says there were more than 500 people there–cathedral could not hold everybody. Town was empty on Thursday, that's for sure. Didn't have one customer all afternoon. Not one. God, that is amazing. It must've been some kind of a grudge thing or something like that. Freddie, can you tell us anything more than what we read in the papers?"

"Carter, I can't tell you any more than what you've read and what Henry said at the press conference. We're contacting everybody that had dealings with the Meacham family. That's a lot of people. We've been through the hotel. Ida Mae and Charlie have been there to help us. Crime lab people from Lansing are looking at a few things. We've searched the other buildings, and up and down the beach and the woods. The sheriff's people have helped us, and we'll ask them to come back next week."

"Freddie," the old man said, "if something like this can happen to them, it can happen to any of us. It's almost like God was mad at them. I see people leaving their lights on all night. I've heard that hardware stores in three towns have sold out of deadbolt locks. Hell, some people bought guns."

"Jake, I know you're scared, everybody's scared," Freddie replied.

"Freddie, there's a rumor that maybe there's one killer, is that right?" Emmy, the waitress, asked.

"Emmy, I can't comment on that."

"I heard from somewhere that police believe the killer or killers don't live in this town?" Emmy asked.

"No comment."

"Freddie, another rumor says they were tortured. Is that why it was a closed casket funeral?" Emmy asked.

"Emmy, as for the caskets being closed, I think that's what Graham preferred. Other than that, I really can't comment."

"Did you see the victims, Freddie?" Emmy asked.

"Yes, I did."

"And?" Carter asked.

"I won't comment on that."

"Freddie, what about the hotel? Will it stay closed, and, if it opens again, who would run it?" Carter asked.

"That's a decision to be made by Graham. None of us know what he'll do. He's in college in California, and we don't know if he'll go back to school or stay here. Graham has lost his entire family. He made the decisions about the funeral, and now he's going to be facing the world alone."

The room fell silent. Freddie pulled a cigarette from the pack on the table, took off his glasses, and wiped his eyes with a napkin. "This's hit," he said, "awfully close to home. I'll miss them all terribly."

Carter brought over another cup of coffee. "Dinner's on the house, Freddie."

"Thanks, I appreciate that."

"A couple more questions, Freddie?" Emmy asked.

"Shoot."

"What about Mary Meade Saltonstall? She wasn't at the funeral," Emmy asked.

"She's in the hospital in Ludgate Hill. She's under Dr. Oliver's care, and that's all we know."

"She's shattered?" Jake asked.

"Totally."

"Reward's up to $10,000. That's a lot of money. Any leads?" Carter asked.

"Brought in a bunch of calls. We followed up. That's all I can say."

"What about Charlie Putnam and Ida Mae Murphy? What'll happen to them?" Jake asked.

"Don't know, at this point. They're shutting the hotel down. That's a big job. After that, I don't think anyone knows."

"This's a terrible thing to ask at time like this, but does anybody think tourists are going to start coming back next week? This is the summer season," Jake asked.

"Henry sat in on an emergency merchant's association meeting for a while this morning. Pen was president of that group, and they've not elected a new leader. The feeling is that Stamford Bridge will go on as best it can for the rest of the summer. The association hopes that people will be coming back as early as next week. They're expecting more sightseers and there's nothing anybody can do about that."

"Another thing, a very ugly thing we've got to guard against," Carter said, "would be if we start suspecting each other."

"That worries Henry. We've got to keep our eyes open, but we've got to stay as a community and not start suspecting each other."

"Why did all of this happen anyway?" Emmy asked. "Does anyone know why this happened in the first place?"

"Emmy, we don't know. It looks like the intent was to kill somebody, maybe anybody, we don't know. None of us have any idea why. In this case, it was the Meachams. I can't figure it. Carter, thanks for the dinner. I'm going back to the office."

"Anything we can do, Freddie? We're all scared out of our wits?" Emmy asked.

"Lock your doors, don't do anything foolish, keep your eyes open and report anything suspicious to us. That's all I can say."

Shannon and Brian sat at a table close against the wall near the front door. They listened to Freddie, looked through the window by their table, and saw the terrace. It was windy and raining hard. A man and a woman walked by under the street light, they were wearing yellow raincoats and rain hats. A waitress came to the table and brought them coffee. Shannon preferred black coffee and Brian put sugar in his coffee and broke the lumps with his spoon.

"It's raining hard," Shannon said.

"I'm glad we're inside," Brian replied.

"These people," Shannon said," have a lot to deal with. This whole thing's threatening to turn the town upside down. People could turn against each other. People are scared. I've been scared too, all week. They're very, very uptight, and they admit it, about dollars and cents. If tourists don't start coming back next week in a big way, this town could lose a lot of money. This's their big season, right now. Did you meet any of the Meacham family?"

"No, I didn't," Brian said, looking down at his coffee. "Did you?"

"Yes, I did. I met Cooper. He was tending bar with Mary Meade Saltonstall on Saturday night. A perfect couple. You could tell they were totally in love with each other. I met Geraldine in the Tea Room Gallery, also on Saturday night. She was attractive, and I enjoyed talking with her for a few minutes. She seemed like a fun person. I've heard so many nice things about them, I can't believe they're gone."

"I'm curious. When you get back to Saginaw, are you going to write this whole vacation off as a bad experience all the way around? One you'd like to forget?" Brian asked.

"It's been interesting and tragic, I guess I'd say. I sure didn't expect the trauma that turned the town upside down. I'll never come back here for any reason, I know that for sure. How about you?" Shannon said.

"I'd say the same thing. I'll never come back here. This week has been traumatic for me, too. It's time to get back to Chicago," Brian said.

"Looking forward to getting back to work?" Shannon asked.

"I guess so, I don't know, I guess so. I came up here to…" Brian said with an abrupt silence and an empty stare.

Shannon stirred her coffee. "You don't sound," she said, "very enthusiastic."

"I've got some issues I need to deal with. I came up here to sort some things out and then everything hit the fan. This vacation hasn't worked out," Brian replied.

"I'm sorry."

"We're both sorry."

"So tell me," Brian asked, as he sipped coffee and looked at her left hand, "have you been or are you married?"

"No, and you?"

"No, never. You've been close to getting married before?"

"Couple of times, "Shannon said. "The closer I got, the more the idea fell apart."

"Fell apart? I'm not sure I know what you mean, fell apart?"

"As I think I said, I've been gone from Kansas for ten years. I struck out from my little hometown into the world by myself. It was hard to leave home. I don't know why I left. Really, deep down inside, I still don't know. Having said that, if I knew then what I know now, I would never have left home in the first place. Whatever I thought was out there, beyond the horizon or wherever, was not there. Anyway, to answer your question, I got to be independent, more so after college, like I had all the answers, doing what I wanted to do. If I were married, I wouldn't be able to live like that. Both times, I knew it wouldn't work."

"Its good you realized that before it was too late."

"I suppose so, what about you?"

"I've been around the block a few times, and now I'm kind of focusing on one person."

"Sounds serious."

"I don't know," Brian said. "You still have family living in Wheatstone?"

"One of my aunts still lives there. My folks are both gone."

"I'm sorry. Long time ago?"

"My dad's been gone for 16 years, and mom for a little over six years."

"You were young."

"Losing Dad so early was terrible. I know now that medical science did everything it could to save him, but he was not checked early enough. Our priest, of course, gave him Absolution. So, I know everything that could have been done for him on earth was done. I know that Dad and later Mom went into eternity with Absolution from the Church."

"You take the church business pretty seriously."

"I don't wear it on my sleeve."

Brian said nothing.

"I go home less and less. Mom and Dad are not there. The life I lived there is pretty much gone. The house where I grew up was sold. I always think of it as my house, but other people are living in it. Does that make sense?"

"Sort of, I grew up without a home."

"Sorry."

"No problem."

"Okay, do you like what you're doing in Chicago?"

"I'm not sure I want to work with numbers for the rest of my life. But, for right now, it's fine. I'm making reasonably good money, so it's fine. I'm not rich, but I'm doing okay."

"You don't sound thrilled."

"That's probably right. I'm not thrilled, but I have an okay life."

"Just okay?"

"Yeah, pretty much just okay, and you?"

"I'm in the same boat, just okay."

"It sounds like this's been a bad trip for you all the way around?" Shannon asked.

"I don't deal with idle time, and driving up here from Chicago was empty time. I'm scatterbrained. My mind wanders. On Saturday, my mind went to

Vietnam. I was one of those dumb bastards sent off to kill gooks. I saw some very bad stuff over there, and once in a while…" Brian was abruptly quiet, and Shannon again noticed an empty stare, a look without focus.

"Vietnam bothers you, doesn't it?"

"No, I work out a lot, and I forget about it."

It was still raining hard, and the waitress brought more coffee. Shannon and Brian were quiet.

"You want something to eat?" Brian asked.

"No, coffee's fine, but order something if you're hungry."

"No, I was just checking on you."

"I'm fine," Shannon said. She touched the coffee cup and saucer and they were hot to her fingertips. *Why am I here?* she asked herself. *This's a strange person,* she thought. *He is angry, moody, and strange. He seems in and out of this conversation. Something is bothering him.* She did not understand how he could have been at the party on Saturday night, as he said, for three hours, and not have spoken to or at least seen one of the Meachams. She remembered speaking with Cooper and Mary Meade, at the main bar during the evening. Brian said he had been drinking gin and tonics during the evening, so he must have talked to Cooper or Mary Meade at the bar.

"You're preoccupied," Brian said.

"Sorry, I'm thinking about what's happened and going home," Shannon replied.

"You're ready to go home?"

"Oh yes. I'm ready."

"Question?"

"Okay."

"You've been a Catholic all your life?"

"Yes, why?"

"I don't know, just curious."

Shannon did not answer.

"Maybe the Jesus story was some kind of a publicity stunt that got out of control and none of it's true? Like somebody just made the whole thing up, maybe just for laughs or something? Maybe the whole thing was a story of some sort, and, after it was translated a million times, nobody even knows what the original story was or even if there was an original story in the first place. If that person, Jesus, did actually exist, maybe he was just an ordinary guy. Then one person made up something about him and told somebody and then, as the story was repeated and repeated and repeated, each person added something more to it, until it has no connection to the ordinary guy at all."

"I wouldn't go as far as you do, but I've got doubts."

"Okay, after saying everything I just did, I'm going to put a very basic question to you. "

"Okay."

"Assuming He did exist, in your opinion, was Jesus Christ the person He said he was?"

"I don't know how this conversation drifted into religion; I'm not a member of the clergy."

"You're sharp. I'm curious."

"Yes."

"Yes, that's it?"

"Yes, He is the Messiah."

"You believe that? Troublemakers in the streets everywhere at the time, raising hell with the Romans. Lots of people, some really strange, claiming to be the savior or whatever of the world, the messiah the Jews had been talking about since day one."

"Sunday school kids know that."

"Romans crucified thousands, they did it all the time."

"Everybody knows that. How's that germane?"

"Why focus on this one rabbi?"

"It's the only thing any of us have. If He was not who He said He was, we've got problems."

"In what way."

"Because without Him, life's meaning disappears totally."

"Camus said–"

"I've read Camus. I know what he said. A person alone is responsible for themselves and for all meaning. That leaves me cold."

"You're saying, since the beginning of time or beginning of whenever, that this one person, again if there really was this one person– nobody knows what he really said or how he died or if he just didn't just pass out or faint instead of dying and woke up later—is the meaning of everything in this whole universe. Is that what you're saying?" Brian asked.

"He either walked on the water or He didn't. I doubt if you would ever do this, but think about everything in your life, everything you've ever done, or not done and then set it all aside and focus on one thing: the Mass."

"You're right, I can't see myself doing that," Brian said.

"Okay, let me continue anyway," Shannon said.

"Sure."

"The Mass is the central act of faith, the perfect sacrament. It does not matter to me what you or the rest of the world believes or does not believe. It does not matter that the celebrant is flawed and imperfect, which is always the case. For me, the Mass is the primary reality of all of life itself. The central focus of all that has been and all that will ever be. The sacrament itself may not and probably does not mean a thing to you. It may sound stupid to you or whatever, but for me the sanctity of the Mass, the Eucharist and the presence of Jesus Christ at the Mass is the only thing I can literally hang on to in this world. There is nothing else. It is the beginning and the end of everything."

"You believe that?"

"Yes."

"Okay."

"I won't belabor the point or try to convince you that I'm right and you're wrong, and I won't presume to question your thinking. Now, having said that, I imagine you're going to ask why, if God's so wonderful, why didn't He protect those people from being killed and the answer is I don't know."

The restaurant was quiet. Brian stirred his coffee, and Shannon noticed his blank stare.

"You're tired?" Brian asked.

"It's that obvious? I know it's early. I'll have one small glass of red wine, and then I've got to go to bed."

The waitress came to the table, filled their glasses with red wine, and took the large bottle back to the bar. The man in white clothes stopped reading the paper, left it on the table, and walked back to the kitchen. The couple at the bar finished their brandy, put on their coats and left.

"You're pondering something? Did I get under your skin?" Brian asked.

"No, I told you how I feel, and I got some idea how you think. That's fine," Shannon said.

"I understand."

"I don't usually talk about religion. People get bent out of shape, so I don't talk about it. Actually, I was still thinking about last Sunday morning. It happened right here in this town, three blocks away. Those poor people must have been shot like animals. God, the hotel looks scary. I'll be glad to get out of here."

Brian said nothing.

"Something like this happened out in western Kansas," Shannon said, "years ago when I was probably twelve. It was horrible. Two guys went into a farmhouse out in the country in the middle of night. They tied up the people in the house, a man, his wife, son, and daughter and shot them. The killers got about $40."

"Did they find them?"

"They were caught, but it took a while. As I remember, there were no clues. I take that back; there was a boot print or something like that. I remember reading somewhere that the two guys thought there was a safe or money in this farmhouse, so the motive was money. Here, at least from what everybody's heard and what's in the papers, there aren't any clues at all, and I guess nobody has any idea about a motive."

"Police know more than they're saying?"

"I would think so."

"How were those guys in Kansas caught?" Brian asked.

"My memory's fuzzy, but I think one guy or both had been in prison, and there was a tip or something from an inmate," Shannon said.

"What happened to them?"

"That I remember, they were both hanged."

Brian was quiet.

"There's something else I remember, now that I think about it. The killers, both white men in their 30s or so, weren't sorry for what they did. There was no remorse. I remember hearing that on the radio. The papers later said they were impulsive, paranoid schizophrenic killers, who had no feeling one way or another for the people they killed. They were animals."

"Do you buy the rumor of one killer in this town?" Brian asked.

"Somehow, it's hard to image two complete psychos in one town," Shannon said.

"Do you think it was a man?"

"I guess I do; it's hard for me to imagine a woman doing this."

"Do you think it was a local person?"

"I have no idea. I think an out-of-town person might have done it. The paper said the homicide had the characteristics of a military man who knew how to hide his tracks. I guess that means no fingerprints, no footprints, no shell casings, maybe like a sniper or military person would do it. The hotel lobby was never locked, so it was easy for somebody to get in there day or night. I've heard people say they don't think anybody will be caught."

"People are scared as hell, nobody seems to have any idea about a motive," Brian said.

"The motive, the paper says at this point, was simply to kill these people, that was it. Why kill those particular people, for God's sake?"

"Because of the storm, nobody heard the gunshots."

"Seems incredible. The paper said the food service person, Ida Mae somebody, discovered the victims. She'll never be the same."

"That thing about the broken picture is strange."

"Picture?"

"I heard it was somewhere in the apartment, the living room, I heard, or some place."

"How do you know that?"

"I don't know. I just heard somewhere or from somebody that the police found a broken picture," Brian lied. He was looking at Shannon, at her eyes and the freckles on her nose and the shape of her mouth as she talked and the curve of her beautifully proportioned cheekbones. She was wearing a green crew neck sweater and a white shirt with a wide collar, her raincoat was on the nearby chair. Her blond hair was pulled back from her forehead and from the sides of her face and her wineglass was almost empty. Brian could not believe his own stupidity. There was a cold sinking feeling in his stomach, and his mouth suddenly felt dry. *So, to hell with it,* he thought, *absolutely to hell with it. I should not have said anything about the stupid, asinine picture, but to hell with it. If she notices that, to hell with her.*

WHY DID I GROW SO COLD?

"Another wine?" Brian asked.

"No thanks, I'm tired," Shannon replied; she was uneasy.

"Something to eat?"

"Can't do it. I'm just not hungry. I want to get back to my room."

Brian paid the waitress, and they put on raincoats and hats. Outside, it was still raining They looked through the window by their table, and the sky was dark. Cold rain was coming in gusts through the woods from the lake. Water was standing on the terrace patio. They walked side by side down the south side of Campbell Street and did not see a person. Streetlights looked like candles in the mist. They passed four blocks and came to Canterbury Lane and turned north to Chestnut Brook, neither had spoken since they left Christie's.

"Have your key?" Brian asked.

"Yes, I've got it here in my hand," Shannon said.

"Want me to get the door for you?"

"No, that's fine. I'd better hurry."

"You don't feel a bit good, do you?"

"I think I'm about ready to throw up. Good night, Brian."

Brian stood outside Chestnut Brook in the rain and saw her room light come on. *Cahill, you stupid son of a bitch,* he thought to himself.

Chapter 35

It rained for days. The sky was overcast with a cold gray mist and the trees were soaking wet with dew. More rainstorms from Wisconsin were coming ashore. A small white cottage was across the pathway from Chestnut Brook. Porch furniture had been put away and smoke was coming from the chimney. Wet leaves covered sidewalks and streets. Shannon had been in and out of sleep since Friday night. In her dreams, she saw Brian Cahill's face, and something was wrong.

Shannon ate chicken soup brought to her room by Polly Brooks. Dr. Oliver gave her a shot of penicillin on Saturday, and her arm was sore. The thunder on Monday night was so loud she woke, and for a few minutes, she was frightened. The table next to her bed was covered with medicine bottles and towels. Curtains were closed; there was a single light coming from the bathroom. Her used clothes were on the bathroom floor and the rocking chair by the fireplace. Clean clothes were still in the chest of drawers. It was evening now and her fever and nausea had passed, her face was quite pale and there were circles under her eyes. She felt cold and isolated from the world around her and wished again that she had never come to this town.

Shannon was out of bed, made coffee, and sat down in the chair next to the bed. She listened to the rain. She remembered talking with Brian on Friday and assumed he left for Chicago on Saturday. *He was a strange and dishonest person, she thought. There was coldness about him, and why,* she asked herself, *did he appear to lie?* She still could not understand how he spent three hours at the hotel party a week ago Saturday, if he really was there for three hours, and had not met or even seen any of the Meacham family members. *So,* she thought to herself, *was he really in Vietnam and is he really an orphan?*

Shannon picked up the newspapers by the front door and laid them down on the bed. She read the articles about the Meacham killings. They agreed with what Freddie Martin said at Christie's Friday night. There was no new information. The hot coffee was good. She leaned back in the chair and thought for a long time about what she had heard from the deputy and the articles in the papers. After pouring another coffee, she looked at the night through the front window. It was raining very hard, and she heard thunder and wind in the trees outside. Shannon checked the door lock and then sat down on the edge of the bed and read the papers once more. She put her head down on the pillow, and she knew something was wrong and fell asleep.

She awoke in the night and heard hail falling on the roof and listened until it stopped. Shannon went back to sleep. In the morning, just before dawn, the wind was still blowing, and she remembered what was wrong. It was something Brian said.

Late that morning, she dressed, put on her raincoat and drove to the police department on Campbell Street.

Chief Henry Plunkett's office was small and Spartan with hardwood floor and gray walls. His desk, with only a telephone, was free of papers. In an adjoining room, files were arranged in rows on a long wooden table. A bulletin board on one wall was covered with notes about the Meacham investigation and crime scene photographs. A state police dispatcher was working in a room down the hall.

"Yes, Shannon, I'm Henry Plunkett. Have a chair. How can I help you?" he asked.

"Thank you for seeing me, Chief. I know you're busy," Shannon said.

"You're right."

"This isn't why I came to see you today, but first I want to say how sorry I am about everything. The Meachams were close with a lot of people in town, weren't they?"

"Yes, they were. Pen Meacham was the best friend I've ever had."

"I'm so sorry."

"Thank you."

Conversation stopped, and Henry pressed his mouth together and rubbed his eyes. Shannon heard the dispatcher's voice down the hallway.

"I'm sorry."

"Not a problem, Chief."

"So, you're here on vacation or what's left of your vacation?" Henry asked.

"Yes," Shannon replied.

"I'm sorry. You couldn't have come to our town at a worst time, but tell me what's on your mind?"

"I'm a reporter with the *Saginaw Journal.*"

"Shannon, I'm sorry, but we don't have anything more to release. Everything we're going to say right now has already been said. It's going to be that way until something breaks loose. Was there anything else?"

"I'm not here as a reporter."

"All right, but I want you to know that if we say anything about the investigation, it will be off the record. Do I make myself clear?"

"Understood."

"Okay, shoot."

"I don't know if the information I have is of interest to you or even if it's worth mentioning, but somehow in the back of my mind, I think it might be. I'll not waste your time."

"Let's hear it."

"I wasn't feeling well last Saturday, and I stayed in my room at Chestnut Brook until late in the day. It was raining, and I walked down to the beach. I ran into a person from Chicago. His name is Brian Cahill and, interestingly enough, in a certain light he reminded me of Cooper Meacham."

"Also here on vacation?"

"Yes."

"Like Cooper looked, really?"

"Yes."

"Interesting."

"Yes, we talked for a while and then went for coffee at Christie's."

"This was last Saturday, the 2nd?"

"Yes, that's right."

"Okay, go ahead."

"Deputy Martin was there having dinner. As I'm sure you already know, everybody was asking him about the Meacham investigation. People are really scared."

"Freddie knows everything the state police and I know."

"I understand. Well, there were a lot of things he said he couldn't comment on, and what he did say, as I found out, was already in the papers anyway. After 20 minutes, the deputy left. It was after Freddie Martin left that Brian and I started talking about the investigation. It was kind of strange, but the guy seemed to get kind of caught up in the conversation around us, and I think he maybe said something that he didn't mean to say. I was feeling so lousy at the time I really wasn't paying that much attention to what he was saying. I told Brian I needed to go back to my room."

"What happened then?"

"Brian paid the bill, and we left, and I went to my room. I think he probably left for Chicago the next day. Since that time, I've been sick in bed, until today. I got up this morning and read all of the newspaper accounts about the investigation, and it hit me. There really was something strange that Brian said at Christies about the Meacham investigation. It finally dawned on me early this morning. Just to make sure, I read the articles again before I came over here."

"What did he say?"

"He mentioned a broken picture."

"A broken picture?"

"Yes."

"A broken picture?" Henry asked, as he pulled a legal pad out of his desk drawer and laid it down flat on the desk. He leaned forward on the desk and looked at Shannon and said, "I want you to think very carefully before you answer a couple of questions for me."

"Okay."

"I want you to tell me exactly what this Cahill person said, word-for-word if you can recall."

"As I said, Chief, I wasn't feeling well, but as I now remember, he said, 'That thing about the broken picture is strange.'"

Henry wrote the sentence down on the legal pad and then looked at Shannon and said, "See if I have this right: 'That thing about the broken picture is strange?'"

"Yes, that's right."

"You're sure?"

"Yes, and I didn't know then, and I still don't know, what he was talking about, and I said, 'Picture?'"

"Picture?"

"Yes."

"Did he answer you?"

"Yes, I believe he said something like, 'I heard it was someplace in the apartment, the living room, I heard, or some place.'"

Henry looked up from writing and said," I heard it was someplace in the apartment, the living room, I heard, or some place,' is that right?"

"Yes."

"What did you say then?"

"I think I said, 'How do you know that?'"

"What did he say?"

"I think he said, 'I don't know, I just heard somewhere or from somebody that the police found a broken picture.'"

Henry looked up. "'I don't know I just heard somewhere or from somebody that police found a broken picture,' are those his words as closely as you can recall?"

"Yes, that's right."

"What did he say at that point?"

"His expression was suddenly different. He changed the subject and seemed angry with himself that he had mentioned anything about a picture."

"What did he then talk about?"

"I don't know, as I said before, I wasn't feeling well, and I told Brian I was sure I was going to be sick, and I had to leave right away. I thought I was going to throw up. We left, and I went back to my room, and I guess he went back to Chicago the next day."

"That was the end of any discussion with him?"

"Yes."

"Do you know if he left for Chicago last Saturday?"

"No, I don't."

"Do you know where he was staying in town?"

"He said he was staying at The Parsonage."

"Okay, The Parsonage," Henry said, as he wrote Brian's name on the legal pad.

"Chief, I've read the news stories and I did not find any mention of a broken picture in what I guess is the Meachams' living room. Did I miss something?"

Henry's face had the look of a man who might be coming close to a discovery that seemed unimaginable. His voice suddenly sounded unnatural and he spoke slowly. "Shannon, I do not know what's going on. I sure as hell do not have any idea what this Cahill guy is talking about, but I am damn well going to find out. I am going way the hell out on a limb here. You seem like an honest person, so I'm going to trust you, but I want to remind you, until I say otherwise, everything that comes up or might come up is off the record."

"Absolutely."

"I'd like you to stay here while I check on a couple of things."

"Yes, for sure."

Henry picked up the phone. "Freddie, I want you to go over to The Parsonage and talk to Michael Carter for me. We want to know if his guest, Brian Cahill, has left town, and if so, we need his address in Chicago. Tell Michael that your inquiry cannot be discussed with anyone. Then, I want you to go over to the hotel and go up to the Meacham's apartment and look in the living room and see if there's a broken picture anywhere in that room. I have no idea where it might be in that room. It could be a framed picture of some sort. If you find it, please be very careful with it and bring it back over here as soon as you can. It might be something crucial."

Chapter 36

Deputy Freddie Martin came into Henry's office at noon and he was carrying a framed picture in a plastic bag.

"Here it is, Chief. It was right there in the Meacham's living room."

"Well, I'll be damned. Where was it exactly?" Henry asked.

"Okay, as you walk into the Meacham's living room from the kitchen, there's a big wooden cabinet with drawers on your left, which is, let's see, okay, it's against the south wall."

"Okay, right, it's just inside the hallway from the kitchen, there's a lamp next to it."

"Right!"

"I know the spot you're talking about. Was it, on top of the cabinet?"

"No, it must have fallen to the floor behind the cabinet at some point. As I looked down, I could see the edge of the frame. The picture was on the floor."

"Freddie, this is Shannon Fitsimmons. She has been staying with Polly Brooks. Shannon's the person that said this picture might be in the Meachams' living room."

The deputy was smoking a cigarette. He came into the room, took off his hat and sat down in a chair facing Henry's desk. "Hi, Shannon. You were at Christie's last weekend," Freddie said.

Shannon nodded. "Hi, Freddie. Yes I was. I'm glad to meet you."

"Thank you."

"Chief, is it okay if I take notes?"

"Not a problem, but your notes are off the record."

"Positively. Also, I've got a question."

"Shoot."

"Freddie, does it look to you as if this picture had been hanging on the wall at some point?" Shannon asked.

"That's interesting. Yes, it does look like that. There's a small picture hook still there on the wall, and there's kind of like an indentation or outline, I guess you'd say, on the wall, where it looked as if the picture had been pushed or, I guess, slammed or hit against the wall, if you know what I mean."

"Freddie, is there broken glass on the cabinet?" Henry asked.

"Not that I saw."

"How about on the floor?"

"I didn't see any."

Henry stood up behind his desk and put on plastic gloves. "Okay, letsa see what we've got."

Shannon stood up as Freddie placed the plastic bag in the middle of Henry's desk. Henry unsealed the top of the bag, reached in and slowly removed the picture. They found an 8x10, black-and-white photograph of Pen Meacham and his brother Paul at about age 15 or 16. The frame was black, and the matting was powder blue. The glass was broken.

"I'll be damned. This's an old picture of Pen Meacham and Paul, his identical twin brother. I remember it now. None of us had ever seen Paul until we saw him at the funeral. The glass is cracked, but still in place. It looks like the glass was smashed or hit in the center with a hand or fist or something. There is blood at what I guess was probably the point of impact. It also looks like there is some kind of a fingerprint or a print of someone's fist. This is very strange, but it looks like we might be on to something. Freddie, what do you think?" Henry asked.

"Chief, I don't know what to make of this. We missed this picture last week because it wasn't in an area where we thought one of the crimes had taken place. We weren't looking for it."

"I remember, we didn't think the living room and some of the others rooms were important," Henry said.

"But, Chief, even if we had found it, I'm not sure what we would have done with it. Why is this important now?"

"Shannon, would you tell Freddie why you came over here today?" Henry asked.

"Sure. Freddie, you might remember that I was at a table with a man at Christie's the other night?"

"Right, you were sitting not far from the front door."

"Correct, and that man's name is Brian Cahill."

"Okay, he's the man from Chicago, I just got his address from Michael Carter. Do you know him?"

"Not really; we just met on the beach and decided to have coffee. The important thing is that after you left the other night we talked for a few minutes about the Meacham investigation and your answers to all the questions you got."

"Okay, I hope I was making sense."

"Perfectly, but the incredible thing is that while we were talking, Brian Cahill brought up the subject of a broken picture that he said was in the apartment, probably the living room."

"He said that? How would he know that unless he had been in the Meacham's living room?"

"That's the whole point of what we're talking about," Henry said. "We don't know how Cahill could possibly have known about the picture unless he had been in the Meacham's living room. But when was he there and why? The Meachams were friendly people, but their apartment was private. Only close friends and family were ever up there. Even Charlie and Ida Mae, who worked at the hotel for years, had never been upstairs."

"Jesus, Chief, this might be something," Freddie said.

"Okay Freddie, I want you to put the picture back in the bag and take it up to the lab in Lansing for prints and blood, and do it right away."

Freddie put his cigarette out in the ashtray next to the chair and then reached over and carefully put the picture back in the plastic bag. "I'm on the way."

"Thanks, Freddie."

Henry was up from his desk, walked over the window on the far wall and looked at the lake. "Shannon, it's difficult to imagine, but it seems possible that this Cahill guy might have had it in for my friend Pen Meacham for some reason. I'm thinking that Pen may have been the real target, and Cooper and

Geraldine were killed just because they were there. Tell me, what did Cahill seem like to you?"

"Chief, I'd say he's handsome, polished and looks like an athlete. He said he'd been in Vietnam. He said he was an orphan and never knew his parents. He seemed glib about that, almost as if it did not matter to him, which I didn't believe at all. I think it matters to him a great deal. His tone changed sharply when he referred to himself as just some poor bastard sent off to kill gooks in Nam. He had a very odd way of starting a sentence and then stopping with an empty stare, like there was something more he wanted to say, but couldn't. He seemed in and out of our conversation, like something was really bothering him. He said he was at the hotel party last Saturday night for three hours and he did not see or talk to any member of the Meacham family, which seemed impossible. What, I thought, a very odd thing to lie about."

"So, he apparently knew the family owned the hotel and that they must have been there somewhere, even though he denied seeing them. That is strange, if he had no idea what they looked like, how would he have known if he saw them or not? Did you notice if he had a bandage on either one of his hands."

"I didn't notice. But Chief, here's something else, now that I think about it, that is maybe more curious than everything else."

"Shoot."

"Cahill said that he drank gin and tonics at the party on Saturday night. Cooper Meacham and Mary Meade Saltonstall were the bartenders at the main bar. At least that's where I met them."

"Cooper and Mary Meade worked at the main bar probably every Saturday night."

"I don't see how Brian Cahill could have avoided the main bar all evening unless he was drinking only on the terrace, which I doubt. I think Brian must have ordered a drink at least one time during the evening at the main bar. Cooper and Mary Meade were so friendly, I can't imagine that if Cahill went to that bar, which I think he did, that he could have avoided meeting them. At least that my theory."

"That's interesting. Unfortunately, Mary Meade's in the hospital, and we can't confirm with her if she and Cooper actually met Cahill, which would confirm that Cahill is lying. I'll check with her as soon as she's well enough.

I understand she's in a very bad way."

"That's so sad. They looked like such a nice couple."

"I'll check with her as soon as possible. In the meantime, we changed the hotel locks on Sunday, and the building is sealed off. Freddie and I've got the only keys. I've been to the hotel every day. There has been no sign of forced entry. Cahill could not have gotten into the hotel after the discovery of the victims. Up to this point, we've had nothing–no weapon, no shell casings, no robbery and no motive."

"What happens now?"

"Freddie will be in Lansing the rest of the day. We already have the victims' blood types, and we have their fingerprints on file. He'll get the blood type and prints on the broken glass and check it against the victims' and Cahill's military records. Then, tomorrow, we'll contact Chicago police and put the wheels in motion to have Cahill brought up here for questioning, or we'll go down there. One way or another, we're going to talk with him. Cahill's going to need a damn good explanation how he came to know about that picture and my guess is that it's his blood on the glass. Cahill probably didn't mean to say what he said to you and he may not even remember telling you. Who knows? We have to make damn sure he's left town before you go back to your room. You have a card?"

Shannon pulled one from her purse and handed it to Henry.

"Shannon, I've got a feeling we might get somewhere with this, at least it's starting to look that way. We'll see. If it looks like we're on to something, I'll give you first look at everything you want to know because you came forward and because everyone else's gone. That is down the road, but we'll see how things work out. Thank you so much."

Chapter 37

In the fall, it was cold in Stamford Bridge, and the dark came early. The sun was behind the horizon, there were shadows across the water. Empty summer homes faced the beach, and the hotel on Campbell Street was still closed. Streetlights were on and a few people were looking in shop windows. Trees were bare. Leaves were gathered in stacks near curbs and sidewalks and the wind across the lake from Wisconsin blew many of them down to the beach. Snow would soon powder everything.

Mary Meade Saltonstall thought about her death. She had seen it coming for months and she was afraid. Her eyes were listless, she never smiled and seldom talked to anyone; her face was white and puffy, she no longer used makeup, and there were dark circles under her eyes. She wore the same sort of clothes she had always worn, but they were no longer pressed, and her blond hair was often uncombed and held in place with a rubber band.

The trauma was there exactly as it had happened in July–Cooper was dead, he had his life, it was finished, and he had not lived long enough to lose hope. There was a cold emptiness inside her where happiness had once been. She walked to Cooper's grave site every day and there was now a headstone next to the other two. Freddie had once seen her there as the sun was coming up on a cold morning. Mary Meade planned, if she lived until spring, to plant flowers near Cooper's grave.

The wind picked up as she turned on the road to St. John's Woods. A small white parish church was on Tenby, off Main Street. It was at the end of the street. There was a cottage nearby, with smoke coming out of the chimney. The cemetery on the west side of the church was old and carefully trimmed. The grass was turning and flowers were spread on a new grave. Winter mulch covered a large flower garden next to the front of the building. Mary Meade passed through an iron gate and walked up a new flagstone sidewalk, up wooden steps and into the church. Inside it was dark and quiet. A narrow communion rail was close to the front altar and a few candles were burning at a side altar. Wooden pews were old, the center aisle was of polished marble, and the smell of incense filled the sanctuary.

She saw the priest's head outlined against the grille as she sat down.

"Are you here for confessional?" a whispery voice asked.

"Father, I came to ask for Absolution," Mary Meade said.

"You are Catholic?"

"Yes. I'm asking for Absolution from the Church."

"I see," the priest said after a long pause. "Tell me what troubles you so deeply."

Mary Meade wiped her eyes with a white handkerchief. "You probably heard about the murders in Stamford Bridge last summer?"

"Yes, of course, a senseless tragedy. A terrible, terrible thing, but why does that bring you here?"

The priest listened in silence while Mary Meade told him about Cooper, the life they had together, and the shattering impact of his death and the depth of her sadness. She said God must hate her–why else would he have allowed Cooper to be killed?

"I am so sorry for you, child. You are so young to carry such a great burden of grief. It is often said that our Lord never gives us a greater burden…"

"That's wrong, Father! Completely wrong! I've heard it a hundred times, and it's wrong. Cooper's loss is unbearable to me. Nothing can change that; I can't live on earth without him. That's why I'm here."

"Surely, child, as a Catholic, you must know that everything is in accord with God's great mercy and His love for each of us. Take the sacraments and pray to the Lord. Thank Him for the time you and Cooper did have together. Ask Him why this has happened to you, and an answer will come to you. It may take time, but there will be an answer for you. Your anger and sorrow are very great. Pray to the Lord, and ask Him to forgive you for being angry with Him."

WHY DID I GROW SO COLD?

Mary Meade was defiant and wiped tears from her face. "Father, I hear what you're saying, but why does God always get off the hook? You say He really is a nice guy after all, although He stood by and let Cooper and his parents be slaughtered like animals, and now you're telling me to ask Him to forgive me for something He shouldn't have allowed to happen in the first place. Catholic or whatever, I'm not that stupid. I don't get it. Do we just say, well God, that's okay, it's okay if You hate me. Just kill whoever in the hell you want to, and we're really sorry to have offended You? But God, why do you hate me?"

The priest was old and spoke slowly in a whisper, "I so thoroughly sense your great anger and bitterness and sadness. I read somewhere long ago that none of us can understand the appalling strangeness of God's mercy. We must pray and hope and take the sacraments and know that Christ is there with us during the Mass, knowing that everything we ask of Him will ultimately be fulfilled."

"If I ask Him, will he return Cooper to life?"

"There is always the hope for everlasting life for you and Cooper together."

"Father, I want to be with him in death, now."

"Do you mean take your life?"

"Yes."

"That's very serious, a very serious matter indeed."

"Yes, Father, I know. I want Absolution from the Church. There's nothing for me here."

"Child, you're so young, and your whole life is in front of you. Such an act would be a very great travesty in God's eyes. Surely, Cooper, whom you loved so deeply, would not want you to do that, surely not."

"I'm terrified that if I don't act soon, I might not find him on the other side.
"

"Cooper was a Catholic?"

"Yes."

"Please tell me if Cooper took the sacraments all of his life?"

"Yes; I have also."

"I'm glad, but please listen to me very carefully. I must tell you, child, if you do what you say, if you end your own life, which I pray you won't, you will die in a state of the most dreadful mortal sin. You may be cast into outer darkness with no hope of redemption. There may be only eternal darkness, and you may never find Cooper again."

Mary Meade broke down. "What am I to do?"

"The Church does not believe that any soul is forever damned if one is truly repentant, but I must tell you that the risk you would be taking would be very great. In your anguish, look deeply into your heart and try to find forgiveness for God and his Son Jesus Christ and ask for forgiveness for yourself."

"There's more, Father, oh, God, there's more, "Mary Meade whispered.

"Yes."

"There will be a child."

"I see. I sense that your desperation is compounded by the fact that you and Cooper never had the chance to marry?"

"Yes, yes, that's right."

"You would be taking two lives then, your life and also the life of the child of you and Cooper."

"Yes."

"I cannot give you Absolution in the face of a planned mortal sin. Again, Cooper, as the person who loved you, I am sure would not want you to do the terrible thing you are considering. Surely, he would not want you to travel down that very dark passage where the outcome would be so uncertain. Now, with two lives in the balance, I am sorry, child, Absolution is impossible. Maybe another priest in another parish, if he did not know your plans, would give you Absolution, but I cannot. Surely, you would not deny your unborn child a right to life. I am sure Cooper would never forgive you. Come back tomorrow and let's talk again."

Mary Meade said nothing and she heard the priest turning pages in his prayer book.

"Shall we pray, child, and ask God, in His wisdom, to help you?"

"No, Father, not now."

"As you wish."

She was silent and heard the priest clear his throat.

"I want you to promise me that if you think of this dreadful step, you will call me, day or night. Is that understood?"

"Yes."

WHY DID I GROW SO COLD?

"Will you come back tomorrow at this same time?"

"Yes, yes. It's so difficult, but I'll try."

"Perhaps God will give you a son and he could be named Cooper Jr. You would live for him and he would be, in a real sense, the incarnation of the man you loved so deeply."

Chapter 38

The steel door closed and the room was quiet. Cell 1437 measured 10x10, and there was a cot, chair, wood table, and a small bathroom. Brick walls were painted white, the floors gray concrete. A narrow window, covered with bars, faced north. Brian could see a school playground in the distance and a small square of sky. He was allowed out of his cell for a shower on Saturday and given clean clothing and sheets each week. Breakfast was brought to his cell at 7 and dinner at 5. Lights burned day and night in the hallways, and cell lights turned off at 10. Brian was almost alone in the world. Charmon did not write or visit, and his Chicago friends deserted him. He thought about being dead and doubted if anyone would miss him. Brian's only visitors were his attorney and Shannon Fitsimmons. He refused to see the prison chaplain.

Brian's friendship with Shannon Fitsimmons began simply enough. He remembered coffee with her at Christie's and seeing her at Holy Cross and the Inn party. Brian knew she was now a reporter on assignment. He knew Shannon was responsible for his arrest and it did not matter to him. Brian told Shannon he knew it was hopeless when they brought him back to his cell, and he had walked back and forth and stopped to look through the window. He said there were no sounds or shapes in the darkness and he knew this was final. Brian began sleeping 15 hours a day and soon lost track of time. After a few weeks, Brian heard voices in the night, and he discovered that he was talking to himself. Escape, he knew, was out of the question, and he thought of suicide. After the trial, Brian told Shannon that he remembered only parts of it. The talking had bored him, and he stopped listening.

WHY DID I GROW SO COLD?

The trial itself, in the circuit court for Barry County, Michigan began on May 2, 1977.

"People versus Brian Cahill," Judge Patterson said. "The charge is murder in the first degree."

"Appearances?" the judge asked.

"J. P. Halligan for the defendant."

"Are the People ready?"

"We are, your honor," the chief prosecutor, F.K. Crews, said.

"Is the defense ready?"

"Yes, your honor."

"Very well. A plea of not guilty has been entered."

The small courtroom was hot and crowded. Judge Patterson was a young man with a mustache. The court would take an impartial view of the trial and the conduct of the attorneys. Outbursts would not be tolerated, he said. Every seat in the courtroom was taken, and some people stood next to the walls. Brian had been in his cell for a year and at first found it hard to believe that these people were in the courtroom because of him. Most stared at Brian, and he knew they hated him. Bailiffs in brown uniforms stood at each door. Brian's attorney, J.P. Halligan, was a older man with short red hair who spoke quietly. Halligan told Brian the best he could hope for would be life in prison without possibility of parole. He said the law in Michigan stipulated that a punishable crime must be committed by a person knowing the difference between right and wrong at the time the crime was committed. He hoped to demonstrate to the court that Brian was insane at the time of the crimes and the burden to prove him sane would fall to the prosecution. He discussed *People versus Durfee*, Michigan 4876, with Brian, in which the court held that, "If the defendant was not capable of knowing he was doing wrong in a particular act or if he had not the power to resist the impulse to do that act...that would be an unsound mind." Halligan explained that this law was their only hope to avoid the death penalty. Halligan said he would do his best, but it would be up to the judge, the judge's instructions to the jury and the jury.

In the opening statement, Halligan said he would demonstrate to the court that his client was not guilty of any crime associated with the deaths of Penfield Meacham, Geraldine Meacham or Cooper Meacham. Brian Cahill was legally insane at the time of the crimes.

Henry Plunkett's testimony recounted Brian's confession. There was no cross-examination regarding the facts of the case. Copies of the 49-page, typed confession were given to the court the day before. Halligan would not attempt to deny that Cahill killed the three members of the Meacham family.

Ida Mae Murphy, Frank Scott, Freddie Martin and the county coroner, Dr. N.V. Stocker, described what they found at The Promontory Inn on Sunday, July 27: the empty lobby, Penfield Meacham on the second-floor landing with a shattered skull, laying on his right side. Cooper Meacham sitting upright against the nearby wall with wound on his forehead and eyes closed, and Geraldine Meacham in a pool of blood in the third-floor bedroom, laying on her side. Dr. Stocker demonstrated with charts where the bodies were found and described how they looked. He explained the nature of the injuries each victim sustained: Penfield and Geraldine's deaths were caused by a severe trauma to the brain and cranial structure inflicted by a shotgun, fired at point blank range. A single severe blow killed Cooper Meacham probably with a rifle barrel, to the forehead. Stocker estimated time of deaths of the victims and said all three victims died instantly, not more than five minutes apart. At the request of Graham Meacham, autopsies were not performed.

Dr. Stocker, also an expert in scientific crime detection, analyzed the two pieces of physical evidence connecting Cahill to the crime–the murder weapon and the smashed picture found in the Meacham's living room with the defendant's blood on the glass. Over Halligan's objections, black-and-white photographs of the victims were shown to members of the jury; there was a gasp and several reacted in shock and disgust, some stared at Brian with outrage and contempt.

Next, Shannon Fitsimmons told the court of her conversation with the accused on the night of August 1. Halligan waived cross-examination.

Psychiatric testimony from two defense therapists was given in an afternoon session. Testimony was long. Both examined Cahill; the defendant revealed severe symptoms of emotional deprivation, paranoia and periodic extreme manifestations of post traumatic stress disorder. Brian Cahill, according to both physicians, was irresistibly compelled to do what he did. He was unable to control himself.

WHY DID I GROW SO COLD?

Halligan presented five character witnesses: Brian's 1st Cavalry commanding officer, platoon Sergeant Selby, a college counselor, highway patrol officer C.J. Adams and Brian's VA psychiatrist. Brian did not testify. Charmon Le Carre attended for two days. Darby Staltonstall, Mary Meade's older sister, and her parents attended the trial. Graham Meacham was in California. Paul Meacham, from Chicago, attended on behalf of his twin brother, Pen. Brian looked at his father and knew he had killed the wrong person.

Paul Meacham told a reporter before the trial began: "I want to see the son of a bitch that did this, and I hope he gets the death penalty." The twin brother was stunned by Brian's appearance.

On the second day, Brian almost forgot what the trial was about. His face was ashen, and there were dark circles under his eyes. He grew tired of people talking about him and thought of going back to his cell and sleeping.

Halligan told the court that his client's mental condition was never stable. Further, his condition had deteriorated over many years: the pain of growing up alone, of having nothing, of having no family, of never knowing his father or mother, of jail and detention centers, of conflicts with those around him, of loneliness, of combat in Vietnam. The shock of confronting the man he believed to be his father, on top of everything else, drove him to a state of madness on July 27, 1975. When the crimes occurred that early morning, Halligan said, making reference to psychiatric testimony, Cahill felt as if he was a spectator watching the events take place, and was unable to stop the killing. He had entered a mental state with an almost dream-like character, only to discover as he emerged from the trance that he had killed the Meacham family members.

"Your honor, I really do not see the need for Cahill's life history," F.K. Crews, a tall, thin man with rimless glasses, interrupted. "I don't see how this information is at all relevant to this trial."

"Mr. Halligan?"

"This information is completely relevant your honor. It is central to our defense. I am trying to demonstrate to the court that Mr. Cahill has had a long history of mental illness caused, as it were, by a series of traumatic events which led him ultimately, against his will, to the events of July 27."

"Your honor, I'm sorry the defendant has had a difficult life, but we all have problems. The People object to this litany as a waste of the court's time. I really do not see the merits of this sob story, and we really have no sympathy for this monster whatever," Crews said.

"I object to this characterization by the prosecutor," Halligan shouted.

"You know better than that, Mr. Crews. You are out of line," the judge said.

"I'm sorry, your honor. I apologize to the court."

"I'm going to allow defense counsel to continue, but I warn you, Mr. Halligan, stay focused," the judge said.

"Thank you."

The court was shown pictures of the orphanages where Brian was raised and abused; the court saw a picture of the truant officer convicted of assaulting Brian; there were pictures of the Ia Drang and American and enemy dead; another photo showed the devastation caused by American artillery fire, as described by Sergeant Selby, called in on top of the American position in the Ia Drang. Brian had suffered some hearing loss, serious shrapnel wounds, and a severe concussion. Halligan then quoted one of the psychiatrists, Dr. Bill J. Evans of the Veterans Administration Hospital in Chicago: "The horror of the Ia Drang has not left Brian for a day since November of 1965."

Halligan stopped for a drink of water and set the glass down on the table next to his notes. He told the jury about the mysterious photo album arriving at Brian's apartment in Chicago on Friday night, July 25. It arrived 36 hours before the crimes. He described Brian's shock at seeing pictures of his mother and perhaps his father for the first time, and the nightmare that followed. The attorney paused again and gathered his notes. Halligan retraced Brian's movements after leaving Chicago on Saturday, July 26: "Brian Cahill, exhausted from a sleepless night, left Chicago in the morning and at 10:46, four miles south of Benton Harbor, Michigan, narrowly missed causing a multi-car accident on Highway I-94. Highway patrol officer C.J. Adams has testified that he found Brian almost incoherent, with obvious symptoms of very severe post traumatic stress disorder."

"Objection–Highway Patrol Officer Adams is not qualified to determine if the defendant was suffering from post traumatic stress disorder or not. It is incorrect for Mr. Halligan to present Officer Adams' testimony to the court as the opinion of a qualified observer of human behavior," Crews said.

"The court agrees," the judge said. "Will the court reporter read back what Officer Adams said in his testimony?"

"Yes, your honor: 'Mr. Adams said. I had seen other guys in Nam suffering from what we were told were post traumatic stress disorders. It was the same thing I'd seen in guys over there in country and I saw the same thing back in the States at the vet centers. Some guys were and are still really messed up. Cahill looked to me that morning like a classic case. He was almost incoherent.'"

"Thank you, your honor. I will rephrase my statement by saying that, 'It appeared to Adams that Cahill was suffering from the same disorder that he had seen in other veterans.'"

"Proceed."

"Thank you. The officer did not issue a ticket or warning. Mr. Adams has testified that he guessed that Brian was apparently experiencing a traumatic Vietnam combat flashback. From what he personally observed that day, it was only the sound of a trucker's air horn that saved Cahill and others on the highway from disaster. To all intents and purposes, according to Mr. Adams, the defendant was out of control and, at the very least, temporarily insane at that hour."

"Objection! Again, your honor, the highway patrol officer cannot determine if Cahill was insane or not. Again, and I repeat, it is incorrect for the defense to present Adams as an expert."

"Your honor, C.J. Adams has been trained as a counselor with the Vietnam Veterans Association of America and he has seen, observed and spent time with other veterans with these same symptoms. We are presenting his views, as an observer of other veterans, which are vital to our defense. In any event, psychiatric testimony has already confirmed to the court that my client does suffer from this disorder," Halligan said.

"The court will allow you to continue, Mr. Halligan, but the jury will disregard any reference to Mr. Adams as an expert in human behavior," the judge said.

"Thank you. To his credit, the highway patrol officer, as noted, a Vietnam veteran himself, had, as I said before, seen these same symptoms in other Vietnam veterans and was somehow able to guide Cahill back into the real world. After talking with Adams for perhaps an hour, Brian evidently improved to the degree that he was able to continue driving. All of this happened about 14 hours before the crimes were committed."

The attorney stopped to see the reaction of the jury; there was none.

"Brian Cahill then drove several miles north toward Stamford Bridge and stopped for drinks at the Blue Arrow Bar & Grill, near South Haven. It was by then early afternoon and the bartender at the Blue Arrow has testified that Brian seemed angry and on edge, about 12 hours before the crimes. Brian stayed at the Blue Arrow for probably half an hour, left and arrived at Stamford Bridge in the middle of the afternoon and checked in at The Parsonage Bed & Breakfast. This was his first visit to Stamford Bridge; his reservations were for 4 and he arrived early. He then changed clothes, left his room, jogged through Stamford Bridge neighborhoods and through downtown, and then made his way down to the beach at Lake Michigan. While walking on the beach, probably at about 4 p.m., Cahill happened to look up from the beach and noticed to his complete astonishment that he recognized, facing the lake, the White Sands Boarding House. There was a picture of the White Sands in the photo album he received the day before. To his knowledge, he had never been to Stamford Bridge in his life and found the sheer coincidence of seeing a building pictured in the photo album almost unbelievable. He found himself at a total loss to understand such a strange turn of events; the arrival of the album of family pictures after 30 years with no explanation and then the incredible fact that the album, from God knows who or where, somehow connected him to Stamford Bridge! In that same boarding house picture, Brian had also seen the woman identified by him as his mother, Ruth Cahill, and an unidentified man. This was the man Brian believed to be his father. That picture had been taken at the same White Sands Boarding House 30 years ago. These strange, bizarre, almost macabre developments, without foundation or explanation, were unsettling. Brian now realized that one or maybe both of his parents had lived in Stamford Bridge before he was born. I am now showing that picture to the court, Exhibit 7, of Ruth Cahill and the unidentified man taken in 1945."

"Your honor, I fail to see the relevance of all this. Defense counsel is speculating about what was on the defendant's mind," Crews said. "This is pure speculation on his part and I object. I don't understand where Mr. Halligan is going with this?"

"Counselor?" the judge asked.

"Your honor, I am trying to demonstrate to the court the frame of mind of the defendant as he moved closer to 3 a.m. Sunday morning, July 27."

"Objection is overruled. Mr. Crews, this seems to be information the court wants to hear. I'll allow it for now."

"Thank you, your honor."

"Your honor, I fail to—"

"That's it. Mr. Crews, Mr. Halligan continue."

"Thank you."

"At this point on Saturday, the 26th," Halligan continued, "Brian Cahill made his way to the White Sands Boarding House and went inside. He evidently met and spoke for some time with Cooper Meacham and Mary Meade Saltonstall. Cooper Meacham looked shockingly familiar to Brian."

Halligan stopped speaking and held photos of Brian Cahill and Cooper Meacham side by side for the jury to see. The jury was impassive.

"My client then discovered another picture of Ruth Cahill on a bulletin board in the boarding house hallway. That additional photograph seemed to confirm to him that she, the person he was certain was his mother, had lived in that building in Stamford Bridge some 30 years ago. Cahill was upset and bewildered and confused by all of this, and he went back to his room at The Parsonage at about 6:00, about eight hours before the crimes."

"Your honor, I again fail to see—"

"Overruled. Continue, Mr. Halligan," the judge said.

"Brian looked at the album of pictures again and thought he was losing his mind."

"Objection!"

"Overruled."

"Cooper Meacham, whom he had just met, looked exactly like the man in the 1945 photo that you, members of the jury, now see on the chart. The mystery man in this picture was about the same age as Cooper Meacham in 1975 when the 1945 picture was taken. The longer he looked at the 1945 photo of the unidentified man and the more he thought about Cooper Meacham, the more astonished and upset and nervous he became. Brian then realized that he himself looked like Cooper Meacham–a person he had never met before that day. Since he looked like Cooper, and since the man in the photo you see before you looked like both of them, Brian concluded that Cooper could somehow be his own brother or perhaps his half brother. Could Ruth Cahill possibly have been the mother of both of them? Other pictures, which you now see as Exhibits 8, 9, and 10, revealed that Ruth Cahill had been a barmaid in The Promontory Inn in Stamford Bridge in 1945 and perhaps 1946."

Halligan stopped for a drink of water and continued.

"Saturday, July 26, was a day of immense tension for the defendant. At about 7 that evening, Brian Cahill left his room at The Parsonage for the party at The Promontory Inn on Saturday night, July 26. Cahill went to the main bar and again talked with Cooper Meacham and Mary Meade Saltonstall. Later in the evening, Brian saw C.J. Adams, the highway patrol officer he had seen earlier in the day, at the party. Adams has testified that he again found Cahill in a state of what appeared to be extreme distress, about five hours before the crimes. Brian did not mention Pen Meacham or Ruth Cahill, but he appeared to Adams to be on the verge of exploding. Adams has quoted Brian Cahill as saying that he thought about violence every day and had periods of rage that he was barely able to control. Adams felt, as he has testified, that Brian Cahill was truly disturbed, and some form of violence seemed imminent. As noted earlier, Adams has testified that he has seen these same types of symptoms in other Vietnam veterans. Adams left the hotel to call a therapist he knew in Chicago. He had hoped to set up an appointment for Brian the following week. When Adams returned to the hotel after half an hour, Cahill was gone. Cahill had gone alone to the bar, located near the hotel's long hallway. Cahill saw for the first time the man he took to be his father, Penfield Meacham. According to psychiatric testimony we have heard, Pen Meacham's presence immediately created a traumatic configuration in Cahill's mind. He now believed that Pen Meacham was the unidentified man in the 1945 photograph with Ruth Cahill. In Pen Meacham, he saw a man who was popular, successful, and happy, and he hated him for what he was. He saw Geraldine Meacham, Penfield Meacham's wife, and was confused and wondered what must have become of Ruth Cahill. He saw, in Pen Meacham, a man surrounded by friends and money and a happy family, a man who was the host of a huge party and who owned a wonderful hotel. Cahill thought about growing up alone with no money, no family, and no decent place to live; about detention centers, a Salvation Army center, jail, and finally the horror of Vietnam. All during those years, Pen Meacham had had everything. Pen Meacham, in Cahill's mind, as Dr. Evans has testified, was the immediate source of all his problems. He had abandoned the other woman in his life and his bastard son at birth. A lifelong hatred of his father and mother came to the boiling point."

Halligan stopped again for a drink of water

"Brian left The Promontory Inn party somewhere around 12:30 and walked in the rain down to the Lake Michigan beach. He does not remember how long he was there, but it must have been for at least an hour, perhaps longer."

Halligan stopped and picked up a copy of court testimony from May 2.

"At this time, I want to refer to Dr. Evans' testimony. As the court will recall, his testimony was presented to the court after psychiatric examination regarding Cahill's probable state of mind on Sunday morning, roughly an hour and a half before the crimes."

"Your honor, we've heard this before!"

"Counselor?"

"Your honor, the most crucial point of our defense is here. We want to establish as clearly as possible for the court, my client's probable state of mind immediately before the crimes were committed. Our defense cannot continue, we believe, without putting this vital testimony in its correct time sequence before the crimes. We ask the court's permission to allow us to repeat this critical testimony which reveals, we feel, the dramatic decline in Cahill's mental condition and his state of mind that Sunday morning."

"I'll allow this, Mr. Halligan. The court understands the direction of your argument and has granted you the time you have asked for, over Mr. Crews' objection. However, I want you to come to your conclusion soon and focus your information on the evidence at hand."

"Thank you, your honor. Dr. Evans, you will recall, in his testimony said, and I am quoting him directly, 'In all probability, Mr. Cahill was suffering from dissociative reaction, which in and of itself indicates to me that there had been a series of massive psychological shocks to Mr. Cahill's emotional equilibrium. Moreover, these traumatic shocks created an overwhelming sense of apprehension and anxiety in his mind. In this state of mind, a person will resort to almost any activity of any nature in an effort to reduce the sense of rage, the sense of anxiety and the sense of apprehensiveness. In this context, there would be no concept of right and wrong. This man has also suffered from episodes of post traumatic stress disorder over a period of years. This fact alone has contributed hugely to his alarming degree of instability. Indeed, the unpredictable nature of the disorder itself tends to create an ongoing sense of apprehensiveness, which can and does severely interrupt normal cognitive functions. Mr. Cahill's life history indicates that he had been capable of extraordinary violence, and it was natural, in his state of mind, that he should turn to violence. Indeed, in his state of mind at the time, there probably was no alternative to violence. When facing Pen Meacham, the man Brian believed to be his father, the man he believed abandoned him so many years ago and, thus, the man responsible for all of his difficulties, real or imagined, there was no alternative in his mind to do other than what he did. Additionally, he almost certainly was not able to consider the consequences of any course of action he might take. If he had been told of the possible consequences of any possible act, he would not have been in a state of mind to appreciate or accept the advice. He was in a spell, much like a trance-like condition. His overriding concern at that time was to relieve himself of the existing unbearable anxiety created by the many factors previously outlined for the court. In psychiatric parlance, the condition is referred to as a state of irresistible impulse. The only option available to him was to resort to violence. This, then, was Brian Cahill's state of mind when he entered The Promontory Inn at 3 in the morning on July 27.'"

Crews started to object and then sat down.

"Thus," Halligan said, "as Dr Evans has told the court, and I again quote directly, 'Brian Cahill was in an uncontrollable state of dissociative reaction when the crimes were committed,' close quote. Members of the jury, I ask you to look at this unfortunate man who fought for his country in not one but two tours of duty of in Vietnam, a recipient of three Purple Hearts, the Vietnam Service Medal, the Vietnam Combat Medal and the nation's second highest award for military service to his country. Raised as an orphan without family, without friends or money or possessions of his own, he has made his way in life. His history indicates a history of emotional and psychiatric difficulties. This man grew up without love or guidance and without any established standards with respect to moral or ethical behavior. The abandonment by his parents, the evidence of that they had once lived in Stamford Bridge and the unremitting horror of Vietnam combat combined to put him in the unbearable sate of mind at the time of the crimes. I ask you to spare his life and allow him to be sent to a state psychiatric facility for as long as treatment is necessary. Nothing that we can do here today can bring the three members of the Meacham family back to life, and we miss them. Surely that tragedy cannot be abated by the execution of Brian Cahill."

Halligan thanked the jury and sat down.

In the People's opening statement, F.K. Crews said, "The defense has claimed that Brian Cahill, the defendant, was insane at the time of the crimes. We believe that Cahill was sane at the time, and that the crimes were premeditated and the results of malice aforethought. Cahill is guilty of three counts of first degree murder, and the People will demand the death penalty."

Crews then called the People's rebuttal psychiatrist, Dr. William M. Jakeway of Detroit State Hospital.

"Your position, Dr. Jakeway, at Detroit State Hospital?"

"Chief of staff."

"Have your reviewed the findings of Dr. Bill J. Evans regarding the state of mind of Brian Cahill at the time the homicides were committed on July 27, 1975?"

"I have."

"Did you have the opportunity to personally examine the defendant?"

"I did."

"How long were those examinations?"

"My examinations were extensive. Actually, there were two sessions of four hours each. My findings including a personal history and notes are included in the report given to the court the day before yesterday."

"Dr. Jakeway, do you now have an opinion regarding the sanity of the defendant at the time the crimes were committed?"

"Yes I do."

"Please tell the court."

"In my opinion, Mr. Cahill was not suffering from dissociative reaction at the time of the crimes. Mr. Cahill did, in fact, know the difference between right and wrong at the time and it is my opinion that he fully understood the consequences of what he was doing. Dissociative reaction is generally a long-term condition, which manifests itself over a period of years. I did not find evidence of post traumatic stress disorder. While I found some abnormalities in Mr. Cahill's psychological profile, I found nothing to warrant the conclusion that he was insane at the time the crimes were committed."

"Thank you Dr. Jakeway, your witness," Crews said and sat down.

"I understand, Dr Jakeway, that Detroit State Hospital is psychiatric hospital of long standing, is it not?" Halligan asked.

"It is," Jakeway replied.

"You, as chief of staff, have the overall responsibility for the psychiatric services provided by the hospital?"

"That is correct."

"How long have you held that position?"

"Seventeen years."

"It is a state hospital funded by the State of Michigan is it not?"

"That is correct."

"Are patients of all ages treated at Detroit State Hospital?"

"It would be unusual for us to treat a patient under the age of 65."

"Detroit State Hospital is, in fact, a geriatric psychiatric hospital, isn't that right?"

"Yes."

"Do you recall, Dr. Jakeway, if patients in the age range of, say, 25 to 35, or even 25 to 40 or 45, have ever been treated at your hospital?"

"No, not that I recall."

"I understand that you are regarded as an expert in the field of geriatric psychiatry. Indeed, you have published articles on geriatric psychiatry in academic journals, and you have written three books on the subject. Isn't that correct?"

"Yes, that's right."

"Have you or does the hospital deal with or treat patients that you might describe as violent?"

"Only insofar as violence might involve geriatric patients, which does not happen often. Older patients can get violent, although agitated is a better word for it."

"Thus, it is fair to say that you personally have never treated a patient that would be described as violent or perhaps potentially violent?"

"Within the usual definition of the term, violent, I would say that is correct. I have treated many patients suffering from various mental disorders, many could be described as disturbed, but not necessarily violent."

"None of the journal articles you have written deal with post traumatic stress disorder?"

"That is correct."

"Post traumatic stress disorder is not mentioned in any of the books you have written?"

"Correct."

"Thus, I take it that you have never treated a person suffering from post traumatic stress disorder?"

"That is correct. I am familiar with the disorder as it relates to the general practice of psychiatry."

"Have you ever treated a man or woman with any other combat-related psychiatric disorders?"

"No."

"Is my client the first person you have ever examined with manifestations of this disorder."

"Yes."

"Have you ever been associated with any VA hospital in any capacity?"

"Your honor! Where is this line of questioning going? Dr. Jakeway's reputation is impeccable."

"I see no harm in this questioning. Overruled, sit down Mr. Crews. Go ahead Mr. Halligan," the judge said.

"Thank you. It is fair to say, is it not, doctor, that your practice is devoted entirely to geriatric psychiatry, that you have no experience whatever in treating anyone other than geriatric patients, that you have no experience whatever with military personnel, let alone combat veterans, you have never even been inside a military hospital and this week, as you yourself have admitted, has been your first experience ever in dealing with the disorder commonly known as past traumatic stress disorder, which you as much as admitted you know very little about–"

"Objection! Objection!" Crews shouted.

"And yet, here you are, with my client's life at stake, testifying as an expert in an area of psychiatry you've as much as admitted you are practically ignorant."

"Objection!"

"So, in a matter of eight or so hours of examination, you've suddenly become an expert, and, with your testimony, you may help to write off a man's life. Is that the way it is with you, Dr. Jakeway?"

"Objection! This is outrageous! Defense counsel is out of line!"

"That's enough, Mr. Halligan," the judge said.

"I hope you can live with yourself, Jakeway–"

"One more remark, and I'll hold you in contempt!"

"I have no further questions of this witness," Halligan said.

"Your honor, may we approach?" Crews asked.

"There is no need for that counselor, proceed with your questioning!"

The prosecuting attorney then called Henry Plunkett to testify again.

"Chief, the Meachams were friends of yours, weren't they?"

"Yes, they were. Pen Meacham was probably the best friend I ever had."

"This case has been difficult for you?"

"Yes."

"I'm sorry."

"Thank you."

"I have a couple of questions."

"Yes, sir."

"Chief, please tell the court how the defendant appeared to you when you first saw him after the arrest?"

"Mr. Crews, I'm not sure I understand the question," Chief Plunkett said.

"How did Cahill seem to you? Was he upset or angry or sad?"

"Chicago police picked Cahill up for us and held him downtown in the lock-up for about half a day until Deputy Martin, Frank Scott and I got there."

"Okay."

"How did he seem to me? Well, that's interesting. I'd say he was indifferent."

"Indifferent?"

"It was strange. Well, he's a strange one, anyway."

"Objection!" Halligan said

"Sustained; the jury will disregard."

"Sorry, your honor. Please go ahead, Chief," Crews said."

"It seemed like he knew what was going on. But, it was almost like what had happened and the fact that he was in the lock-up and now heading to jail in Michigan was not important to him one way or another, like maybe he expected us to pick him up. I read the charges against him, and all we got was a strange far-away look in his eyes, kind of like he was somewhere else, and then he kind of laughed like maybe the whole thing was some kind of a sick joke. He's a strange one, all right."

"Objection. The police chief is not a psychologist. I object to the Chief's use of the words 'sick joke.'"

"Sustained. The jury will disregard."

"Go ahead, Chief."

"There were four of us in the squad car on the way back, and I'll bet he didn't say one word for the first hundred miles. He did say he thought the handcuffs were a little tight, but that was about all."

"The car was completely quiet?"

"Yes, it was spooky for a long while, and then he just kind of laughed and looked out the window and said something like, 'I suppose you want the whole story' or words to that effect."

"Then what happened?"

"Well, he was quiet for maybe half an hour or so and then he just started talking about the Meachams and the hotel and how he got there. I interrupted him and warned him that anything he would say could be used against him."

"What did he say then?"

"Then he was quiet again."

"Okay."

"Then Deputy Martin read him his rights."

"Then what happened?"

"I have read Cahill's signed confession, and you have my testimony from yesterday about his confession. We heard most of his confession from the back seat of the squad car while we were driving north. However, there were a couple of things Cahill said that are not in the confession. I do not know if it is important or not. It's been mentioned before in this trial."

"Your honor, is the prosecutor on a fishing expedition? We have heard Chief Plunkett's testimony before. How has he suddenly remembered something he left out before?" Halligan said.

"Mr. Crews?"

"Your honor, the chief of police has been deeply involved in this case since the beginning, perhaps more than anyone else. I would like the court to listen to any other information that may have a bearing on this case," Crews said.

"Mr. Halligan, I don't have a problem with this. I will allow it. Go ahead Mr. Crews, but stick to the facts," the judge said.

"Thank you, your honor. Go ahead, Chief. Is this something concerning the facts of the case?"

"No, nothing like that. Freddie and Frank and I think he was faking being borderline nuts anyway,"

"Objection!" Halligan said.

"The jury will disregard that remark," the judge said.

"Sorry, your honor. Go ahead, Chief," Crews said.

"Well I know there's no doubt about what he did, and he doesn't deny what he did. But he said something like 'When I fired at them, it was like I was watching myself in a movie or on television, and I couldn't stop it.'"

"Objection! Is the police chief guessing at or outright fabricating what the defendant said?"

"Chief?"

"Cahill said, and I heard it distinctly, 'It was like I was watching myself in a movie or on television, and I couldn't stop it.'"

"Thank you, Chief, that has been mentioned before. Anything else?"

"Well, I think he's fooled all of us. His act was deliberate."

"Objection, The police chief is not a psychologist," Halligan said.

"Overruled. Go ahead, Chief Plunkett."

"Objection, counsel is leading the witness. Chief Plunkett is talking about his impressions, not the facts about the facts," Halligan said.

"Sit down, Mr. Halligan, I've already ruled on your objection."

"Go ahead, Chief."

"Okay. Well, Cahill told us in the car that he knew what he was doing when he got the weapon from his car and headed for the hotel in that rainstorm. Then he looked up and said, 'I did not believe that I would shoot any of them until I did it. The gun went off and it seemed to wake me up.'"

"Objection; this is hearsay. I move to strike this entire line of questioning and dialogue."

"What the hell is the matter with you, Halligan? Three other people in the car heard exactly the same thing. Question them, and you will get exactly the same answer. He's a cold-blooded killer, pure and simple, and he's made a fool out of you," Chief Plunkett said.

"Plunkett, you are out of control, I move to strike," Halligan said.

"This court will not tolerate any more outbursts like this from either one of you. I warn you, I'll hold you both in contempt. Chief, there will be no more flare-ups, and Mr. Halligan you are overruled. Go ahead, Mr. Crews."

"Tell the court, Chief Plunkett, did you see any sign of remorse? Do you think he regretted what he did? Was he at all sorry?"

"Objection. Crew is calling for a conclusion from the witness. He is soliciting an unqualified opinion. The police chief is not an expert on human behavior," Halligan said.

"Overruled."

"Thank you, your honor," Crews replied. "Go ahead, Chief."

"No, not at all. I do not think he regretted what he did at all. Freddie and Frank would tell you the same thing."

"Thank you, Chief, anything more?"

"No, nothing more."

Crews stopped for a drink of water, gathered up his notes and faced the jury: "Members of the jury, you have heard Mr. Halligan's dramatic plea for mercy for the defendant, Brian Cahill. It is fortunate for Mr. Halligan that he himself was not at The Promontory Inn on that terrible Sunday morning of July 27, 1975, because he would also almost certainly have been slain by this violent killer, and we would have had a funeral for four instead of three. While it is true that religion and politics do not mix, I think it is important for the jury to know that Cahill is a man who does not believe in God. As we have all seen over the past several days, he has not exhibited the slightest sign of remorse for what he has done. Members of the jury, this man is not sorry in any way for the terrible things he has done. As you have no doubt noticed, this trial appears to have bored him. Cahill is an atheist. He does not believe in God and, as such, does not live by any generally accepted standards of behavior. In your deliberations, I ask you to remember, members of the jury, the Biblical admonition that comes down to us from Genesis: 'Whosoever sheddeth man's blood, by man shall his blood be shed.'"

Crews stopped and looked at his notes.

"The People call upon you, members of the jury, to enforce the laws of our state as they are written. The punishment for murder in the 1st degree is death by hanging or life in prison, without any possibility of parole. It is your sworn duty to enforce the laws of this state to the maximum. The People want this evil man put to death. These were not ordinary crimes by any means. These were crimes of such horrendous magnitude, of such sheer horror and cruelty that the human mind recoils at the very thought of them. Three of our most respected citizens, indeed our most popular citizens, liked by virtually every member of our community, were slaughtered like animals. We ask ourselves, why did this happen? We don't know of God's reasoning, but we do know that the assailant killed out of pure hatred, because of a belief of some kind that he was killing his father, Penfield Meacham."

F.K. Crews stopped speaking and walked over to the table nearby. He put his notes down and stopped for a drink of water. He turned and pointed his finger at Brian Cahill: "There he is. This is the man who made his way into The Promontory Inn, in the dead of night, during the rainstorm, in the early hours of July 27, 1975, and shot Penfield Meacham in the face and almost blew his head completely off. Cahill then turned and delivered what must have been a sledgehammer blow to Cooper Meacham's face, which killed him instantly. Cooper Meacham, a straight A-student, an acolyte, a football player and former class president, with his entire life in front of him, is now dead and buried.

"Now think of Geraldine Meacham. She must have heard the shot. She must have heard Cahill coming up the stairs, and she must have waited in her room in terror until Cahill came through the door and pointed the shotgun at her. She must have begged for her life. Cahill pulled the trigger and absolutely destroyed that beautiful woman's face.

"Now think of Mary Meade Saltonstall, cheerleader, class secretary, athlete, also with her entire life in front of her–is now dead. During the last months of her life, she was treated at Ludgate Hill Hospital, suffering emotional damage from Cooper's violent death from which she never recovered. The damage and sorrow that this evil man caused is widespread and has reached so many lives, indeed the lives of all of us. Members of the jury, the People call on you to put this horrible, vile man to death, or he will surely kill again. The next time it might be your mother or father or brother or sister or son or daughter."

Crews paused and walked near the jury.

"We believe that all appropriate and admissible evidence bearing on the innocence of guilt of the accused has been presented to the court. These killings were not the action of an insane man. These were the actions of a deliberate, cold-blooded killer who savagely struck his victims without warning and with no justification whatever. He is a cunning, devious person whom we believe may have outwitted his lawyer, but we will not allow him to outwit this court. This person took for what he perceived to be personal revenge into his own hands. There is, members of the jury, a difference between insanity and rage. This was not insanity. This was pure, calculated vindictiveness, and this man has no place in a civilized society. The People confidently await your verdict, the only verdict possible–that of murder in the first degree. And finally, I ask you to remember the Commandment, unmistakable in its certitude, from God Himself:' He that smiteth a man, so that he die, shall be surely put to death.'"

Crews thanked the jury and sat down.

"We will now hear summation by the defense," the judge said.

"Thank you. Members of the jury, as we have seen, Mr. Crews has introduced personal opinions, unsubstantiated facts and some completely undocumented assumptions that have obscured the true nature of this case. Consider if you will, members of the jury, that the defendant, Brian Cahill is a man who has faced death many times. You may remember that many young men in our country, because of privilege or position, escaped the responsibility of serving our nation. Brian Cahill made no such attempt to escape the service of his country. Indeed, he volunteered for the most difficult and most dangerous combat assignments in Southeast Asia, not once but two times. Mr. Crews has made a point of saying that Brian Cahill is a man who does not believe in God. I suspect that has not always been the case, because it is said that there were no atheists in foxholes in Vietnam. In light of the fact that he was surrounded by death in the jungle for two years, he may have believed in something beyond himself at some point. In Southeast Asia, Brian Cahill faced the terrible fury of hand-to-hand combat; he endured night patrols deep in the center of darkness and ferocious firefights with an enemy that did not take prisoners. Who among us in this very room could long endure such trauma? What we can say is that Brian Cahill endured with a determination that not many of us have. Mr. Cahill's beliefs or lack of beliefs should have no relevance to the outcome of this trial and I am sure that the judge's instructions to you, members of the jury, will confirm this with you."

Halligan walked across the courtroom and faced the jury.

"With Vietnam tenuously behind him, Brian Cahill tried to find a place for himself in society. After graduating from college, Brian worked for a public accounting firm and did his best to survive in what he perceived to be the real world. However, as Dr. Evans has testified, the terror of the Ia Drang has not left him for a day since late 1965. The years of early neglect and abject poverty, of abuse and the wrenching ordeal of killing and killing and killing all but destroyed any semblance of emotional stability. As we have learned during this trial, there were many periods in Brian Cahill's life of devastating post traumatic stress disorder, and he eventually sought vindication for all that he believed had happened to him."

Halligan stopped, looked at his notes, and continued.

"Brian Cahill became obsessed with the man he believed responsible for all of his misfortune. He was enraged at the father he never knew, the father that abandoned him in infancy. Then, the photographs arrived on Friday night, July 25. Who sent the pictures and why, without a word of explanation? What terrible disturbance they caused in Brian's mind! How would any of us in this room react, if we had never known our mother or father, to such a cruel way to learn of your parents, if they really were your parents. Then, Brian saw the Meacham life style at The Promontory Inn, a lifestyle ostensibly thrown in his face and denied him. His grasp on reality, never secure, began to disintegrate. Brian Cahill felt abandoned by his mother, by his father and by the Army, which taught him to do horrible things to survive. He knew what the Army had taught him–problems could be solved by violence. Brian remembered being called a pothead, a loser, a baby killer. There were no parades, there was no welcome home, the nation was not grateful for what he had done. There was only shame and a demand for vengeance for all that had happened, and it was all directed against one person, on July 27, who when Brian Cahill's mind crossed the breaking point and went out of control."

Halligan walked over and put his notes down on the table.

"Members of the jury, the evidence is clear. Brian Cahill committed these acts. Was he responsible for these acts? The testimony presented to the court proves that he was not. He was driven insane by duty to his country and by events and circumstances beyond his control. Brian Cahill was insane at the time of the crimes and is not guilty by reason of insanity. Thank you."

The judge then asked Crews if a final rebuttal is in order.

"Thank you, your honor. Members of the jury, your duty is clear. Weigh the evidence and review the testimony. Three outstanding members of our community are dead, and Brian Cahill is responsible for their deaths. Your duty to God and your community are clear. As God is our witness, this man must pay the extreme price for his actions. Thousands of Vietnam veterans have returned to the 'real world,' as defense council calls it, and they live socially responsible lives. Mr. Halligan would have you believe that other forces were at work in these deaths. That is complete nonsense. The only forces at work in these crimes involved the use of a shotgun and simple blind rage, not insanity. Members of the jury, remember the faces of the victims as you knew them in life, and then remember the horribly disfigured images you saw in the pathology photos. Can there be any doubt in your mind about the verdict? Brian Cahill should pay the ultimate price for his terrible actions."

Following the instructions of Judge Patterson, the jury deliberated for less than an hour and returned to the courtroom.

"Members of the jury, have your reached a verdict?" the judge asked.

"We have, your honor," the jury foreman said.

The bailiff handed the sealed verdict to the judge.

"Count One, Count Two, and Count Three, we the jury find the defendant, Brian Cahill, guilty of murder in the first degree and the punishment is death."

Later that afternoon Brian looked at a shadow near the cell window, pulled the gray blanket from the cot, wrapped it around himself, and sat in the chair by the window. There was a humming sound and a soft voice. He did not know if it was from a person outside the cell door or if he was losing his mind. He listened again, and the sound vanished. He later told Shannon of his life and that long forgotten faces and sounds came to him in the night and then left. Sometimes there were meaningless images, without a beginning or an end that came in rapid succession and disappeared. Brian said he often shut his eyes and imagined Charmon there in the cell with him, and he knew it was pointless.

The nights were worse than the days, and often he did not sleep at all through the night, only to fall asleep for 15 hours into the next night and day where time was of no consequence. When Brian was not sleeping, reading, walking back and forth in his cell, or talking with Shannon during her monthly visit, he would often stand at the window and watch children on the school playground nearby. In the beginning, he had thought about running outside on a bright sunny day, but that was a few years ago. The past could overwhelm him; he would fall into deep depression, and silence would seem to swallow all sound.

As his execution date neared, Brian said he would lie awake in the night and remember the arrest he had known was coming. He knew then that it was all over; there was nothing more to do with life. Brian told Shannon he had tried to settle the score and failed–Paul Meacham still lived, and he now knew that Ruth Cahill was dead. Brian knew he should feel remorse about what he had done, but he did not; he saw no difference between killing the Meacham family members and killing in Vietnam. Brian knew he had lost his way early in life, and he was approaching the end. Being dead wouldn't be so bad, he thought, but he was afraid of dying and often sat in the darkness and wondered when they were coming for him. The only certainty, he said, was that he was alive and death was coming, but death was coming for every person. Some will die sooner than others, but what did it really matter? He thought about being hanged and wondered what would happen if the knot was not tight enough or if the rope broke and he fell to the ground. Did that mean he would have to go through it all over again? What, he asked, had been the point of all this? Why was there no God or something to give it meaning?

WHY DID I GROW SO COLD?

Brian said he would lie still on the cot and wait for death. Sometimes he felt death in his cell, waiting for him at the foot of his cot. Death had haunted him for years. Now, as it moved closer, he told Shannon, death had lost all meaning.

Chapter 39

Day after day, sunlight came through the dining room window and reflected off the Calder painting over the fireplace. Furniture had not been used in years, and white sheets covered tables and chairs. Geraldine Meacham's coffee cup was still on the dining room table by the window. The hotel kitchen was white and spotless, and dishes, pots, pans, and utensils were put away in cabinets. Pen Meacham's clipboard with notes and cigars were on the counter where he had left them. Living room furniture was still grouped around the large fireplace and covered with white sheets. The lobby's check-in register, in Cooper Meacham's handwriting, was dated July 26, 1975. The hallway landing near the second floor, where Penfield and Cooper Meacham were slain, had been repainted and looked new.

Tea Room Gallery paintings, returned to artists years ago, left the room empty. Errol's pieces were still in the long hallway, and the door to the main bar was closed. Sometimes at odd hours, voices in the long hallway whispered from the past. Guestrooms, where there had once been laughter, were quiet but ready for visitors. Furniture pieces in the Meachams' apartment were draped with sheets, pictures were displayed throughout, and window shutters were closed. The bedroom where Geraldine Meacham had been killed, was repainted and looked new. Clothes and shoes were still in closets and drawers, storage boxes were aligned, undisturbed, in the attic. Outdoor furniture was stored in Charlie Putnam's shack. Tennis nets were in storage; pool, porches, and patios were empty; the lawn and gardens were still tended with care. Four graves, covered with red and white carnations and impatiens in good weather, were on the crest of the hill not far from Gerry and Charlie's flower garden.

WHY DID I GROW SO COLD?

The hotel was empty for six years and no one knew if The Promontory Inn would be sold. Charlie Putnam and Ida Mae Murphy shared a devotion to the Meachams and the hotel and they maintained the Inn as if it might open. Graham Meacham, practicing law in San Francisco, had not returned to Stamford Bridge since the funeral; but he sent money to Ida Mae and Charlie every month to keep the hotel as it was in the summer of 1975. Ida Mae and Charlie were soon close. They went to the Inn every day; neither would go alone. Only the quiet sounds of their work broke through the veil of silence around the old building. In autumn, leaves would fall in the yellowish light to the ground, as Charlie and Ida Mae prepared the hotel for winter. During months of darkness, snow quietly blanketed the grounds, and the building looked forlorn and forgotten.

In spring, Charlie and Ida Mae opened windows and cleaned, dusted, painted and repaired for weeks. Charlie planted new flowers and trimmed and cut the grass and cleaned gutters and downspouts. Chief Henry Plunkett and Deputy Freddie Martin checked on the hotel's security every few days. Tourists came by every day, stopped, and took pictures, but none walked on the grounds and the hotel stood by itself. Merchants and friends wrote to Graham often asking him to return, and he did not write back. By late April each year, the hotel was ready for guests, and the town hoped it would open again, but the Inn did not open.

Chapter 40

In the fall of 1981, the snow came early and Graham Meacham returned to Stamford Bridge.

Graham practiced law in California for six years after the death of his family. He missed Darby Saltonstall and The Promontory Inn and Stamford Bridge and knew that home was where he ought to be. Graham's relationship with Darby began simply enough. She liked Graham as they grew up in Stamford Bridge, but when he left for college, she almost lost track of him, and neither knew when their love started. After the funeral, they were together and talked about building a life together, but then Graham left for California. They were sometimes together in California, but Darby always returned to Stamford Bridge alone. After being gone so long, Brian had not dealt with his sorrow. He had only made it more painful. He had seen them in death and his mind had shut down in the face of unbearable agony. For years, he could not talk about what he had seen, and he avoided Mass and the holy days. Whatever he was looking for in California was not there. What point was there in being away from Darby? He did not know, and she did not know. They wrote, and he could not stop missing her. Finally, Darby said it was time to come home.

Mary Meade Staltonstall, Darby's younger sister, died in April of 1976 giving birth to Cooper Meacham Jr. and the boy had lived for five years with his aunt, Darby. Graham and Darby were married in December of 1981 at Holy Cross and made their home in an apartment on the hotel's second floor. They adopted Cooper Jr.

Ida Mae Murphy's parents died in 1980, and she lived alone in the small cottage with the white picket fence. Charlie Putnam still lived in the maintenance shack at the edge of the hotel property. Both had worked at the hotel every day for years, but nothing had really changed. Pen's clipboard and cigars, left on the kitchen counter, were finally put away. Geraldine's coffee cup, still on the dining room table where she had left it, was put in the china cabinet. The hotel log in Cooper's handwriting was put with his things in his room on the third floor. The Meachams' third-floor apartment looked as it did on July 26, 1975. The broken picture of Pen and Paul Meacham, People's Exhibit 11, was returned to the hotel. Charlie repaired it and put it back on the south living room wall. Ida Mae dusted the third floor apartment once a week. Graham and Darby never went there.

Graham and Darby tried to work through the tragedies that time had laid down on them year after year: the violent deaths of Graham's family, the premature death of Mary Meade and the years apart. The sadness lingered. Both knew, in their hearts, that they would never come to terms with what had happened.

Paul Meacham visited his nephew, Graham Meacham, in California late in 1980. Paul told Graham that he had worked in Stamford Bridge during the summer of 1945. Brian Cahill, was the child of he and Ruth Cahill, and he had had no knowledge of a son until the trial. He had not seen Ruth since that summer. Paul's wife had been dead for many years, and he had never told her of Ruth Cahill. They had had no children. Paul Meacham knew he was responsible for the son he never knew and the deaths of Graham's father, mother, and brother. Paul's son, his only son, Brian Cahill, then in prison awaiting death, refused to see his father. Brian Cahill was executed for his crimes by hanging in May of 1982.

It was after the death of Brian Cahill that Paul Meacham ended his own life in June of 1982.

The Promontory Inn opened again in the summer of 1982, and it seemed as if the passage of seven years had never happened. Graham, Darby, Charlie, and Ida Mae ran the hotel. There were no Saturday night parties. The Tea Room Gallery opened again and there were crowds for dinner most nights.

Cooper Jr. became the image of his father. Once a month, and sometimes more often, he, Graham, and Darby walked up the hill to the four graves overlooking the lake. When the weather was warm, they brought flowers. Cooper Jr. idolized the father he had never met. Although it was never said, he always longed in his heart for his real mom and dad.

Shannon Fitsimmons could not put events behind her. So, when she got back to Saginaw in late August of 1975, she could only think of Stamford Bridge. Shannon reported on the investigation, the trial, and the prisoner. Brian Cahill liked Shannon and saw her each month after the trial. Brian read what she wrote about him and wished things had been different. Brian asked her to be there when the end came.

Shannon's book, *Incident at Stamford Bridge*, was published in 1984. She left for Kansas that fall and drove back through the years to Wheatstone. She missed the Labor Day picnic at Ruder Park. Leaves were falling on the stone sidewalk where she and her mother walked 14 years before. Shannon walked alone through the park and could not account for the years she had been gone. She drove by her girlhood home, and there were strangers on the front porch. She stopped near the narrow gravel road. The two gray tombstones almost matched, and it seemed inconceivable that her mom and dad were both gone. What had been the point of all this, she asked herself. Shannon wished she had never left and wished she had never come back.

Printed in the United States
36648LVS00005B/103-111